This
Marquess
of Mine

ROMANCING THE ROGUE

SERIES

SYLVIE SINCLAIR

CHAPTER ONE

LONDON — JUNE 1821

LADY OLIVIA BLAKELY WAS not, and never would be, one of the great minds of her time. She had, however, learned a thing or two in her twenty years on this earth, and one such lesson was the power in a good accessory.

Knowing precisely the right moment to wield such power was another.

"Thank you for a most enjoyable outing, Your Grace," she said as the Duke of Paxton escorted her up the sun-lit steps to the front door of her Mayfair townhouse. Her lady's maid, Nellie, stood on the pavement below, watching the carriages go by while she waited.

"The pleasure was all mine, Lady Olivia," the young duke replied with a gallant bow of his head. "Will I see you tonight at Lady Tobin's ball?"

With his thick auburn hair and handsome, friendly face, the Duke of Paxton was precisely the sort of man every young lady hoped to marry. Olivia included.

Donning her most fetching smile, she fanned her gloved fingers across the simple strand of pearls resting above the swell of her breasts, gratified when the duke's dark eyes flared with interest. "I will be there, yes," she said.

He grinned. "Then you must save me a waltz."

"Must I?" she teased, arching a playful brow.

"I will be devastated if you do not," he said, pressing a hand to his heart. "And there is no telling what I might do if you refuse."

"Oh, dear." She twisted the pearls around her fingers, battling a smile. "Then I suppose I have no choice but to agree."

Lifting her free hand to his lips, Paxton brushed a kiss across her knuckles, his admiring gaze never leaving hers. "Thank you, my lady. I will ensure you do not regret it."

Olivia watched as Paxton bounded down the steps and hopped into his canary yellow phaeton, a satisfied smile turning her lips as he waved farewell and set off down the street in a clatter of wheels and hooves.

Another successful outing, she thought, as she turned to the door. *It is only a matter of time now.*

She let herself inside, slipping into the cozy entrance hall with Nellie only a few steps behind her.

"Forgive my forwardness, my lady," the young maid whispered as she shut the door behind her, "but His Lordship seems to grow more and more smitten with you every day. Why, for a moment there, I actually thought he was going to kiss you on the front steps for all and sundry to see."

The exhilarated gleam in Nellie's pale green eyes brought a smile to Olivia's lips. "Good," she said as she worked at the buttons on her powder blue spencer jacket. "That was precisely what I was hoping he would want to do."

Nellie giggled as Olivia handed her the spencer before moving on to her bonnet strings, pulling them free with an impatient tug. "Lord above, this bonnet was beginning to make my head ache," she muttered, lifting the beribboned torture device from her skull. "It is amazing, isn't it? The things we women will endure to snag a husband?"

Nellie nodded, her brown curls swaying beneath her plain white cap. "Aye, my lady, it is," she said. "Though I expect it will all be worth it for you, in the end."

"I certainly hope you're right, Nellie." Olivia handed the girl her bonnet and kid gloves before making her way to the drawing room, her heeled slippers clapping on the spotless marble floor.

She'd been after the Duke of Paxton for weeks now, and she was fairly certain she had him in the palm of her hand. Of course, she *should* already have a wedding band on that hand, and she would have, if only...

Her lips pursed. *If only I hadn't bungled the whole thing last Season.*

Paxton had asked for her hand once before but, like a fool, she'd turned him down. A fact his mother seemed unable—or unwilling—to forget. Or forgive. And if there was one person Paxton might hold in higher regard even than Olivia, it was the Duchess of Paxton.

The duke adored his mother, and because he adored her so much, he could not bear to see her unhappy and did everything in his power to please her. If the duchess did not approve of her son's wish to marry Olivia, it was unlikely to happen. Paxton did not go against his mother's wishes, which made the duchess the sole obstacle standing between Olivia and a second proposal of marriage.

Try as she might, though—and she *had* tried—she could not seem to win the woman's forgiveness.

A frustrated sigh escaped her as she reached the drawing room door. She needed more time.

Time, however, was in short supply. This Season was her last chance to nab the duke. If she could not manage it within the next few months, she would be forced to marry another man.

Someone of her father's choosing.

Pasting a bright smile to her lips, she shoved all thoughts of her father's ultimatum to the back of her mind as she walked through the door into the sunny drawing room with its pretty floral furnishings and cheerful, pink-and-white-striped wallpaper.

"Good afternoon, Aunt Augusta," she said, bending down to buss her guardian's cheek before taking a seat beside her on the chintz sofa.

Lady Augusta Crenshaw, a tall, handsome woman with graying blonde hair and a regal bearing, looked up from the letter in her hand and gave Olivia an affectionate smile. "Good afternoon, dearest. How was your drive with the duke?"

"Excellent, as always," Olivia quipped before kicking off her nankeen slippers. She rubbed her stocking feet on the dense wool rug, her soles still aching from all the dancing she'd done last night. "And how was your visit with Lady Keswick? Is she faring any better today?"

Aunt Augusta's hazel eyes dimmed as she blew out a beleaguered sigh. "She is faring as well as can be expected, considering she has a sprained ankle." Her mouth firmed into an unhappy line. "I feel so guilty. I *hate* feeling guilty."

Olivia gave her aunt a comforting pat on the arm. "It was an accident," she said soothingly. "You mustn't blame yourself."

"As it was *my* walking stick that brought the poor woman down, how can I not blame myself?" She threw a glare at the offending article, which sat propped against the rosewood armchair beside her. If a single look held the power to kill, that walking stick would be nothing but a pile of ash.

Biting back a smile, Olivia snagged a lemon biscuit from the tea tray on the sofa table and curled her legs beneath her skirts.

At sixty years of age, Aunt Augusta was still spry and fleet of foot, and only used the walking stick because she thought it paired so strikingly with the bold velvet gowns she favored.

A perfectly good reason, so far as Olivia was concerned.

Still, she could understand why her aunt was upset to have injured someone—her dearest friend, no less—with a walking stick she didn't strictly need. And in front of a ballroom full of people, no less.

Never in a thousand years had Olivia imagined the stately, elegant Marchioness of Keswick would one day wind up sprawled on the floor with rum punch dripping down her face and her skirts nearly up to her knees.

"Well, I am certain Lady Keswick does not blame you," Olivia said, trying not to grimace at the memory of that night. "And even if she does, she is a forgiving woman.

She will not be cross with you for long." She bit into the still-warm biscuit, savoring the tangy lemon flavor coating her tongue.

"That's just it," Aunt Augusta said. "She isn't cross with me at all. And it's driving me positively *mad*."

Olivia couldn't help but smile at the disgust in her aunt's voice. "But why? Do you want her to be cross with you?"

"Yes!" Aunt Augusta threw her arms out in exasperation, crinkling the letter she still held in one hand. "I want her to shout at me or refuse to speak to me for a week or two, like a reasonable person would do. Instead, she's been nothing but kind and gracious and it's making me feel worse. *Diabolical woman*."

Olivia took another bite of biscuit, smothering the urge to laugh. Aunt Augusta and Lady Lavinia Keswick had known each other for years, ever since Lady Keswick married the Marquess of Keswick, who was close friend and cousin to Aunt Augusta's husband, the Earl of Crenshaw.

Both gentlemen died many years ago, but the two ladies remained as close as sisters to this day.

"In any case," Aunt Augusta went on, "I promised Lavinia I would do everything in my power to make it up to her. Even if it kills me." She huffed out a sigh then held up the letter in her hand. "At least your cousin is having a good week. She writes from Venice and says she and Dearborn are having a marvelous time on their wedding trip."

Olivia smiled as she brushed the biscuit crumbs from her lap. "I'm glad to hear it," she said, reaching for the stack of correspondence lying on the sofa table. "They certainly deserve to be happy after everything they went through."

Aunt Augusta hummed her agreement. "Indeed, they do."

Sophie, Olivia's cousin and one of her two dearest friends in the world, had just married James, the Earl of Dearborn, a man they knew as children and met again earlier this year at a country house party hosted by Lady Keswick.

Sophie and James fell in love, but a man from James's past bent on revenge had nearly ruined their chance at happiness together. Olivia was so grateful it had all worked out in the end. If anyone deserved to be happy, it was Sophie, and Olivia loved that her friend—her sister, really—had married a man who cherished her as she ought to be cherished.

Sophie's parents died when she was just a little girl, which thrust her under the guardianship of Earl Blakely, her mother's brother and Olivia's father, an uncle Sophie had never laid eyes on before. Olivia, two years younger than Sophie, was thrilled to have a new friend to play with, and even more ecstatic when her great-aunt Augusta took over the girls' care.

Before that, it had always been just Olivia and her father, a man who could barely stand to look at her. When Sophie and their aunt came along, Olivia finally knew what it was to have a family who loved her.

"I've always wanted to visit Venice," Aunt Augusta murmured as she munched on a biscuit. "Your cousin's letters leave a lot to be desired in the way of details, but I suppose that is to be expected with a wedding trip. I intend to ask her to elaborate when I see her next."

Olivia smiled. "I am sure Sophie will be more than happy to tell you all about her trip," she said as she riffled through the stack of letters and invitations. She paused when she came upon a letter with her name on it, the address written in a familiar, swooping hand.

"Oh, look. A letter has come from Caroline," she said, referring to her stepmother. She broke the seal and began to skim the letter's contents. "I wonder how her sister is faring after the..." Her words trailed off as the words she read began to sink in.

"Olivia? Is something the matter?" Concern edged her aunt's voice.

Lowering the letter to her lap, Olivia slowly shook her head. "Yes. No." She drew in a calming breath. "No, everything is fine. I—I've just received some surprising news, that's all."

"Oh? What news?"

She swallowed, her mind oddly numb. "Caroline is going to have a baby."

A baby. Her stepmother was pregnant.

It was silly to be so bemused by the news. Her father married Caroline more than a year ago. She knew this day would come eventually. Still, the image of her father with a new little family had always seemed strange and abstract, a reality for the distant future.

That it was nearly upon her now...

She could not seem to wrap her mind around it.

"I see," Aunt Augusta said softly, her gaze trained on Olivia's face. "Well, your father will be pleased."

Olivia huffed out a humorless laugh. "He certainly will be if the child is male."

The words stung her throat, and her chest ached, though she knew it shouldn't. Not anymore. She'd had these last twenty years to accept her father's disregard, after all. *So why did it still hurt so much?*

"Are you all right, my dear?" Sympathy shone in her aunt's eyes.

Olivia forced a smile she knew would fool no one, and chirped, "Of course! I knew this news was imminent. It is the reason my father decreed this will be my last Season, and the reason I must find a husband before it ends. Father needs to *economize*."

Her gaze fell to the letter in her lap, and she absent-mindedly smoothed her fingers along the creases in the paper. She hated that her father was forcing her hand this way, making her choose a husband to keep him from choosing one for her, even as a part of her understood his reasons. A London Season was not inexpensive, and he'd granted her three of them. Three Seasons ought to be plenty of time for an earl's daughter to make a satisfactory match.

Still, it hurt that he didn't seem to care who she married. And that his new family mattered to him so much more than she did.

"I'm sorry, dearest," Aunt Augusta said with a squeeze to Olivia's shoulder. "I wish I could talk some sense into your father. I wish I could change things for you."

Olivia nodded. "I know you do," she said. "But there is no sense in dwelling on that, is there? And I'm thrilled for Caroline. Truly I am. I know how much she longs to be a mother."

"Yes," Aunt Augusta said. "She will be a wonderful mother. And you will be a sister soon."

Olivia stilled as the words penetrated her brain. The thought hadn't occurred to her. How strange. "Yes, I suppose I will," she said softly. Though how well she would come to know her new sibling remained to be seen.

Aunt Augusta's gaze was assessing, her silence probing, and Olivia rose to her feet, eager to escape. "Well, I think I shall change out of this gown now and do a little pruning in the garden."

With her letter in hand and her smile firmly in place, she headed for the door, hopeful that some time spent in her little garden amongst the marigolds and lavender and the warm spring sun would set her to rights again. Or, at the very least, distract her.

"Olivia, dear..."

Aunt Augusta's voice beckoned her to stay, but Olivia did not pause on her way to the door. She already knew what her aunt would say, and she had no desire to listen to words of comfort. Not when her emotions were so close to the surface.

She *was* happy for Caroline. She'd meant that. She did not know her stepmother well, but she liked her, and liked that she seemed to make her father happy when he'd had so little happiness since Olivia's mother died.

Caroline would make him happier still with the birth of this child. Perhaps it would be the boy he'd always wanted, the boy he'd always wished Olivia had been.

Perhaps Earl Blakely would finally get his heir. And then, perhaps, he would finally stop hating her.

CHAPTER TWO

THE FRONT DOOR TO Mrs. Morris's townhouse swung closed with a thud, rattling the door knocker. Griffin, the Marquess of Keswick, sighed and turned to face the quiet, lamp-lit street where his carriage with matching bays awaited him, blanketed in misty evening fog.

"Well," he murmured, glancing down at the tiny bundle of black fur nestled in the crook of his arm. "That didn't go quite as we'd planned, did it?"

"*Meow.*"

The kitten's bright yellow eyes blinked up at him and a smile touched Griff's lips. "Exactly so."

Descending the stairs with slow, measured steps, he approached the carriage and called up to his coachman. "It's a fine evening, John. I think I'd like to walk home. Follow behind me, will you?"

"Yes, m'lord. And what of..." The driver tipped his chin at the cat. "Shall I put it in the carriage?"

Griff shook his head. "No, I'll keep her with me. I think she fancies a walk, as well."

John nodded. "As you say, m'lord."

Shifting his furry cargo to his other arm, Griffin started up the pavement with brisk steps, enjoying the cool caress of the evening mist on his cheeks. He thought he'd be spending the evening with Jane and had brought the kitten as a gift for her, but she'd taken one look at it and promptly ordered him to take it away. Her response surprised him, and he'd asked her if kittens made her sneeze.

No, she'd said. *I simply don't like cats.*

Griffin frowned. "How could she not like you?" he asked the kitten, stroking her soft black fur. She purred and snuggled deeper into the crook of his arm.

Truth be told, he knew next to nothing about cats. He'd never kept one as a pet before and, apart from the toms that prowled the barn and stables at Keswick House, he had very little experience with them. Still, he couldn't fathom disliking an entire species of animal. He hadn't bothered to ask Jane why she didn't like cats. It hardly mattered. He'd been waiting for an excuse to end their arrangement for some time now, and hating cats seemed as good a reason as any.

Honestly, he'd been growing bored with her for some time.

Although, if he was even more honest with himself, he would have to admit that just about everything bored him lately. He didn't know why.

Dragging in a deep breath, he glanced up at the night sky, surprisingly clear given the fog at his feet. He could even see some of the constellations hanging up there. Cassiopeia, Ursa Major, Andromeda.

"No Orion tonight," he murmured, scratching the kitten's chin. "My father would have liked that. Orion was his least favorite constellation, you know. He always felt that of all the Greek characters of myth, Orion was the least deserving of those who'd been immortalized in the sky."

A worthless scapegrace, he'd liked to call him. Griff smiled. "The only thing that seemed to make my father feel better was that every story written about Orion ended the same way: With Artemis killing him."

His smile faded as a sharp pang of sorrow pierced his chest. The same pain of loss that struck him even now, twenty years after his father's sudden death. He was only ten years old when his father died, but he still remembered him, still missed him, though the feeling had softened some over the years.

Sometimes, though—not often, but sometimes—he hated his father for leaving them. Logic told him he hadn't left intentionally, that he would have stayed had he been given a choice, but logic and grief rarely shook hands.

And he couldn't help feeling cheated. He would never speak with his father again, would never know him as an adult, would never again have the chance to discuss mythology and astronomy or share his worries or go to him for advice. Life could be deuced unfair sometimes.

The kitten squirmed and Griffin glanced down to find feline eyes peering up at him with keen interest, almost as if she craved more of Orion's downfall.

"Bloodthirsty little thing, aren't you?" he said with a chuckle.

The kitten mewled again then stretched a tiny paw out to swipe at the folds of Griff's silk cravat. He caught her paw gently in his hand and sighed. "What am I to do with you, then?" he mused.

It had never occurred to him that Jane would reject his gift, and he'd made no contingency plan. "Perhaps Mother will take you. Or Emmy."

So far as he knew, neither his mother nor his sister hated cats. He'd never heard them utter a disparaging remark against them, at least. And he was certain all it would take was one look at her furry little face and any misgivings would fade away.

He arrived home a few minutes later, reaching the top step just as the front door swung open, revealing Winters, the family butler of some forty-odd years.

"Good evening, my lord," he said, "and welcome home."

"Thank you, Winters," Griffin said as the door was shut behind him.

Winters eyed the cat as he collected Griff's hat and gloves, his curiosity almost palpable in the silence of the entrance hall.

"She's a gift," Griff explained. "For my mother."

"Ah." Winters stepped back, fussing with the gloves before clearing his throat. "Forgive my impertinence, my lord, but I do hope your gift will lift Her Ladyship's spirits."

A smile tugged at Griffin's lips. "Been a right terror today, has she?"

A mildly pained expression crinkled the older man's brow, but all he said was, "I will leave you to draw your own conclusions, my lord. She's been asking for you."

"Thank you, Winters."

Griffin turned and carried the kitten up the stairs, shaking his head at his mother's behavior. Not that he could blame her for being out of sorts. She was cranky because of her injured ankle, and the mandatory bedrest forced upon her. This would make anyone cranky, but it was especially irksome to a woman as active as the Marchioness of Keswick.

Unfortunately, her injury wasn't the only reason for her ill temper. Guilt tightened his chest and he grimaced. She was displeased with him at the moment and had made little secret of it. She had grown rather desperate for him to marry and his disinterest in taking a wife seemed to confuse her as much as it irritated her.

"I hope you can cheer her up, little one," he muttered under his breath. Perhaps the kitten would distract her enough that she would forget to lecture him. *A man can hope.*

Lady Keswick seemed to think she would wear him down, that if she kept asking and prodding, he would finally come to realize she was right, that it was time for him to marry. That, in fact, he couldn't wait to take a wife and start a family.

The truth was, he simply wasn't ready for marriage. He had nothing against the institution, and when he was ready to take a wife, he hoped they would be happy together. He had no illusions that he would marry for love, but he knew it could happen. He knew love existed. He'd seen evidence of it with his own parents, before it was all ripped away without warning.

He knew he would have to marry eventually, and he was prepared to do his duty. Someday. But not just yet.

He wasn't ready to give up his freedom, his *fun*. He was only thirty years old, for God's sake; hardly a relic. There would be plenty of time for marriage and begetting heirs later.

He would take a wife when he was good and ready, and his mother would simply have to accept it.

Shifting the kitten to his other arm, he drew in a fortifying breath. What he really wanted was a stiff drink, maybe two, but that would have to wait. It was best for everyone not to keep his mother waiting.

He reached the door to her chambers and, bracing himself, rapped his knuckles on the dense oak.

"Enter," came her reply.

Griffin went in wearing a smile. Lady Lavinia Keswick did not return it.

"Ah. There you are," she said coolly from her enormous four-poster bed with its damask drapings and mauve silk coverlet. "I wondered when you would finally pay me a visit. I thought perhaps you had gone to bed without seeing me first."

Griff swallowed a laugh as he shut the door behind him. Even laid up in bed, wearing a lavender-hued nightdress and a white cap covering her dark hair, Lady Keswick was as imperious as a queen.

"Come now, Mother," he said, turning to face her with his most disarming smile. "Have I ever done that before?"

She sniffed. "No. But considering your behavior of late, I wouldn't be a bit surprised by the change."

The room was dimly lit and smelled of chamomile tea, the fire blazing in the hearth heating the room to near-sweltering, but Griffin knew better than to mention it. *Never poke a cranky lioness.*

"What is that?" she asked, pointing to the kitten, who was peering about the room with avid interest.

"It's a cat," he said. "For you."

He crossed the room to the bed and gently transferred the little fluffball into his mother's outstretched hands. She cooed, turning the kitten's face to hers so she could get a closer look. "Well, aren't you a precious little thing?" She looked at Griffin, skepticism sharpening her pale blue eyes. "A cat? For me?"

"Well, I, ah..."

Lady Keswick sighed. "Never mind. I don't think I want to know."

Relieved at having avoided discussing his mistress with his mother, Griffin sat down beside her on the downy mattress, mindful of her injured ankle. "Now," he said, "what is it I can do for you?"

"Pardon?" she asked, looking up from the kitten playing in her lap to meet his gaze.

"Winters said you've been asking for me. He said you've been in an ill temper all day."

Her gaze fell away, and she lifted one shoulder in a half-shrug. "Can you blame me? I'm bedridden and my own son barely visits me. What is there to be cheerful about?"

"I visited you this morning, didn't I?"

"Only because I summoned you."

Griffin bit back a smile. "Well, you've summoned me again, and here I am." And before she could argue further, he reached over and took her by the hand. "Now, is there anything I can do for you? Fluff your pillows? Ring for more tea?"

She hesitated then nodded. "More tea would be nice," she said. "And...there is one other thing you can do for me."

Griffin rose to ring the bell for the maid. "Yes? What is it?"

He reclaimed his seat on the bed and his mother pursed her lips, a clear sign of danger to come. "With my injury, I will be laid up for some time," she said slowly. "And this means I will be unable to act as your sister's chaperone. Therefore, I will need you to take on the task until I am well again."

Griffin's brow knit. "What about Lady Augusta? Can she not escort her around?"

His mother's gaze was on the kitten, her fingers scratching her chin. "Lady Augusta will be too busy helping me. She feels responsible for my injury and no matter how hard I try, I cannot convince her otherwise. She practically begged me to let her care for me until I am well, and I felt I had no choice but to give in. I could see it was the only way to make her feel better. So, over the next few weeks, she will be here with me."

The kitten began to move about the coverlet, exploring her new surroundings with unabashed curiosity.

"Would you like me to speak with her?" Griffin asked. "Perhaps I can convince her to abandon the idea."

Lady Keswick shook her head. "I shouldn't bother if I were you. Her mind is quite made up."

"But surely it would be worth a try," he argued. "I can be rather persuasive when I try."

She smiled. "I know you can, darling, but not this time. Lady Augusta will not be persuaded."

"But—"

"Griffin, I am surprised at you," she scolded, her lips puckering. "It is such a little favor to ask, and I would think you would be happy to spend this time with your beloved sister."

Well, hell. There was simply no argument against that. "Very well," he said, suppressing a sigh. "I will do as you ask."

"Oh, splendid." Lady Keswick clapped her hands together, a smile gracing her lips. "Emmy was hoping to visit the shops tomorrow. I'll let her know you have agreed to take them."

Griffin stilled, a wisp of unease brushing his nape. "Them?"

She nodded, chuckling softly as the kitten attacked a loose thread on the coverlet. "Yes, I believe Olivia would like to go, as well."

A muscle ticked in his jaw. *Damn.* He could just about tolerate an afternoon at the shops with his sister, but Olivia Blakely was another matter entirely. *She* was insufferable.

He'd already promised to go, however, and he always kept his word, so he swallowed the argument on his tongue and gave his mother a tight smile instead. "Fine. I'll be here."

Lady Keswick patted him on the hand. "I knew I could count on you."

Griff huffed out an exasperated laugh. Guilt was a powerful weapon and Lady Lavinia Keswick brandished it like a master.

"Well," he said, rising to his feet, "I'm tired. I think I'll retire now." He leaned down and kissed his mother's forehead, catching the subtle scent of mint and rose water that never failed to comfort him.

"Sleep well, dear," she said. "And don't forget to take your kitten with you."

"She isn't my—" The words died the moment his gaze landed on the tiny ball of fluff trotting after him, her tiny paws silent on the coverlet. She looked up at him expectantly and his heart melted a little. A masculine sort of melting, of course.

With a resigned chuckle, he leaned down and scooped the kitten up before turning for the door. "Good night, Mother."

"Good night, darling."

Shutting the door softly behind him, Griffin paused in the corridor and glanced down at the purring little mongrel in his arms. He shook his head and sighed.

Damn, but he was a soft touch.

Chapter Three

"She's beginning to try my temper, Livvy," Lady Emmaline Keswick complained as she fell back against the pale green sofa cushion with a dramatic sigh. "If this goes on much longer, I'm afraid I might do something desperate."

Olivia chuckled softly from the seat beside her, mindful of the tiny kitten curled up on her lap, dozing like a sweet angel.

"You ought to be battle-hardened by now," she said, arching her brows at Emmy. "Your mother has been trying your temper for years."

"I know." Emmy frowned and brushed a dark curl from her cheek. "But I don't usually feel so guilty about it."

Olivia smothered a smile. She and Emmy were gathered in the warm, comfortably elegant drawing room at the Keswicks' townhouse, sharing a light repast of tea and scones before heading off to Bond Street to visit the shops, weather permitting. A light, late spring storm had blown in overnight, covering the sky with a flimsy quilt of clouds, portending a potentially drizzly day.

Emmy was not as fashion-minded as Olivia, but she hoped an afternoon out would help to lift her friend's spirits. At least it would provide a respite from her grumpy mother.

"Your mother's ankle will be good as new in a few weeks," she said, "and then you can go back to being irritated with her *sans* guilt like you're used to."

Emmy sighed. "I only hope I can last that long."

"I shall say a nightly prayer for you," Olivia teased, patting Emmy on the knee.

The kitten lifted her head, yawned adorably and with a smack of her lips, promptly went back to sleep.

"I should probably do the same for my aunt," Olivia mused aloud, stroking the kitten's fur. "Your mother is driving her mad, as well."

"Is she?" Emmy's head came up, her gray eyes alight with curiosity. "Why?"

Olivia's smile turned wry. "Because she's being too nice. Aunt Augusta feels awful about the accident, and I think she would feel better if Lady Keswick were angry with her, but instead she's being the soul of charity, and it's making my aunt feel worse. She thinks she's doing it on purpose."

Emmy snorted a laugh, her smile deepening the dimples in her cheeks. "Well, of course she's doing it on purpose. My mother is a very shrewd woman. She knows precisely what she's doing to your aunt."

Olivia blinked. "Goodness. I had no idea Lady Keswick was so devious."

"Well, I wouldn't go so far as that," Emmy said. "But I will own that she can be rather...*creative* when it comes to getting what she wants."

Olivia chuckled. The way Emmy spoke of her mother, one might almost believe she disliked the woman when, in fact, the opposite was true. Emmy adored Lady Keswick and the feeling was mutual. Although they were unalike in nearly every way, the love between them was genuine.

If not for Lady Keswick's determination to marry Emmy off and Emmy's total disinterest in cooperating, the two would probably be the best of friends.

Olivia couldn't help envying their relationship. It was by no means perfect, but it was a far cry better than the one Olivia shared with her father. At least Lady Keswick cared for her daughter. Would Olivia's mother have cared for her? Would the two of them share the same closeness Emmy shared with her mother? She liked to think they would but, of course, she would never know for sure.

"By the way," Emmy said, reaching out to pet the still-dozing kitten, "how was your drive with the duke yesterday? Has the idiot proposed to you yet?"

Olivia's lips pursed at the insult—*the idiot* was the man she hoped to marry, after all—but she didn't bother to scold. Emmy was only trying to be supportive, in her own brash way.

"No," she said with a sigh. "Not yet. We had a lovely time, though, and at one point I'm certain he would have kissed me if we'd been alone. Even Nellie noticed it."

"And you would have let him kiss you? If you had been alone?"

Olivia notched her head to one side. "What an odd question. Of course I would have let him. If a handsome duke tried to steal a kiss from you, wouldn't you let him?"

Emmy shrugged. "I've never been tempted to do so before."

"Really? Not once?"

Emmy shook her head. "Not that a duke has ever tried to kiss me, of course. But other men have, and I've always declined."

"Why?" Olivia couldn't fathom being three-and-twenty and still unkissed. Kissing was one of life's greatest pleasures, so far as she was concerned.

"I didn't see the point, I suppose," Emmy said. "I cared nothing for any of them, and if I didn't feel anything before kissing them, why should I feel anything after?"

Further proof that Emmy had never been kissed. In Olivia's experience, kissing was about giving pleasure as much as receiving it. She liked kissing, and being desired, knowing her kiss brought pleasure to the gentleman in her arms. Perhaps this made her wicked, but she'd accepted long ago that she was no angel.

"Well," Olivia said, "perhaps you simply haven't met the right gentleman yet. When you do, I'm certain you will feel differently about kissing him."

Emmy's nose wrinkled. "Maybe," she said. "But he will have to be someone truly spectacular."

Olivia nodded. "Like Paxton."

A peculiar noise sounded in the back of Emmy's throat, and then her gaze fell to her lap, and she began plucking at the lace overlay of her skirts as an unusually fraught silence fell over the room.

Olivia frowned down at the top of Emmy's head. "What was that noise?" she demanded.

Emmy's gaze met hers, innocence personified. "Hm? What noise?"

"The noise you made with your throat," Olivia said, throwing her a pointed look. "It is obvious there is something you wish to say, Em, so say it."

Emmy shook her head. "It's nothing. Really."

"Come on. Out with it."

Emmy's gaze turned wary, and she pressed her lips together, finally huffing out a breath. "Oh, all right. If you insist." She clasped her hands in her lap. "You know I have nothing against the Duke of Paxton. He is a decent man with impeccable manners and an unimpeachable family line, but, well..." She frowned. "Don't you think he is just a little too...nice?"

Olivia's brows shot up. "Too *nice?*"

The sharpness in her words roused the kitten from her nap, and Olivia stroked her fur in apology. "What do you mean, he's too nice?"

Emmy pursed her lips. "He's always smiling, always spouting off compliments and waxing optimistic. It's too much."

"It is *not* too much."

"Well, it is for me."

Annoyance had Olivia's lips dipping into a frown. "Well, you are not going to marry him. I am. And I don't think he's *too* anything. I like his optimism, and I am certain we will share a long and happy marriage together."

Just as soon as he asks me.

"I hope you're right, Livvy."

"I am," she said firmly. "I know I am."

25

Emmy nibbled her lower lip, her eyes shadowed with concern. "I know you have your heart set on marrying the duke, but time is not exactly on your side and, well, I'm worried you might be putting all your eggs in one basket."

Olivia's stomach clenched, but she would not give credence to Emmy's fears. Even if they mirrored her own. "It's true, Paxton has not proposed marriage to me yet, but I know he wants to. And he will. I'm certain of it."

"But if he doesn't—"

"He will."

"But *if he doesn't*," Emmy said, holding up her hands. "If he should—I don't know—suddenly fall ill and die, what will you do? Have you an alternative option? Another gentleman waiting in the wings?"

"I don't need an alternative option," Olivia insisted. "Nothing is going to happen to Paxton. He *will* offer for me, and I *will* marry him."

She had to. She *must*.

"There are other men, Livvy," Emmy said, her voice tinged with exasperation. "Men who are just as handsome, just as charming, just as rich."

Olivia sighed. "But there is only one duke."

And it had to be a duke. Only a duke would do. Marrying well—marrying *the best*—was the only way she could make her father proud of her. She'd already tried everything else; excelling at her studies, mastering the pianoforte, mastering everything, and none of it had worked. Her father barely knew she existed.

Perhaps he would never care to know her better, perhaps he would always resent her for her mother's death, but she would never stop trying to curry his favor. She couldn't help it. He was her only parent, and she wanted his love. She wanted him to be proud of her and, as a woman, there were very few ways in which to achieve this. Marriage was just about the only avenue left to her, and she intended to use it.

"*Meow.*"

The tiny squeak broke into the tense silence, and Olivia smiled as the kitten clumsily leapt from her lap to the floor and stretched her limbs with a lusty yawn.

"She is so darling," Olivia said, as the little ball of black fluff flopped onto the floor and began chewing on her paw. "What on earth possessed your brother to bring a kitten home?"

Emmy shook her head. "I really don't know. He says he found her and thought to give her to me and Mother for a pet."

Olivia's brows dipped. "He found her? Where?"

Emmy popped a bite of buttered scone into her mouth and shrugged. "On the street, apparently."

"Hm." Olivia looked down at the kitten, now playing hopscotch on the patterned Persian rug. "It is difficult to picture your brother in the role of savior. Even for a tiny, helpless kitten."

"But, of course, I only saved the thing so I could fatten it up and eat it."

Her head snapped up at the sound of Griffin's droll voice, and she watched him, her pulse thrumming, as he strolled into the room with confident ease. Her cheeks warmed as her eyes met his, dark gray, beautiful. Mocking.

Always mocking.

"Good afternoon, Olivia," he said, the words polite, even as his eyes teased.

Her toes curled in her striped satin slippers, and she sniffed, her gaze falling to her lap as she brushed at the fur clinging to her skirts. "Griffin."

Her mind whirled and her heart leaped, as it often did when Griffin was near, and she mentally admonished the fact that she'd just been caught talking about him. It didn't matter that what she'd said had hardly been complimentary. She worked hard at making him think she didn't speak of him, or even *think* of him, and the dratted man had caught her doing just that.

"And good afternoon to you, too," Griffin said to the kitten as she trotted across the carpet to greet him.

He scooped her up into his arms, his smile affectionate, his eyes soft, and Olivia's heart practically melted into a puddle on the floor.

The man was far too handsome for his own good. Certainly too handsome to ignore, no matter how hard she tried. Her gaze flicked over him. Dark hair cut short, broad shoulders, strong thighs. Distractingly large hands.

He wore a dark gray coat and burgundy cravat over black trousers and boots. The image of the perfect marquess, ruggedly elegant, effortlessly assured. Entirely irresistible.

Olivia swallowed and looked away, her lips thinning. Drat it all, she wasn't supposed to melt over him. Not anymore. Not after what happened last December when she'd humiliated herself before him at the Stevensons' Christmastide house party, when he'd called her a silly, spoiled brat.

Not after he took such care to show me how little he thinks of me.

"Are you two ladies ready to leave?" Griffin asked, and Olivia looked at him, confusion crinkling her brow.

"I am," Emmy said, pushing off the sofa and smoothing the wrinkles from her pale peach gown. "Are you ready, Livvy?"

Olivia slowly rose to her feet, her perplexed gaze on Emmy's face. "I am, but what..."

Emmy gave her a wide smile. "My mother asked Griffin to be our escort during her recovery," she said cheerfully. "And he agreed. Wasn't that sweet of him?"

Olivia looked at Griffin and found him watching her, absentmindedly scratching the kitten's ear as a smile tugged at his lips.

"Oh, yes," she said faintly. "Very sweet, indeed."

And very, very unwelcome.

"SHALL WE, LADIES?" GRIFFIN swept his kitten-free arm toward the door, eager to leave and get this deuced outing over with as quickly as possible.

Emmy gave the kitten's ears a scratch before heading for the door, humming to herself. Olivia followed, tugging on her as she glided past Griffin, a serene smile pasted to her lips, her blue gaze resolutely avoiding his.

He sighed. She didn't want him here, just as he knew she wouldn't. And though she tried to hide it, he'd caught the brittle edge to her smile.

Too bad, sweetheart. You're stuck with me, just as I'm stuck with you.

He followed after her and made his way into the corridor, the scent of jasmine and the subtle sway of luscious hips threatening to annihilate his peace of mind.

Ignore her.

Admittedly, ignoring Olivia Blakely was not an easy thing to do, but neither was it impossible. He'd had plenty of practice these last two years, ever since he'd realized how beautiful she was. On the outside, at least.

He was there the night she made her debut, just eighteen years old, looking quite different from how he'd remembered her. Elegant and mature with her blond curls swept up and her pink satin dress accentuating womanly curves he'd never seen before. Or, at least, never noticed before.

The first lick of desire low in his belly had caught him totally unaware, and he'd shifted on his feet, uncomfortable with the idea of lusting after little Olivia Blakely, the girl he'd known since she was eight years old. His sister's longtime friend. She'd never been anything more than that.

Until that night.

He'd watched her all evening, a blonde goddess surrounded by slavering admirers, all of them hungry for her attention. He'd been hungry for it, too, but he'd kept his distance. She was beautiful, yes, and she knew it. She reveled in the attention she received, teasing and toying with every man in her orbit, though none were good enough for her. Countless proposals, countless rejections.

Olivia, his sister's sweet little friend, had grown up, and grew into a shallow, title-chasing flirt.

"Have you named the kitten yet, Griff?" Emmy asked over her shoulder, interrupting his reverie as the group made their way into the entrance hall.

He cleared his throat and shoved all thoughts of that long ago night from his mind. "I haven't," he said. "I thought I would leave that to you and Mother."

"But she's your cat," Emmy pointed out, turning to face him with raised brows.

Olivia stood a short distance behind her, busily situating her velvet cloak around her shoulders.

"She is not my cat," he returned. "I brought her home for you."

Emmy smiled. "Be that as it may, she likes you best. She *chose* you. Therefore, she is your cat, and you should be the one to name her."

Griffin frowned and glanced down at the kitten in his arms. "But I wouldn't know what to name her. I've never named anything before."

Emmy threw him a speaking glance, clearly disappointed in him. "It is hardly a monumental decision. If you name her something awful, she won't care. She won't even know."

Griff hesitated, unsure exactly why he was so reluctant to give her a name. She was only a kitten, after all. Hardly a life-altering commitment. Still...

"Oh, very well," Emmy said, throwing her hands out. "I shall name her. Let's see..." She scrunched up her nose and eyed the kitten thoughtfully. "What about...Pudding? Or Pumpkin? Parsnip? Persimmon? No, no, I have it! *Princess Plum Cake.*"

"Oh, I like that last one," Olivia said, her lips trembling with mirth.

She would choose now *to speak.*

Griffin scowled. "Don't be absurd," he said. "That isn't even a real name."

Emmy shrugged. "If you don't like it, I suppose you'll have to name her yourself."

Griff sighed and looked down at the kitten's furry face. She returned his gaze, her yellow eyes bright with mischief, and then one eye winked, reminding him of a flickering star in a sky black as night.

"Artemis," he said promptly.

The kitten mewled, as if affirming his choice, and Griffin smiled. "Yes. Artemis."

"Artemis?" Emmy notched her head to one side, considering the name. "Artie. Yes, I like it."

Griffin shot her a stern frown. "No, not Artie," he said. "*Artemis.* A strong name befitting the feline goddess of the hunt."

The feline goddess in question chose that moment to grip her tail between all four paws and gnaw on it as if it were a furry sausage.

"Goodness me," Emmy said, her voice dry as dust. "You had best arm yourself, Livvy. A fierce and terrifying predator walks among us."

"Fiercely and terrifyingly adorable, you mean," Olivia quipped, her gaze on Artemis, a soft smile curving her plump, wine-red lips.

Forcing his gaze from that irritating smile, Griffin turned to Winters, who hovered near the front door. "Take Artemis to my mother's rooms," he instructed. "Thank you, Winters."

With a bow, the butler collected the kitten and carried her from the room.

"Shall we, then?" Emmy asked, pulling on her pelisse as she headed for the door. "Where shall we go first? I know we need to visit the plumassier for your costume, Livvy, but should we stop at Madame Adelasia's first?"

"Yes, let's," Olivia said, following her out the front door. "Her shop is on the way, and I would like to see if any new earrings have arrived. I still need to find the perfect pair to go with my costume."

Emmy nodded. "And I need a pair of red gloves to go with mine."

Grabbing his beaver hat from the coat rack, he donned it and followed the two chattering ladies down the front steps toward their awaiting carriage. He inhaled deeply, willing the damp spring air to clear his thoughts, and cleanse the scent of jasmine from his addled senses.

"Have you chosen a character yet, Griff?" Emmy asked once the trio were settled and the carriage had set off, Olivia and Emmy seated side by side on the bench opposite his.

"Character?" he asked, crossing one leg over the other. "For what?"

Emmy threw him a frown. "For Lady Henley's costume ball, of course. It is next week."

Griffin shook his head. "I don't do costume balls."

"Well, you will be attending this one," she replied crisply. "You are to act as my escort. Remember?"

Bloody, bleeding hell.

Olivia's head dipped and she appeared to be fighting a smile, almost as if she'd read his mind. Or perhaps she'd simply read his expression.

He cleared the frown from his lips and turned to the window, looping his hand through the leather strap attached to the upholstered wall beside him. He gazed out at the passing carriages and strolling pedestrians, though he barely noticed the view as images of costume balls and musical soirées and God only knew what else flashed through his mind. *Bloody sprained ankle.*

"I cannot wait to see everyone's costumes this year," Emmy said, clacking her heeled slippers on the carriage floor. "There are sure to be some excellent efforts. Lydia Tuttenham told me last night that George Milton will be in attendance and apparently, he has a real treat in store for us." She chuckled. "Although, I cannot imagine he will be able to best his wolf in sheep's clothing costume from last year's ball."

Olivia groaned. "I had forgotten all about that night."

"It was rather a clever creation," Emmy said, still chuckling, "but I don't think he considered how warm it would be, poor man."

"Well, I say he deserved every miserable moment," Olivia said with a sniff.

Griffin raised a brow, curious despite himself. Olivia wasn't usually so mean-spirited. He held his tongue, though, and continued his feigned interest in the passing scenery.

"Oh, let it go, Livvy," Emmy said, her tone more than a little exasperated. "It's been nearly a year! I can't believe you are still sore with him after all this time."

"Let it go?" Olivia scoffed. "The man proposed marriage to me that night, Em! And when I asked him how I could possibly agree to marry a man with a large, red tongue hanging down the middle of his face, he behaved like a petulant child and called *my* costume boring."

Griffin couldn't help himself. He turned from the window and looked at Olivia, who was gaping at his sister, her color high, her full lips parted in indignation. *Gorgeous*, he thought. *Even with her bristles up.*

"To be fair," Emmy countered, "you had just rejected the man's proposal."

Olivia sniffed. "That is no excuse for such ungentlemanly behavior."

"I'd wager his behavior would have been less offensive to you if he'd been a rich duke," Griffin drawled before he could stop himself.

Olivia's bright blue eyes met his, and he caught the barest flash of emotion there—indignation? hurt?—before her expression cleared. "Well, of course it would," she said brightly. "One can forgive almost anything for a duke. Isn't that right, Em?"

"Er, well…" Emmy shifted uncomfortably in her seat.

"If only there were more of them to go around," Olivia went on, her voice mournful now. "Alas, single dukes are in tragically short supply these days. It almost renders the lesser titles more appealing." She shot Griffin a treacle-sweet smile. "*Almost.*"

Arching a brow in reply, he said nothing, fighting the urge to laugh. She irritated the hell out of him, but she amused him, too. Always had. Spending time with Olivia Blakely could give a man whiplash.

The carriage rolled to a stop in front of Madame Adelasia's shop, and a moment later the door swung open. Olivia exited first, her head high, her back ramrod straight, coolly regal in her snow-white gown as she descended the steps with the assistance of a liveried footman.

Griffin looked at Emmy, expecting her to follow suit, but instead he found her watching him. Her gray eyes, so like his own, teemed with a mixture of exasperation and curiosity.

"What?" he asked, his tone more defensive than he'd intended.

"Why do you say things like that to her?" she asked, her voice low. "You never behave that way with anyone else. I don't understand it."

Griff grunted, resisting the urge to tug at his cravat. "She's hardly an innocent lamb. She insults me every chance she gets."

"True," Emmy said, nodding. "But her insults are nearly always provoked. The same cannot be said for you."

She exited the carriage then, leaving him with the echo of her words, unwelcome but undeniably accurate. He did provoke Olivia and, worse, he enjoyed doing it. He'd like to pretend he didn't understand the reason why, but he knew damn well what it was.

Olivia Blakely was a frivolous, spoiled, title-chasing flirt and he did not like her.

But that didn't stop him from wanting her.

He hated himself for the weakness, hated that he couldn't eradicate the feeling, that no amount of reasoning or self-admonishment could kill the attraction. He'd tried it all and still he wanted her.

Disgust soured his belly and, with gritted teeth, he stepped down from the carriage and headed toward the shop, his steps clipped and impatient.

Ignoring her used to be easier, he thought as he pushed the shop door open. Before December, before the Stevensons' Christmastide ball where a tipsy Olivia had found him in the library and angled for a kiss beneath the mistletoe. He thought of the mischievous twinkle in her bright blue eyes, the shy, sweetly seductive smile curving her generous lips. How tempted he'd been to say yes, to give her what she wanted—what he'd wanted, too.

Thank Christ he'd come to his senses in time.

And that was why he pushed her buttons, wasn't it? Because if he could keep her at arm's length, and make her believe he found her company undesirable, she would be less likely to turn her considerable charms on him. Charms he knew he would be powerless to resist. He had no defense for them, and he knew it.

He thought of that sweet, tipsy smile again and his gut clenched. And then he remembered his cutting words, and the way her smile had withered on a mortified gasp.

It was for the best, of course.

But he wasn't proud of it.

CHAPTER FOUR

Madame Adelasia's Fashion Boutique was small yet tidy and always busy, and today was no exception. With its variety of unique goods from bonnets and parasols to incense and rouge, the shop was highly favored amongst the fashionable ladies of the *ton*.

Standing before the giltwood mirror in an empty corner of the noisy shop, Olivia turned her head this way and that, admiring the bonnet's little pink bows and delicate lace trim.

It was frilly and feminine, a decadent pink concoction that would pair beautifully with her silk slippers with the pink and white stripes. A covetous sigh escaped her lips. She wanted it.

She'd always loved pink, ever since she was a little girl, though she'd worn very little of it this Season. Paxton preferred her in blue, so she wore blue. Lots and lots of blue.

Not that he'd asked her to, of course. The duke seemed to admire her no matter what she wore, but when a girl was attempting to snare a husband, she must use every weapon in her arsenal.

Men were visual creatures. They liked to look at beauty, liked knowing the effort was made for them.

Olivia knew she was pretty. Or, rather, she knew men found her pretty. She'd heard more than enough odes to her beauty over the years to understand there was something about her that men found pleasing to the eye, something that blinded them to her faults.

Yes, she was blessed with a creamy complexion and large, blue eyes. A pleasing figure, full lips, a dainty nose.

An English rose, or so she'd been called.

But she'd also been gifted crooked front teeth, too-pale eyebrows, and one ear that stuck out a fraction more than the other, which she carefully masked with a strategically-pinned curl. Of course, not one of these features had ever found its way into a sonnet.

Men—most of them, at least—seemed to notice only the picture as a whole, missing the details.

How like her to fall in love with one of the few who missed nothing.

Olivia pulled a face, and the looking glass caught it, reflecting it back to her. She was *not* in love with Griffin. At least, not anymore. Not ever, really.

Oh, she thought she was once, for a little while, but she'd realized soon enough it was nothing more than a girlish infatuation, and only a fool would love a man who did not feel the same. Olivia was no fool.

Still, there is no denying he is a handsome man, she thought, catching sight of him in the mirror. He stood some distance behind her, staring out at the street with his hands clasped behind his back, his strong jaw and big, powerful body illuminated by the muted sunlight streaming in through the windows.

Her heart stuttered. While she'd vowed never to pine over him again, she hadn't quite managed to eradicate his effect on her. Not completely. The sight of him still made her pulse skip and when he smiled at her—or at a kitten, apparently—her knees weakened. But only a little.

His new role as Emmy's chaperone was an unforeseen and wholly unwelcome surprise, but there was no reason for her to lose her head over it. She could behave normally—*would* behave normally—as if this was nothing but a routine shopping trip with Emmy. She needn't speak to Griffin. Indeed, she would pretend he wasn't even there.

And she would definitely pretend she hadn't embarrassed herself before him last Christmas. The incident—that moment of utter madness—never should have happened, but it had, and there was nothing she could do about it now except pretend she'd forgotten all about it and hope Griffin would continue to do the same.

"That's a pretty bonnet," Emmy said, coming up behind Olivia and eyeing her reflection in the glass. "Will you buy it?"

"I don't know," Olivia said. "Perhaps." She turned to face Emmy and lowered her voice. "Why didn't you warn me that your brother would be our escort today?"

Emmy had the grace to look mildly ashamed of herself. "Because I knew if I told you, you wouldn't come."

"Yes, I would."

Emmy raised a brow.

"Probably." *Maybe.*

"Well, I thought it best if you had no choice in the matter," Emmy said, glancing at the front of the shop where her brother still stood. "You'll have to get used to being around Griffin again someday. You might as well start now."

Olivia turned to face the mirror again, biting back a frown. Get used to it? *Impossible.* But she knew Emmy was right. She would have to try. She would have to accept the fact that he disliked her, and ignore it, and refuse to allow his disregard to injure her any further.

She would be a duchess soon, after all, the wife of a powerful duke. What did she care what a mere marquess thought of her?

From now on, she would simply be herself. Silly, spoiled, flirtatious—unabashedly herself. Perhaps even obnoxiously, if the mood should strike.

Plan set, she shoved Griffin from her mind and studied the bonnet again with a critical eye. "Do you think this bonnet suits me?" she asked Emmy. "You don't think it's a touch too...frilly?"

She adored the bonnet, but even she had to acknowledge that frills could be overdone.

Emmy cocked her head to one side, studying Olivia's reflection. "No, I don't," she said. "But perhaps we need a third opinion. A male one."

Before Olivia could stop her, Emmy turned and called out Griffin's name, beckoning him over.

"Emmy, no," Olivia hissed. "That isn't necessary—"

But it was too late. Griffin was already walking over to them, his gaze on his sister. Olivia drew in a breath and turned, clasping her hands at her front.

"What do you think of this bonnet?" Emmy asked him. "I think it is lovely. Simply perfect for a drive through the park with a certain gentleman caller, but Olivia isn't so sure. What do you think?"

Griffin's gaze flicked from Emmy to the bonnet to Olivia's face, and she could feel her cheeks warming beneath his perusal. The seconds felt like hours as he considered his answer, and suddenly, the weight of the moment grew uncomfortable, and the thought of hearing his opinion was simply too much to bear.

She could not stand another of his veiled insults or, worse, an insincere compliment.

"I have no need for your brother's opinion," she said lightly as she removed the bonnet and returned it to its perch. "He and the duke have vastly different tastes, after all." She set about securing the ribbons of her own bonnet, avoiding Griffin's gaze.

"And besides," he said, his deep voice laced with amusement, "if I said I liked the bonnet, she wouldn't want it, and if I said I didn't, she would."

Olivia clucked her tongue and forced a serene smile. "Don't be silly. That would suggest your opinion matters to me and, I assure you, it does not."

The bell on the door gave a pleasant jangle, interrupting the moment, and two women walked into the shop, one older, the other a younger version, clearly mother and daughter.

"It's Miss Stanhope and her mother," Emmy said, heading off to greet them. "Miss Stanhope! What a beautiful shawl. You must tell me where it came from."

Olivia watched as Emmy joined the ladies, well aware she ought to do the same, but she was too aggravated for social niceties.

Ignoring the infuriating man at her side, she stepped around him and wandered over to the display case of earrings, irritation thrumming through her veins.

No one tested her patience like Griffin. No one. And no matter what she did or how hard she tried, she seemed incapable of containing her temper with him.

Dratted man.

She knew he thought very little of her, but why did he have to be so rude? Why did he derive such pleasure from mocking her, and provoking her temper?

Could he not simply suffer her presence in silence?

She stared at a pair of earrings with unseeing eyes and blew out a frustrated breath. He'd called her a silly, spoiled flirt, and maybe he was right, but surely she wasn't the only silly, spoiled flirt in London.

So why did he dislike her so much?

When she was a little girl, he'd tolerated her as his younger sister's little friend, and she'd been fine with that. He'd ignored her more often than not, but he was never mean. It wasn't until she made her debut that his behavior changed toward her, as if he sensed her budding attraction for him and sought to repel it.

A peal of giggles drew her gaze to the center of the shop where Emmy stood chatting with Miss Stanhope and her mother. Griffin had joined the group, though she knew him well enough to recognize that he didn't want to be there. His smile was tight, likely due to the fact that Miss Stanhope was flirting with him, her smile coy, her eyes coquettish. Griffin shifted on his feet.

With a soft chortle, Olivia turned back to the display case, pleased as punch to see him suffering so. Petty, perhaps, but she didn't care. *Just add it to my long list of transgressions.*

Shoving Griffin from her mind yet again, she studied the display of earrings, searching for a pair that would complement her costume, something in deep blue or bright green.

A slash of scarlet caught her eye, a stunning pair of earrings with gems of bright red, violet and orange intertwined like flames. She stroked one with the tip of her gloved finger, her eyes transfixed on the work of art. They were bold and daring and gorgeous. She adored them.

But Paxton liked her best in blue. Indecision warred within her.

"Those are pretty."

Olivia stiffened at the intrusion, Griffin's low voice invading her space. "Yes, they are," she murmured, her tone impassive even as awareness skittered up her spine.

He was close, *too* close, his arm scant inches from hers, and the warmth of him, the scent of him—sugared almonds and bergamot—seemed to be everywhere.

He reached out, his forearm brushing hers, and though it was only their sleeves that touched, she felt it all the way to her toes.

"I like the purple pair, too," he said. "They would make your eyes shine even brighter, I think."

She blinked, captivated by the sight of his gloved fingers skating over the amethyst beads like a caress. *A compliment from the Marquess of Keswick?* Surely she was dreaming.

Bemused, she looked at him, wary of what she might find in those dark gray eyes of his, but for once there was no mockery, no judgment.

"Thank you," she said softly. "I—"

Another peal of giggles erupted behind them, and Olivia turned at the sound, peering over her shoulder in time to catch Miss Stanhope sneaking a glance at Griffin with covetous eyes. Her gaze snapped to Olivia's and her lips thinned before she looked away, her nose in the air.

Ah. There it is. The reason for the anomalous compliment.

"You've found yourself a new admirer, I see," she said crisply, turning back to gaze at the earrings again. "Is that why you're here, paying me false compliments? You're hiding from the girl?"

She shot him a sidelong glance, masking the hurt behind an amused smile. Griffin's gaze met hers then dipped to her mouth and lingered for a beat before falling to the display case.

"Gentlemen do not hide," he corrected. "We *evade.*" His tone was light, though his voice had deepened to gravel.

"Oh, yes. Of course." Olivia nodded with faux solemnity. "How silly of me."

Absently, she reached out and systematically straightened the row of earrings with her forefinger until they all fell in line like good little soldiers.

Another burst of female laughter trumpeted behind them, startling her, and she snorted a laugh, her shoulders shaking with suppressed mirth.

"It isn't funny," Griffin grumbled.

"Oh, but it is," she said through trembling lips. "I feel as though I've walked into the middle of a mating ritual."

A muscle ticked in his jaw. "This is why I avoid places like this. It isn't safe for me here, with all these women around, falling at my feet."

Olivia shot him a dubious look. "Falling at your feet?"

He shrugged. "Practically."

She huffed out a laugh. "Well, you can hardly blame the girl for trying to catch you," she said. "You are single, after all, and—"

"And devastatingly charming? Dangerously handsome?" His half-smile was both in spades, but Olivia ignored it and rolled her eyes.

"Deliriously rich, then," Griffin offered.

She smirked. "I was going to say a marquess."

He cocked his head to one side, his gaze quizzical. "Meaning what? That women wouldn't want me as much if I weren't a marquess?"

"No," she said cheerfully. "Meaning, they wouldn't want you at all."

A reluctant smile tugged at the corners of Griffin's mouth, and Olivia couldn't help herself. She smiled back at him. Their gazes held for a moment, and she allowed herself the luxury of admiring his eyes, stormy gray, mischievous, arrogant. Wholly irresistible.

Resist.

She turned from him, her heart thudding in her chest, ridiculously affected by the man beside her, despite his opinion of her. His rejection of her. *Fool.*

Drawing in a slow, brain-clearing breath, she moved farther down the long table of goods, past the earrings and gloves until she came to the display of hand-painted silk fans nestled into one corner. She paused to admire the colorful assortment of butterflies and blossoms and seascapes, each design unique and expertly painted, and so beautiful people traveled from all over England to buy one.

Olivia treasured her own, a jungle forest of vivid reds and purples and greens. Perhaps she should treat herself to another.

"I'll have you know," Griffin said, coming up beside her. "My company is highly sought after. I'm told I make a charming companion."

His voice was low but light, his big body dwarfing the already crowded space and self-preservation had her shifting away from him, as far as the little corner would allow.

"Are you, indeed?" she asked mildly, picking up a fan painted with purple pansies. "I wouldn't know. You've certainly never tried to charm me."

He cocked his head to one side, slipping his hands in his pockets. "Would you want me to?"

Yes.

The word teetered on the tip of her tongue, but she swallowed it whole. And then she lied. "Of course not," she said, studying the fan with feigned interest. "And, anyway, it would be an exercise in futility. I am immune to your charms."

She could feel his eyes on her, a whisper of awareness prickling at the nape of her neck, and she forced her chin up to meet his gaze.

He arched one brow and a smile toyed with the corners of his lips as his gaze dipped to her mouth. "I think we both know that isn't true, Olivia."

She stiffened as his meaning sank in, and embarrassment followed, flooding her face with heat. He was thinking of last December, of her moment of weakness beneath the mistletoe, and was using it against her. *Awful man.*

"Pardon me," she said faintly, her throat suddenly very dry. "I need to look at the earrings again. The blue ones. Paxton is sure to adore them. He does like to see me in blue."

She brushed past him, biting her tongue lest it try to run away from her completely.

Her skin prickled beneath the weight of his stare, delving, distracting, and more than a little perplexing. Just like the man.

She reached the earrings display and, with her head down, inhaled a deep, calming breath. Being around Griffin should not be this difficult. All she had to do was act as if he meant nothing to her, as if everything was as it used to be, but all it took was one allusion to that night in December and her composure crumbled like dried rose petals.

Avoidance. That was the answer. She must avoid him as much as possible. Speak only when spoken to, display nothing but cordiality, and *avoid, avoid, avoid.*

How difficult could it possibly be?

CHAPTER FIVE

"VISCOUNT AMBERSON IS CERTAINLY a fine example of the male species," Aunt Augusta said the following afternoon, her walking stick crunching with each step on the sanded footpath. "Handsome face. Strong shoulders. Firm rump."

Olivia choked on a laugh, even as her gaze dipped of its own accord to the retreating man's posterior.

She and her aunt had ventured into Hyde Park and were strolling along the sunny, tree-lined footpath bordering Rotten Row when they came upon Lord Amberson and his two younger sisters. Olivia had danced with the gentleman a handful of times and found his company pleasant, if a bit pedantic.

Her aunt was right about his rump, though. It did look firm, even from beneath the folds of his morning coat.

"You shouldn't say such things, even if they're true," Olivia said with a smile. "He's a man, not a horse on the auction block."

"Oh, tosh." Aunt Augusta waved her free hand in the air, her sleeve a slash of ruby red velvet. "It amounts to much the same thing, doesn't it? He is a man on the marriage mart." She raised a brow at Olivia. "He admires you. I could tell."

Olivia lifted a shoulder, her gaze falling to her feet as she kicked a pebble out of her path. "Perhaps he does."

"He would make you a fine husband, I think."

"I'm certain he would," Olivia said. "But I've already chosen the man I will marry."

A beat of silence passed between them, and then, in a quiet voice, her aunt said, "But has he chosen you?"

Olivia's head came up and her lips parted as if to leap to Paxton's defense, but no words came. She turned her gaze to the bridle path and passed unseeing eyes over the assemblage of men and women on horse-back, her chest suddenly tight.

"The Duke of Paxton is a fine man, my dear," Aunt Augusta continued. "And I know you've made up your mind to marry him, but...is that truly what your heart wants? Are you certain he is the man you wish to share your life with?"

Olivia's nod was instant. "Of course. Paxton is sweet and thoughtful and will provide well for me. He is precisely the sort of man I wish to marry."

"That isn't what I asked, dearest."

Olivia pressed her lips together. She knew it wasn't, just as she knew her answer was not the one her aunt had wanted to hear, but it was an honest one. Mostly.

"The duke is precisely the sort of man most women would like to marry," Aunt Augusta said. "He is everything you said, and rich to boot. But, Olivia..." Her steps slowed and she pulled Olivia to a stop in the middle of the path, turning to meet her gaze. "If Paxton wasn't a duke, would you still want to marry him?"

Olivia shifted on her feet, uncomfortable beneath the weight of her aunt's assessing hazel eyes. She had no idea what to say. The truth was, she didn't know the answer, and she wasn't certain she wanted to. But admitting that to herself and admitting it out loud to her aunt were two very different things.

"What do you think of the man behind the title? Do you like him? Do you care for him?" Aunt Augusta's voice was quiet but firm. "Can he make you happy, Olivia?"

The barrage of questions pelted her like stones, and she swallowed hard, searching for her voice. "I am...fond of the duke," she answered stiffly. "I hold him in the highest esteem."

"But you do not love him."

It was not a question. Indeed, it felt more like an accusation, and Olivia stiffened as hurt and indignation swept over her.

"What does love matter?" she demanded, the words quiet but sharp. "Many marriages are loveless yet still happy and successful. Including yours."

She cast a glance around, careful to keep her expression serene. An argument would not go unnoticed on Rotten Row.

"That is true," Aunt Augusta said with a nod. "But I was never a romantic. Not like you."

Olivia's lips pressed into an unhappy line. She had no defense for that. Her aunt was right. She was a romantic and always would be. But any chance she'd had at love was lost to her now, and wishing for it would be nothing but an exercise in futility.

The realities of life were not always kind, and sometimes they left no room for dreams of love.

"Why are you speaking of this now?" she asked her aunt. "You've never done so before. What has changed?" She'd softened her tone, but she could not mask her frustration completely.

Aunt Augusta's marriage had been arranged by her parents, and although it was not a love match, she spoke of her late husband with affection. By all accounts, she was content in her loveless marriage, and had always seemed perfectly happy to accept the same for her nieces. Until now.

"I suppose I'm getting soft in my old age," Aunt Augusta said with a rueful sigh. "Seeing how happy your cousin is in her marriage to Dearborn, and how much they love each other..." She trailed off, twisting the tip of her walking stick into the sanded path. "I can't help but hope for the same for you."

Longing, sharp and poignant, gripped Olivia's heart until her chest ached with it. "What happened between Sophie and James is wonderful, and I am very happy for them," she said, forcing a small smile. "But their love is a rarity, a happy accident. A *miracle*, really. And miracles are scarce."

Aunt Augusta's eyes softened. "I disagree. I believe miracles happen every day."

Olivia lifted a shoulder, working to keep her smile in place. "For other people, perhaps. But not for me. And so"—her tone brightened—"if I am lucky enough to receive a proposal of marriage from the duke, I shall accept it, and spend the rest of my days as England's most grateful duchess."

Aunt Augusta smiled and, though it was a little sad, she said no more on the subject and the two resumed their stroll up the path.

Olivia drew in a breath, relieved to quit the conversation. It was a lovely day and she wanted to enjoy it. Shoving all thoughts of love and miracles from her mind, she focused on the warm spring sunshine, the scent of wet grass, the breeze brushing her skirts against her legs.

The path ahead was crowded, teeming with the top hats and twirling parasols of lords and ladies dressed in their finest, all out to see and be seen.

A young couple caught her eye, the lady's arm looped through his, their heads bent together in conversation, clearly very much in love.

The lady's bright green shawl suddenly slipped free of her shoulders and took to the skies, a jungle bird in the middle of London. The winds were temperamental today, calm one moment and the next whipping trees and skirts around like flags on Naval ships.

The lady's escort took off after the escaped garment, narrowly missing it not once but twice before finally snatching it up in his fist. He carried the shawl back to his lady, draping it around her shoulders, lingering over the task as if he cherished her, as if he couldn't help but keep her close to him.

Envy knifed through Olivia. She wanted that for herself. She wanted a husband who would look at her like that, who adored her for her, a man who would walk the streets of London with his hand curled protectively over hers, a man who would chase down her favorite shawl on a blustery London afternoon.

The image floated through her mind, of a strong, strapping gentleman walking toward her, a tender, sheepish smile curving his lips...and she realized it was Griff's smile she had conjured, Griff's gray eyes gazing at her so lovingly.

"Idiot," she muttered to herself, dropping her gaze to the ground at her feet.

"Did you say something, dearest?" Aunt Augusta asked.

"No, it was nothing, Auntie."

She tipped her head back, letting the sun touch her face for a moment, as if it might burn away Griffin's image from her mind. Why did she still harbor these feelings for him? Why could she not let them go and forget him?

The idea that the Marquess of Keswick might bestow such a smile on her was absurd. More than absurd. It was *impossible*.

He didn't even like her, for pity's sake.

The duke, on the other hand, did. He liked her very much, in fact, and she was rather fond of him, as well. And why shouldn't she be? He was young and rich and sweet. And rather handsome, too, with his auburn hair and warm brown eyes.

A comforting warmth settled over her as her aunt's earlier question flashed in her mind. Yes, she thought, the Duke of Paxton was *precisely* the sort of man with whom she wished to share her life. Even if she didn't love him.

Love was an indulgence, a luxury only those with time could afford to seek. And time was one thing Olivia did not have.

CHAPTER SIX

ALL OF LONDON SEEMED to have converged on Covent Garden, Griffin observed two nights later as he followed Emmy and Olivia up the steps and past the giant columns toward the Theatre Royal's front doors.

His ears rang with the clatter of carriage wheels and heeled slippers on the stairs, the chatter of excited voices a low and constant hum. The evening's performer, a new soprano from Italy, was being lauded all over Europe for her rare and extraordinary talent, and everyone in Town was here to judge for themselves.

Everyone except Griffin's mother, as she'd grumpily pointed out from her bed only an hour ago. Then she'd made him promise to watch every moment of the performance and report back to her later tonight with a complete and detailed description of the evening while it was still fresh in his mind.

The memory of his mother's stern scowl brought a smile to his lips.

Fortunately for him, he'd always rather enjoyed the performing arts, music and plays and the like. Yes, he would rather trade places with his mother, send her off to the opera instead and spend the evening at home with Artemis, but he was here now, and he supposed it could be worse. It could be *him* with the injured ankle.

"Goodness me, it is an absolute crush tonight," Emmy said as the trio stepped through the front doors and into the spacious lobby teeming with patrons.

Serving girls bustled around the stuffy, opulent room, offering tea and coffee to the guests, though Griffin could think of nothing he'd like less right now than a hot beverage.

"I hope our box isn't as warm as the lobby is," Emmy said, fanning herself with a gloved hand. "It is smoldering in here."

"I brought my fan with me, Em," Olivia said, holding it aloft. "If you would like to borrow it—"

The remainder of her words fell away as an overeager young dandy pushed through the crowd, jostling her arm and knocking the fan to the floor.

"Oh, drat," she muttered, pausing to sweep her gaze over the carpet at her feet.

"Allow me." Griffin bent down and scooped up the fan then rose and held it out to her.

She took it from him, her gloved fingers grazing his, and the slide of velvet against his palm sent a jolt of yearning straight to his groin. He dropped his arm to his side and flexed his fingers, curling them into his still-tingling palm. *Christ above.*

"Thank you, my lord," she said with a polite smile, though her gaze never met his.

She turned and began pushing forward through the crowd with Emmy at her side, and Griffin followed behind them, his gaze trained on the back of Olivia's head.

'My lord'?

His brows drew together. In all the years he'd known her, she'd never called him by anything but his given name, yet tonight she'd *my-lorded* him twice. It was odd.

Her behavior had been odd all evening, though. Oh, she was everything polite and proper, of course, but unusually taciturn, too—when she deigned to speak to him at all.

Evidently she was ignoring him.

He gave a mental shrug and continued weaving through the crowd, keeping an eye on his two charges as they slowly made their way through the packed entrance hall and up the carpeted stairs to the uppermost circle of boxes, where they were greeted with the sounds of the orchestra tuning their instruments.

They had just reached their private box when Emmy paused and touched Griffin's sleeve. "You two wait for me here," she said. "I've just spotted a friend I need to speak to."

Griff nodded. "Fine, but don't wander off. Mother will never forgive me if I lose her only daughter."

"I won't wander off," Emmy said, rolling her eyes as only a sibling could. "I'll be right over there, within sight at all times." She used her chin to point out a skinny redhead in a pink frock standing some distance up the corridor with a graying gentleman and an older lady with red hair the same shade. The girl's parents, presumably.

"We'll wait for you," Griffin said. "But don't be long."

His sister waved a dismissive hand and then she was off, wending her way through the crowd, greeting nearly everyone she passed.

Griffin faced forward and slipped his hands in his pockets, watching the seemingly endless stream of theater patrons go by. Olivia stood beside him doing the same.

The corridor was brightly lit and faintly scented by the gaslight sconces adorning the walls, and despite the chatter of patrons and the noise from the orchestra, the silence between them seemed to grow heavier by the moment.

Olivia was the picture of serenity in her pale blue gown, her gloved hands clasped at her front, a placid smile curving her lips. Her gaze looked every which way but his, and Griffin decided he'd had quite enough of her indifference.

Shifting on his feet, he turned to her with a raised brow and said casually, "Why are you calling me 'my lord' tonight?"

This earned him a swift glance of surprise before she faced forward again, her expression unchanged. "I beg your pardon?"

A smile curled her lips as she exchanged nods of greeting with a passing guest, a pudgy young man with a curling mustache and the most hideous checkered waistcoat Griffin had ever seen.

"You've always called me Griffin," he said, his unfriendly stare dissuading the man from approaching. "Why is it 'my lord' tonight?"

The question was met with a long silence until, finally, she gave an indifferent shrug and said, "Calling you by your

Christian name was acceptable when I was a child, but such familiarity is no longer appropriate. We are not family. And neither are we friends."

Griffin had no ready reply. A small part of him wanted to argue with her, but there was no argument to be made. They were not family, although he'd known her since she was a child, and while they were more than mere acquaintances, he would never call them friends.

They were *something* to each other, though; he just didn't know what. At the very least, their long-standing connection made them familiars, and he'd grown accustomed to her calling him by his Christian name.

Anything else felt odd. Wrong.

A frown marred his brow, and he parted his lips to speak, though he hadn't a clue what he intended to say.

He was given no chance to find out.

"Lady Olivia!"

Griffin glanced up to see the Duke of Paxton headed their way. Annoyance stabbed at him.

The duke's mother was with him, of course, clutching the sleeve of her son's pea-green coat and looking as austere as ever in a long, gray gown, her cool smile in direct contrast to her son's affectionate half-grin.

"Good evening, my lady," Paxton said warmly as he bowed to Olivia. His gaze met Griff's. "Lord Keswick. Good evening."

Griffin inclined his head.

"Good evening, Your Graces," Olivia said, dipping into a flawless curtsy before turning to the duchess. "How lovely to see you again, Your Grace. Your gown is positively divine."

"Thank you, Lady Olivia," the duchess replied with a cool nod of her head.

She did not return the compliment.

Olivia must have noticed it, too. She'd widened her smile, as if by doing so she could infuse some warmth into the older woman, but the duchess appeared unmoved. Her lips thinned as she peered down the generous length of her beaklike nose, and it seemed a cruel pairing; a nose that could devour, a mouth that could only nibble.

"Are you looking forward to the performance?" Paxton asked into the uncomfortable silence. "I hear Giulietta Bianchi is an extraordinary talent."

"Oh, yes," Olivia said brightly. "I've been looking forward to this for weeks. It is sure to be an evening to remember."

The two continued their exchange of pleasantries and Griff, only half-listening, studied the man Olivia seemed so determined to claim.

He did not know the Duke of Paxton well. He'd only spoken with him a handful of times over the years, but he seemed a decent enough sort, if a bit eager to please. With his thick auburn hair and animated eyes, he reminded Griff of a perky Pomeranian.

Paxton's devotion to his mother was well-known amongst the *ton*, and normally Griff would find this trait admirable, feeling as he did about his own mother. But there was something about the man's relationship with the duchess that rubbed him the wrong way. He was *too* devoted to her, too attached, and seemed incapable of making a decision without her counsel.

Griff couldn't help but wonder how much that would change after the duke married. If it changed at all.

Paxton made no secret of his feelings for Olivia; it was clear he wanted her. The adoration was there in his smile for all to see. The duchess, however, did not seem to share her son's opinion, and Griff had to wonder why.

Olivia was sought-after by many and admired by all. It seemed odd that anyone should disapprove of her or find her lacking in any way. Besides him, of course. But then, he knew Olivia better than most, knew of her flaws and foibles. On the surface, she was a prize most men would covet and most mothers—even the mother of a duke—would be more than happy to welcome into the family.

So, what did Paxton's mother have against her?

"...think we should start making our way to our box, don't you?" the duchess was saying as she took her son by the elbow, a tight smile on her lips.

"Of course, Mother." Paxton gave Olivia a parting bow, his smile anything but tight. "Goodbye for now, my lady. I hope you enjoy the performance."

He raised her hand to his lips and pressed a kiss to her knuckles, lingering over the task a beat too long. Griffin's hands clenched with the potent, irrational urge to knock the man on his dukely arse.

"And I you, Your Grace," she replied prettily, returning his smile with one of her own.

Griff watched as the duke and his mother meandered up the corridor on their way to their private box.

"The Duke of Paxton certainly wears his heart on his sleeve," he said, turning to Olivia. "I've never seen a more smitten man."

Her hands flexed around her fan, and she wore a small smile, though it did not reach her eyes. "He cares for me," she said lightly. "As I care for him."

"Yet you are not betrothed."

He left the obvious question unasked, and it hung heavy between them.

"Paxton is courting me as a gentleman should," she said, busily straightening her long white . Her voice had cooled considerably, a warning to retreat.

Griff ignored it. "I'm glad," he said smoothly. "I was worried the delay had something to do with his mother. She seems...less than enthused by the match."

Olivia's hands flexed again, his words striking another nerve. "As usual, you are mistaken."

"Hm." He tugged his pocket watch from his coat and checked the time before glancing down the corridor at his sister. She was still talking with her friend.

He tucked the timepiece away and slipped his hands in his pockets. "So...has he kissed you yet?"

Her gaze shot to his, her lips parted in outrage. "That is *none* of your business."

Griffin smiled. "That's a no, then."

Her fist tightened around the fan, throttling it, and for a moment he wondered if she would hit him with it. "The duke is a gentleman," she said. "Unlike *some* men of my acquaintance, his interests extend beyond mere copulation."

He chuckled softly, amused by both her word choice and her naivety. "I can assure you, even the most gentlemanly of men are interested in copulation, Olivia. And if I were you, I'd be wondering why he hasn't tried to kiss me yet."

"Well, you are not me," she said, her blue eyes flashing. "Paxton will kiss me when the time is right, and when he does, it will be magnificent."

Griffin's brows rose. *Magnificent?* It was hard to imagine the cheery, dimwitted duke doing anything magnificently, least of all pleasuring a woman.

Olivia's eyes narrowed. "And what is that look meant to imply?"

He shrugged. "*Magnificent* is a touch optimistic, don't you think? Your duke is a pleasant enough fellow, but teeming with passion, he is not."

Her chin rose. "Nonsense. Everyone knows still waters run deep."

"But even puddles can be still."

"Well, no one would know that better than you, would they?" The arch of her brow was impressively sanctimonious. "After all, you've dipped your toe in more puddles than I can count."

Griffin grinned, a slow, devilish flash of his teeth. "I'm an adventurous man, Olivia," he drawled, "but even I've never thought to use my toe."

Her cheeks bloomed with color, and she turned from him, in tandem with the slap of her fan against the palm of her gloved hand.

Griffin chuckled. Probably thinking about smacking him with it again.

An image flashed through his mind: Her, on his bed, on her knees, her curvy little body in nothing but stockings and stays, the wicked promise of the slow, sharp slap of her fan against her bare palm.

God. His mouth went dry, desire unfurling low in his gut, sweet and sharp. He forced his gaze to the floor and curled his hands into fists, squeezing until his nails bit.

What in blazes was taking Emmy so long?

He was seconds away from stalking down the corridor and herding his sister into their box when the orchestra began to play, signaling the start to the performance.

Thank God.

He waited for Emmy to make her way to the box and then followed the two ladies inside, purposefully ensuring Emmy was seated between him and Olivia. It was better this way. Safer.

He did not want to lust after Olivia Blakely.

CHAPTER SEVEN

GIULIETTA BIANCHI'S TALENTS WERE not exaggerated. As the soprano's final, glorious note drew to a close, the opera house erupted into thunderous applause and the patrons remained standing long after the singer had left the stage.

Olivia slowly sank to her chair and waved her fan at her wet eyes, struggling to rein in her emotions. Never in her life had she witnessed such a powerful performance, and now that it was over, she was awestruck and contented yet utterly bereft all at the same time.

"Here," Emmy said, handing her a white handkerchief. "Take this."

Olivia accepted the folded bit of linen with a grateful smile. "Thank you."

"Thank my brother," Emmy said. "Occasionally he does prove useful to have around."

Olivia laughed and dabbed at her eyes with the handkerchief. It was still warm and smelled of him. She swallowed, fighting the urge to burrow her nose in the soft linen and breathe him in. Lord, but he smelled good.

"Are we ready to leave?" Emmy asked, glancing first at Olivia then at Griffin on her other side.

"I am." Griffin rose and headed for the box's entrance. Olivia stood and followed him and Emmy into the corridor as their fellow patrons did the same, spilling out from the neighboring boxes.

"Are you all right?" Emmy asked.

"Yes," she said, a watery, embarrassed laugh tumbling from her lips. "I don't know why the performance affected me so. My Italian is terrible. I could only make out a word or two."

Emmy gave her an understanding smile. "You were not the only one moved to tears tonight. It was a beautiful performance."

"It was," Olivia agreed as they moved toward the stairs with the rest of the crowd. "Although, I don't recall seeing *you* shed any tears."

Emmy grinned. "You know what a cold and heartless shrew I am."

Olivia laughed, and then she fell in line behind Emmy and Griffin as they descended the stairs and made their way through the lobby to the front entrance.

Stepping out into the night, she paused on the top step and breathed deeply, her gaze flicking to the nearly-full moon hanging high in the clear night sky. The temperate weather was welcome tonight, as it would be several minutes at least before their carriage arrived to take them home.

Passing her gaze over the crowd, she searched for Paxton, but there was no sign of him or his mother anywhere. The pair must have left before the performance ended, she mused. *Oh, well.* She would ask him what he'd thought of the performance later. A love of music was one thing the two of them had always had in common.

She spotted Emmy on the pavement below, already speaking with another of her many friends. Griffin stood a few feet away, gazing out at the street, his hands clasped behind his back. He was the image of easy confidence, his stance relaxed, his masterfully tailored coat and trousers emphasizing his broad shoulders and powerful thighs.

Olivia sighed. Was there a way to snuff out an unwanted attraction? If there was, she wished someone would share it with her. Lord knows, she'd tried, but so far nothing had worked, and even with everything they'd been through, this dratted attraction to him burned as brightly as it ever had.

He did not like her, though he did seem to enjoy teasing her, a fact she did not understand. No matter his reasons, she could not seem to stay away. Apparently she was a glutton for punishment, at least where the Marquess of Keswick was concerned.

His devilish smile from earlier flashed through her mind, his words seared on her brain.

I'm an adventurous man, Olivia, but even I've never thought to use my toe.

Warmth suffused her cheeks, but it wasn't from embarrassment. It was that cursed smile of his. It slayed her every time, even the memory of it, sucking the breath from her lungs and filling her belly with warmth.

No other man's smile had ever elicited this reaction from her. Only Griffin's.

Avoid, avoid, avoid.

With a little shake of her head, she gathered her cloak around her and headed down the stairs, her gaze on her slippered feet. She had just stepped onto the pavement when she bumped into someone.

"Oh, I do apologize," she muttered. "I'm afraid I wasn't watching where I was going."

Her near-victim, a dark-haired woman in a beautiful crimson gown shook her head and smiled. "No harm done."

Griffin turned to look over his shoulder and the lady's smile widened as she spotted him. "Lord Keswick," she said, her voice soft and melodious. "Good evening. How lovely to see you."

"Cecilia—Mrs. Morris." Griffin took two steps forward to meet her then bowed to the woman. "You are looking well."

Olivia watched the exchange with interest, her gaze flitting back and forth between them. How did they know each other?

"Thank you, my lord," Mrs. Morris said. "And thank you for your generous gift, as well. How is the kitten faring, by the by? Did you gift it to someone else?"

Olivia's gaze flew to Griffin's profile before dropping to her feet as realization dawned, slow and uncomfortable. This woman was his mistress. Artemis had been intended for her, a gift for her affections.

Griffin cleared his throat. "She's doing well," he said. "I decided to keep her myself."

"Oh, I am glad," Mrs. Morris said with a smile. "Well..." She shrugged one shoulder. "I should be going now. Good-bye, my lord." And with a nod of her head, she turned and walked away, a blonde gentleman Olivia hadn't even noticed trailing behind her like a devoted camp follower.

In silence, she watched the woman depart, envy churning in her gut. Mrs. Morris was a beautiful woman. Raven black hair; dark eyes; long, willowy limbs. Everything Olivia wasn't. And she wore the bold red dress with such confidence. The color suited her.

Was this the sort of woman Griffin preferred?

Her gaze flicked to his face, and she watched him as he watched Mrs. Morris's retreating form, his expression unreadable in the moonlight. Jealousy snaked through her insides like venom, biting and bitter on her tongue, and she closed her eyes briefly, as if she could purge the feeling by sheer force of will.

Stop this at once. You do not want him anymore, remember?

She cleared her throat, desperate to fill the silence. "So..." She clasped her hands behind her back. "Found the kitten on the street, did you?"

Griffin turned to look at her, and he shrugged, his half-smile faintly chagrined. "The truth is hardly mother-appropriate."

Olivia nodded. "The truth being that you obtained Artemis as a gift intended for your..." She trailed off, pursing her lips. She couldn't bring herself to say the word *mistress* out loud.

"Intended for and rejected by," Griffin said, thrusting his hands in his pockets.

69

"Rejected?" Olivia shot him a curious glance. "Why? Do cats make her sneeze?"

He smiled. "That's what I asked, too. But no. She doesn't like them, apparently."

"I see." She didn't, though. How could anyone not like Artemis?

"I gave her a necklace instead." His gaze flicked to hers. "As a parting gift."

"I see." It was all she could seem to say. She'd never had a conversation like this one before, and certainly not with Griffin. It was odd, to say the least.

She'd never imagined him with a mistress before, sharing gifts and his bed with beautiful, dark-haired widows. Jealousy flared again, hot and swift, and she gritted her teeth against the sensation, smacking her fan in the palm of her hand. She had no business being jealous. Griffin could do as he pleased, for he meant nothing to her.

Only the duke mattered now.

"You're wrong, by the by," she blurted out before she could stop herself. "About Paxton. He *is* a passionate man, a *wonderful* man, and he will make a wonderful husband and we will have a dozen wonderful children together."

And how dare he imply otherwise? How dare he express any opinion at all on Paxton? She let the anger in, *welcomed* it, a balm soothing away the unpleasant, unwanted jealousy.

She smacked her fan against her palm again, enjoying the sharp *thwack,* and Griffin's gaze dipped, lingering for a moment before he turned to face the street.

"I know you like that Paxton is a duke," he said, his voice low and oddly gruff. "But what else do you like about him?"

She blinked, caught off guard by the question, and then her chin rose. "I like many things about him."

"Such as?" He looked at her, and she was surprised by the seemingly genuine curiosity glimmering in his eyes.

She dropped her gaze to the ground and ran the toe of one slipper over the rough pavement as she considered her answer. "Such as...his kindness, his amiable nature, his sense of honor." She shrugged one shoulder. "I like that he's sweet to me, and that he admires me."

"Of course he admires you," Griffin said, his voice flat. "You're a beautiful woman, Olivia. Every man in England admires you. The only difference with Paxton is that he's a duke."

Any warm glow she might have felt at his compliment cooled and hot indignation brewed in its place. She swiped at a curl tickling her cheek and turned her gaze to the street, battling to keep her temper in check.

"So what if I like that he's a duke?" she asked, her voice mercifully calm. "I am not the only woman with dreams of one day being a duchess." She tugged her cloak snug around her arms and flicked him a sideways glance. "And why do you care, anyway? What difference does it make to you what I do?"

"None whatsoever," he said mildly, his own gaze tracking the passing guests. "I was only thinking of the duke. I believe a woman should marry a man for reasons beyond his title alone."

"So do I," she shot back. "But men marry women for their dowries all the time and no one thinks twice about it. Why is it so terrible for a woman to marry for unromantic reasons?"

She studied his profile for a moment, and then, in a low voice, mused, "Or perhaps it is only terrible when *I* do it."

His gaze met hers, his eyes dark with feeling. But what was it? Shame? Apathy? Annoyance? It was impossible to tell, and she suspected he wanted it that way.

The clatter of wheels and hooves disrupted the moment as the Keswick carriage finally pulled up, and a moment later Emmy joined them, a string of enthusiastic words tumbling out of her mouth as they all climbed into the carriage.

Olivia pasted a smile on her lips and listened with determined interest, forcing Griffin and his poor opinion of her to the furthest corner of her mind.

She did not need his good opinion for he had no place in her life, and it was only a matter of time before she forgot him and this silly, ridiculous attraction completely.

She was sure of it.

CHAPTER EIGHT

"WELL, DARLING, WHAT IS on the agenda for the evening?" Lady Keswick asked the following night as Griffin sat down on the bed beside her. "Lady Chavel's ball, isn't it?"

"I believe so, yes." He sighed and leaned his elbows on his knees, trying not to grimace.

Truth be told, he wasn't entirely certain whose home he was going to tonight. He only knew it wasn't his own.

Three balls in as many nights. A man could only stomach so much ratafia.

"I do appreciate your willingness to escort Emmy and Olivia around," Lady Keswick said, patting his hand sympathetically. "You know I would do it if I could."

Griffin smiled at her. "I know." Guilt speared his gut. He was being a churl. Here his mother sat, bedridden with an injured ankle, and he was feeling sorry for himself. "It isn't so terrible," he said. "I'm just a little envious because you get to spend the evening at home with Artemis."

The kitten was rolling around on the bed with a ball of red yarn clutched in her paws, trying to choke the life out of it. The prey was nearly double the size of the predator, but Artemis showed no fear. Or mercy.

"She has certainly helped to keep me entertained these last few days," Lady Keswick said, a smile in her voice. "She's a sweet little thing."

Griffin nodded. "She is."

It surprised him how quickly he'd grown accustomed to having a kitten around. He had no experience with keeping a cat for a pet, but he found he liked having a little companion close by to keep him company. He kept her in his study with him while he worked, and at night she slept in his bedchamber. He'd set up a pile of blankets for her at the foot of his bed, but the last two mornings he'd awakened to find her sleeping on him instead, curled up on his chest with her nose nestled in her tail.

He knew he should probably discourage that, but he couldn't bring himself to do it. Truth be told, he rather liked starting his day that way.

"I do not believe I've seen this coat before," Lady Keswick said, eyeing Griffin's dark green dress coat. "Is it new?"

"It is," he said, smoothing his hands down the lapels. "Do you like it?"

"I do. You'll have the ladies throwing themselves at your feet all evening." She touched his sleeve, testing the feel of the wool between her fingers before giving it a tug. "I only wish you would pick one of them up and marry her already."

He stifled a groan. "Mother, please..."

"I'm sorry, darling, but I cannot help it," she said with an unapologetic shrug. "It is past time you were married. I hoped seeing how happy James is with Sophie might make you realize what you're missing out on, but since it hasn't, I have no choice but to badger you."

Griff huffed out an exasperated chuckle. They'd had this conversation a hundred times before, and he suspected they would have it a hundred times more. James's unexpected love match with Emmy's friend, Sophie, had surprised them all, and made Lady Keswick even more desperate to see her own children meet the same fate.

"James is a lucky man," Griffin said. "Sophie is good for him, and he deserves to be happy."

He met James nearly twenty years ago at Eton, when they were just boys of ten or eleven, and the two became fast friends. He'd seen everything James had gone through over the years: His father's death when he was barely nineteen, his wife's death only a few years later. If anyone deserved to be happy, it was James.

"You deserve to be happy, too, Griffin," Lady Keswick said, her voice soft.

Artemis mewled and Griff turned, smiling as she trotted across the bed toward him, her teeth clamped around a strand of yarn, the ball dancing and flopping as it unspooled behind her.

"I am happy," he said, scratching Artemis behind the ear.

Even with the fire crackling in the hearth, his mother's silence rang so loudly he could practically hear her objection in it.

In the end, she only heaved another sigh and said, "Well, you would make *me* very happy if you would give me grandchildren. I'm beginning to think Artemis here is as close as I'm going to get."

She couldn't suppress her smile, though, as the kitten embarked on a wobbly ascent up her shin, a diminutive, whiskered tightrope walker.

Griffin smiled. "You could do worse."

Lady Keswick kissed Artemis on the top of her head before setting her on the mattress. "Honestly, two grown children and neither of them with an ounce of interest in marriage." She clucked her tongue. "If I'd known you and your sister would torment me like this, I would have had a dozen more children."

Griffin had often wondered why she and his father hadn't produced more offspring. With eight years between him and Emmy, he suspected his mother had struggled with infertility, or perhaps even lost a child or two, though he'd never asked her about it. She'd been through so much, and he hated to think his curiosity might bring her pain.

"Why didn't you?" he asked. "You were still a young woman when Father died. You might have remarried."

It was a strange thought, imagining his mother with another husband, another man, but as beautiful and charming as she was, she would have had no trouble capturing another man's heart. Many would say she should have.

"I thought about it, of course," Lady Keswick said, smoothing her hands down the coverlet. Artemis tracked the motion with wide, interested eyes. "But I never could find a man who intrigued me like your father did. And if I was going to marry a second time, I was not going to settle for mere companionship or status. I wanted to love my husband, and I simply could not imagine how I could love another man like I loved your father."

Griffin nodded his understanding. He remembered how his parents had been together, the obvious love and affection between them. It was hard to imagine his mother like that with another man. Not that he thought it would have been wrong, it was only that he couldn't fathom another man deserving his mother's love and devotion.

"And as much as I love you and your sister..." Her gaze drifted to the small portrait of Griffin's father which hung on the wall beside the bed, and she smiled. "After your father died, I wasn't really interested in trying for more children. Certainly not enough to marry again."

Her gaze found Griffin's again, and she gave his hand a squeeze. "It's what I want for you, darling. It's why I push so hard. I want you to be as happy as I was with your father."

Griffin nodded, though he wasn't sure it was possible. Their love had always seemed an unattainable standard. "I know, Mother. And I will be. When the time is right."

Her brow crooked. "And when will that be, pray? Before or after I'm dead?"

Griff's lips twitched at her peevish tone. "*After* I've met the right woman."

"And what sort of woman is the right woman?"

Unbidden and wholly unwelcome, Olivia's face appeared in his mind. He nearly choked on the curse that caught in his throat. Olivia Blakely was *not* right. She was all wrong. Shallow, spoiled, attention-seeking, title-grasping. Everything he did not want in a wife.

But she's everything you want in your bed, isn't she?

The thought had him raking a hand through his hair, discomfort settling in his chest like a boulder. How could he want a woman he didn't even like?

He shoved the uncomfortable question—and Olivia—to the back of his mind where they belonged and gave his mother a smile. "The right sort of woman is beautiful, gracious, kind. Patient to a fault." He winked at her. "She's exactly like you, Mother."

Lady Keswick shook her head, clearly battling a smile, and reached up to pat his cheek. "Impudent boy," she murmured. "You do make it impossible for me to stay angry with you."

"Good," he said, leaning down to kiss her cheek before rising to his feet. "I'd best be off now. I'll collect Artemis when I return."

"Right, and do give your cat a kiss before you leave. She misses you terribly when you're gone."

Griffin blew out a breath. "She isn't my—oh, never mind." He scooped Artemis up and kissed her on the top of her head, ignoring his mother's amused gaze.

She knew as well as he did that he was deluding himself. For some reason, Artemis had chosen him, and there was no sense in trying to resist her. They were stuck with each other now.

He left his mother's chambers with a smile on his face.

CHAPTER NINE

"WE SHOULDN'T BE DOING this, Olivia," the Duke of Paxton whispered. "We could be seen."

Ignoring his objections, Olivia herded him toward the rear doors with another tug on his immaculately tailored coat sleeve. "Lady Chavel is renowned for her roses, and I want to see them for myself," she said, "but I don't want to go alone. We'll only be a few minutes. No one will even notice we've gone."

With a resigned sigh, Paxton followed her lead and the two slipped from the ballroom, making their way into the darkened gardens beyond.

"This is not a good idea," Paxton grumbled. "My mother would not approve."

Olivia rolled her eyes but said nothing. Honestly, she was afraid of what she might say if she did speak. She loved the respect and adoration Paxton showed his mother, but sometimes she thought it was a little too much, especially for a grown man, not to mention a *duke.*

Lady Paxton was a formidable woman, yes, but she wasn't Paxton's keeper. He should be able to make his own decisions once in a while.

This decision, however, to visit Lady Chavel's rose garden, was all Olivia's doing. Inspired by a certain marquess's impertinent questions.

Because despite what she'd said to him last night at the opera, Griffin was right. It was odd that Paxton hadn't kissed her yet, and she'd thought of little else since.

She'd had her fair share of kisses, shared with several different men—a few of whom had even tried to steal a kiss the first night they'd met—but she'd known Paxton for months now and he'd made not a single attempt.

Why hadn't he kissed her yet? He was attracted to her, she knew that. So why did he not kiss her? Was he afraid of offending her?

She hadn't a clue what he was thinking, but she'd decided the time had come to take matters into her own hands. There was nothing else to be done. If he wouldn't kiss her, she would simply have to kiss him.

"Oh, look," she breathed, pointing to the gardens beyond. "There they are. Don't they smell simply divine?" She inhaled deeply, the sweet floral scent delighting her nose.

Paxton sneezed. "Oh, yes. Divine." He sniffled.

"The moon is so bright tonight," she said, gazing up at the sky, determinedly ignoring the snuffles and snorts from beside her. She tipped her head to catch the moonlight on one cheek and peered up at him through her lashes. "Quite lovely, isn't it?"

He blinked, his gaze dipping to her mouth. "Erhm..."

She leaned in just a hair, not so much as to be the instigator, but enough to signal that she would not rebuff his advances should he choose to make any.

Paxton's eyes were fixed on her lips, uncertainty warring with desire, and the silence stretched into absurdity.

Olivia leaned in another hair, close enough now to catch a whiff of his musky cologne, and she gave him a smile, soft and encouraging.

Kiss me, you idiot. Kiss me now.

But the kiss never came.

His head snapped up and he cleared his throat before taking a step toward the house. "Come, Olivia, you've seen the roses. Let's go back inside before our absence is noted."

Suppressing a frown, Olivia waved a hand in the air. "You go on," she said brightly. "I'd like to stay for a few more minutes and enjoy the night air. I'll be along in a moment."

Her words were in direct contradiction to her earlier claim that she did not wish to venture into the gardens alone, but she didn't care. She was too irritated to return to the party just yet, so she sent Paxton on his way with the assurance she would join him shortly.

She watched him go before turning to face the garden, a frustrated sigh slipping from her lips. *What a debacle that had been.*

Why was Paxton so reluctant to kiss her? He seemed to want to and yet, something was holding him back. *But what?*

Restless, she moved deeper into the gardens, passing through the rows of roses toward the long, dense hedgerow, the only sounds the soft crunch of her slippers on the gravel path and the hum of crickets singing their evening song.

What was she doing wrong? Why did he not wish to kiss her? It might sound conceited, but she was *used* to men desiring her. She'd heard enough compliments on her eyes and lips and charming ways to know that men found her attractive, and if given the chance, were more than eager to claim a kiss.

Except Griffin, of course.

And, apparently, Paxton. The man she hoped to marry.

An unhappy sigh escaped her as she rounded the hedgerow, the moonlight lighting her path. Her head came up, her gaze trained ahead...

And then she spotted him.

Griffin. Sitting alone on a bench against the hedgerow.

She stopped in her tracks, scattering gravel as her breath caught. "How long have you been sitting there?" she blurted.

Had he heard her exchange with Paxton?

Her cheeks flushed. Of course, he had. The bench was only feet from where she and Paxton were standing. How could he have missed it?

"Not long," he said, shifting on the bench to hook an ankle over the other knee.

His casual posture grated, and she crossed her arms over her chest. "Long enough to overhear my *private* conversation with the duke?"

"I'm afraid so."

Well. She hadn't expected him to admit to it so readily. Her arms fell to her sides.

"Go on, then," she said. "Laugh if you want to. It was a pitiful attempt at seduction, and I will not fault you for mocking it."

She steeled herself, embarrassment knotting and twisting in her gut.

"I don't want to laugh, Olivia." His voice was quiet, almost caring, and she could see the truth of his face as he turned dark, steady eyes to hers.

No, he did not want to laugh at her. It was worse. There was *pity* in his eyes.

Oh, God. She could not abide his pity.

"Why are you out here?" she asked, the words made harsh by injured pride. "Why are you sitting there on that bench, alone, like some sort of eavesdropping lecher? I—"

"Lord Keswick? Where are you?"

Olivia froze, her words falling away as the woman's hushed whisper shot into the garden like cannon fire.

Griffin slowly rose from the bench, his gaze on Olivia's as he slipped into the shadows, a forefinger pressed to his lips in a bid for silence.

There was no need for the reminder, though. She had no desire to be discovered out here alone with an unmarried man. Least of all this one.

Leaning her back into the hedgerow, she ignored the shrubbery pricking her skin and focused instead on shrinking into the darkness.

"My lord?" the lady called out. "Are you there?"

Olivia's lips pursed in annoyance. Who was this woman searching for Griffin? *Why* was she looking for him? And how did she know he would be in the gardens? Had she—

Oh.

Olivia's jaw tensed. So that was why he was waiting on that bench. He and this woman had arranged to meet here. Olivia had interrupted their tryst.

The evening grew better and better by the minute.

Another several interminable moments passed before the unknown lady finally gave up. Olivia listened to her retreating footsteps and waited through several beats of silence before slowly emerging from the hedge.

Griffin did the same, shaking out his coat tails and smoothing his hands through his hair.

"I'm sorry about interrupting your...meeting," Olivia said, filling the silence as she brushed the shrubbery from the back of her dress. "I had no idea you were out here."

It was a lie, of course. She wasn't sorry at all.

Because she didn't care.

"She'll try again," Griffin said with a shrug, apparently unconcerned.

Olivia's lips quirked. "You seem very certain of that."

His smile was his only reply.

She rolled her eyes at his cockiness, but she had to admit, to herself at least, that he was probably right. Griffin was an attractive man, and women wanted him. There was no point in denying it.

Of course, she saw no need to agree with him, either. He was arrogant enough already.

"Well," she said, "I suppose I had best return to the party now. This was more than enough excitement for one evening." She took a step to leave then stilled and turned to face him again. "About what you overheard earlier..."

His gaze met hers.

"Please don't mention it to anyone."

He nodded once. "Your secret is safe with me."

"Thank you, Griffin."

She turned to leave again, eager now to leave and return to the warmth of the house. She started up the path and had taken just three steps when Griffin's low voice stopped her in her tracks.

"Paxton is a fool."

Olivia's eyes fell closed and she swallowed, her throat suddenly tight. "No. I'm the fool," she said. "I thought if I lured him out here amongst the roses and the moonlight, he would finally kiss me and then maybe he would finally ask me to—" She broke off with a shake of her head and wrapped her hands around her chilled upper arms. "But it was a silly thought."

She only hoped it hadn't erased the progress she'd made with him these last few months.

Griffin moved behind her, the crunch of his footsteps growing louder as he neared, and then his evening coat draped over her shoulders, his warmth, his scent, wrapping around her like an embrace.

"You're not a fool, Olivia." His voice was low, comforting in its conviction. "Paxton is not the sort of man to appreciate boldness in a woman. Not with his mother like she is."

Her lips tipped up in a self-deprecating smile. "Or perhaps he simply did not wish to kiss me."

"Bollocks."

She shook her head. "Maybe I misread his feelings. Maybe he is not attracted to me."

"Impossible."

She huffed out a humorless laugh and turned to face him, gripping the ends of his coat in one hand. "I don't know how you can say that when just the *idea* of kissing me horrified you."

His jaw flexed. "That isn't true."

"You know it is. I saw the expression on your face, the disgust—" Her throat caught as the memory of that night besieged her mind, the censure in his eyes, the coldness of his voice. The scornful words that had cut her to the quick.

Silly, shallow flirt.

She'd indulged that night on too much mulled wine, and it had made her brave. And she'd been burned for it.

"Anyhow, none of that matters now, does it?" She forced a small smile. "It was a silly mistake, and you can rest assured it will not be repeated. I know what you think of me, Griffin, and I—"

Her breath stuttered as his hands shot out and hauled her in by the lapels of his coat, his jaw like granite, his eyes ablaze. "You know nothing."

Olivia's heart gave a wild, incandescent leap.

And then his mouth was on hers, his lips shaping, claiming, and her mind went utterly blank. This was no tender kiss, no tentative meeting of mouths. It was nothing at all like her previous kisses.

This kiss was *devouring*. Desirous. Dangerous.

A groan caught in her throat at the first touch of his tongue to hers, and her arms swept around his neck, dislodging his grip on the coat. It slipped from her shoulders and fell to her feet just before his hands curved around her back and her own fingers sifted through the soft hair at his nape.

She'd been kissed before, but never like this. Never had she felt this way, like she couldn't catch her breath, like she'd never truly breathed. Like she was sinking and somehow only this kiss—*his* kiss—would keep her from going under.

She nipped his lower lip with her teeth, and he sucked in a breath, his hands skating down her back to curve around her hips and cup her bottom. He gripped her, tugged her closer, and she gasped at the press of his hard length against her belly.

Desire licked at her insides, and she arched her hips, welcoming the fire, succumbing to it, spurred on by the stark, irrefutable evidence of his arousal. Evidence that he was right there with her. That he desired her, too.

Their tongues tangled, hands gripping and exploring, and Olivia sighed against his lips, breathless but too far gone to care.

Her body was his for the taking. He had only to ask.

"Griffin..." she whispered.

With a rough groan, he tore his lips from hers and stepped back.

Olivia's eyes fluttered open and she pressed the back of her hand to her bruised lips, her heart thudding in her chest.

She raked her gaze over his face, seeking answers, seeking *something*. But there was nothing to see, no hint of feeling, no clue to his thoughts. Even his eyes had cooled.

"Why did you do that?" she asked faintly. *Why did you stop?*

He slipped his hands into his trouser pockets and shrugged. "To prove a point." His tone was casual, dispassionate even, as if he'd proved a thousand points this way. "And to lift your spirits."

The haze of desire lifted, sniffed out by his words, and Olivia swallowed in a futile attempt to ease the ache in her throat. "I see," she said, her voice surprisingly calm considering her heart was at her feet.

What a fool she was, thinking he'd kissed her because he'd wanted to. He'd made his opinion of her perfectly clear, and one kiss—one *pity* kiss—changed absolutely nothing.

"Did it work?" He tipped his head to one side and smiled at her, as if awaiting his accolades for a job well done.

She wanted to throw rocks at his head.

Instead, she returned his smile, compelled by pride alone, and nodded. "It did, yes. Thank you, my lord. That was...most kind of you." She bent down to retrieve his fallen coat then handed it to him. "I really do have to return to the ballroom now. But I shall see you later, yes?"

Without waiting for his reply, she turned on her heel and strode up the path with a straight spine and unhurried steps. *Mustn't let him think we're running away.*

Once she'd rounded the hedgerow, she allowed herself to breathe again, drawing in a slow breath to clear her mind before she reached the ballroom. A dull ache throbbed in her chest, even as her lips still tingled from that kiss. It was an unsettling dichotomy. But then, it wasn't the first time Griffin had unsettled her.

She was determined to make it the last.

Shoving the dratted man from her mind, she approached the house and slipped into the ballroom, scanning the crowd for the duke.

She must find him and apologize for her behavior. She should never have pressed him like that. She would blame it on the moon or something. A romantic mood had come over her, she would say, and it would never happen again.

He would forgive her. He had to.

CHAPTER TEN

GRIFFIN PUSHED HIS PLATE across the dining room table and scowled at his uneaten kippers.

Something was wrong with him. Normally he had the appetite of an elephant, but these last two days, food held little appeal for him.

Coffee, thankfully, did not.

Rising from his chair, he crossed the dense Aubusson rug to the sideboard and poured himself another cup before making his way to the window overlooking the garden. He sipped the steaming brew as he gazed down with tired eyes at the empty, sun-glazed square of greenery.

He sighed. He was up too late again last night, his mind refusing to rest, consumed with thoughts of Olivia and that bloody kiss that seemed to have seared itself on his brain.

He rubbed his aching eyes. He shouldn't have done it. He should never have kissed her. He knew that now.

Hell, he'd known it then, but he'd done it anyway.

And even though he knew it was foolish, he couldn't bring himself to regret it. Not completely. It was stupid, yes, but—*damn it all*—it was bloody good, too. Better than he'd imagined it would be, and he'd done a lot of imagining where Olivia Blakely was concerned.

Just last night he'd imagined her in his bed, her soft hands on his body, her lips around his cock, the hot slide of her tongue as she sucked him deep. And then he'd taken himself in hand and spilled his release on the counterpane.

Even now, the thought of that kiss stirred his blood. It was utter madness, and it had to end.

"Good morning, brother dear!"

Griffin gave a guilty start, sloshing his coffee, and turned as Emmy breezed into the room and made for the sideboard, her ivory gown swishing with each stride.

"Good morning, Em," he said, shifting on his feet. Had his sister really caught him thinking erotic thoughts in the family dining room?

Erotic thoughts of her dearest friend, no less. *God, he needed a good night's sleep.*

"You look tired," Emmy said, as if reading his mind, something she did with annoying regularity. She spooned eggs onto her plate and flicked him a glance. "Were you up late last night entertaining a lady friend?"

Griff shot her a look on his way back to the dining table. "I beg your pardon?" he asked after he'd settled onto his seat.

She joined him a moment later, setting her plate down on the table across from his before sitting in her chair.

"I understand you and Cecilia Morris are enjoying an illicit affair right now," she said casually. "I thought perhaps she might have kept you up late." Gray eyes met his over the rim of her teacup.

Griffin sighed. "Bloody hell, Em. You shouldn't say such things. You shouldn't even *know* such things."

But his sister seemed to know everything about everyone, even him. It was deuced irritating.

Emmy rolled her eyes and bit into a slice of toasted bread. "If you wish to hide such things from me, I suggest you try harder," she said around the bite of bread. "Besides, isn't this what gentlemen discuss with each other? Their mistresses? I only brought it up because I thought you might be missing James."

"Well, you thought wrong."

She took another bite of bread, watching him as she chewed. "So?" she pressed. "Were you up late last night with Mrs. Morris or not?"

Griff heaved a resigned sigh and gave in to the inevitable. He knew his sister, and she would not let up until she received an answer.

"No, I wasn't," he said. "Mrs. Morris and I have ended our arrangement, and now I'm..." He trailed off with a flick of his hand.

"Between mistresses?" Emmy supplied, her grin impudent.

It was Griff's turn to roll his eyes. God, she was a pest. "When are you going to get married so I can finally be rid of you?"

She arched her brows. "I could ask the same of you, brother dear. Shouldn't you be working on producing an heir? Or, better still, a *spare*?"

Griff sat back in his chair and gave his head a slow, mournful shake. "My God," he muttered. "You are sounding more and more like our mother every day."

"Take that back this instant," Emmy said, setting her fork down with a sharp scrape of silver on porcelain.

He smiled. "No."

Her lips pursed and she glared at him. "You are such a nuisance. It is no wonder you're not married yet. No woman would have you."

Chuckling softly, Griffin sipped his coffee. He enjoyed bickering with his sister, nearly as much as he enjoyed goading her into bickering with him. The two had always been close, at least as close as brothers and sisters could be, although, truth be told, they didn't often discuss weighty topics. Their relationship was a good one, despite their bickering, and if asked, he would say he knew his sister well.

If pressed, however, he would have to admit there were things he didn't know, questions he'd never asked. Questions like what she wanted for her future, what she desired out of life.

Was it odd that he didn't know the answers?

"Em," he said quietly, "why haven't you married yet?"

Her eyes met his and he could see his question had surprised her. She shrugged. "I suppose it is because I haven't found anyone I wish to marry."

He nodded then tipped his head to one side. "Are you *looking* for someone to marry?"

Her gaze fell to her plate, and she pressed her lips together, considering her answer. "I am not averse to the idea of marriage," she said slowly, "but I am in no rush to take a husband, either. I am happy as I am now. I like living in the city. There is always something to do here, and my friends are here..." She trailed off with another shrug.

"And you're worried that marriage would change all of that?"

"A little," she said, pushing her eggs around with her fork. "And I've never met a man I liked well enough to risk my future on. I'm not sure I ever will."

Griff nodded again. He could understand her reluctance. Marriage was permanent, final, and husbands held virtually all the power. The idea that his sister might find herself trapped in an unhappy marriage did not sit well with him.

"What about you?" she asked, her gaze meeting his. "Why have you not married?"

He looked at his plate and shook his head. "I don't know."

Emmy waited a beat and then huffed out a sigh. "You don't know? Come now, Griff, tit for tat. I've just bared my soul to you. It is your turn now."

But the truth would not paint him in a flattering light. It sounded so selfish, a man like him, a *marquess*, putting off marriage to keep his freedom. It would certainly sound selfish to a woman.

He knew how fortunate he was, how many privileges his wealth and status—his *sex*—afforded him. For a woman, marriage meant her life was inexorably altered. But it was different for men. If a man wished to carry on as he had before he wed, it was well within his rights to do so. And most men of his acquaintance did.

But that wasn't the kind of marriage Griffin wanted. He wanted a real marriage, a true one, with a wife who loved him as he loved her. As soon as he was ready for it.

"I suppose it's the same for me as it is for you," he said, setting his empty cup on the saucer. "I haven't met anyone I wish to welcome into my life. When I do, I'll marry her."

Emmy's gaze turned thoughtful, quizzical, as if there was a question she wanted to ask but wasn't sure she should. A beat later, her gaze fell to her plate, the moment gone.

Griff leaned his elbows on the table, curious to know what it was she'd wanted to ask him, but he held his tongue. He wasn't sure he wanted to know.

"You don't seem to be searching very hard for a bride," she said when she'd finished a bite of kippers. "I think Mother would appreciate at least the appearance of trying."

He raised a brow. "And what of you? Younger sisters are meant to marry before their brothers, you know."

"Perhaps," she said. "But *I* haven't the fate of a marquessate on my shoulders."

She shot him an arch look then returned to her kippers with relish while Griffin picked at his with his fork, her words echoing through his mind.

She was right. He did have the marquessate to think of. He kept telling himself there was plenty of time to marry and bear an heir, but how could he be sure?

His father was thirty-four when he died, only four years older than Griffin was now. And if his death had taught him anything, it was how temporary life could be.

He might have reservations about getting married now, but was his personal comfort more important than the family line? Would his father be ashamed of him if he were here to see him dragging his feet?

"Well, now that I've eaten," Emmy said, "I have some letters to write." She set her napkin on the table and rose from her chair. "I will see you later, yes? Remember, we have the Henleys' costume ball this evening."

Griffin blew out a long-suffering breath. "How could I possibly forget?"

"Come now," Emmy said, humor sparking her eyes. "You might actually enjoy yourself."

Unamused, he fixed her with a dubious stare.

Her lips twitched. "Then again, you might not."

Griff watched his sister leave and then trudged over to the sideboard for another cup of coffee, his mood considerably dampened. *Bloody costume ball.*

He wished like hell he could get out of it, but it would do no good to dwell on improbabilities. He knew there was no hope. His mother's ankle would never heal by tonight, not without a miracle, and even he wasn't selfish enough to use a prayer for that.

CHAPTER ELEVEN

AUNT AUGUSTA'S SIGH FILLED the carriage as it crawled its way up the gravel drive, one of many in a long queue of carriages following the torch-lined path leading to Lord and Lady Henley's front door.

Turning from the window, Olivia gazed at her aunt's frowning face, her pinched brow illuminated by the oil lamp burning above her head. "Are you all right, Auntie?"

"Oh, I'm fine, my dear," she said. "I only wish Lady Keswick could be here tonight. She was so looking forward to showing off her costume."

Guilt threaded her voice, and Olivia reached over to pat her knee. "I know she was. But there will be other costume balls."

"Exactly," her aunt said. "Which is why I should have stayed with her tonight—"

"No, you shouldn't." Olivia shot her a scolding look. "Lady Keswick will survive without you tonight. She *wanted* you to come. She said so herself."

"I know she did," she replied, but her voice suggested she didn't quite believe her.

"Besides, you *had* to come," Olivia said. "For me, if no one else. I spent far too much time on your costume not to see you wearing it tonight." She swept her gaze over her aunt's colorful gown and smiled. "And I must say, there has never been a more glorious Queen Mab. You look magnificent, Aunt."

"I do, don't I?" She patted the sparkling crown circling her head and grinned.

Olivia had fashioned the crown herself, adorning a simple gold circlet with paste jewels and flowers of every color until it sparkled. She'd even designed her aunt's gown, as well as her own, and she couldn't help feeling proud of how their costumes had turned out.

She only wished she were in better spirits tonight. She adored costume parties, and had been anticipating this evening for weeks, but her thoughts were focused elsewhere, on the letter from her father that arrived earlier today.

Three lines. He'd told her he needed to economize, that his growing family meant this Season must be her last, and yet he'd wasted an entire sheet of new paper to pen her three silly lines.

I hope this letter finds you well on your way to a proposal of marriage. Do write back and tell me how your search is progressing, so I can determine when I should begin my own. Your stepmother and I are eager to see you wed.

Olivia dropped her gaze to the mask in her lap and studied her work, thinking of Paxton as she stroked the beautiful peacock feathers she had so painstakingly attached to the demi-mask. She hoped he liked her costume.

She'd apologized for her forwardness the other night, and he'd forgiven her without preamble, but his disinterest in kissing her was a blow to her pride, not to mention her confidence. Her father's letter certainly hadn't helped.

All she could do now was continue on as before, waiting patiently, praying fervently that Paxton's love for her would win out in the end. She'd designed her costume with just that purpose in mind, and while she had to admit the bodice was a bit low, a bit daring, she felt no shame.

A daring bodice could further a lady's cause as well as anything.

"You look beautiful," Aunt Augusta said, breaking into her reverie, and Olivia realized she'd been fidgeting with her gown. "Your costume is a work of art."

"Thank you, Aunt." Olivia gave her a smile and rubbed a gloved palm on the bench seat, the slide of velvet on velvet oddly calming.

"Are you unwell, dearest?" Aunt Augusta asked, her brows drawing together. "You've been rather quiet today."

She hadn't told her aunt about her father's letter. It would only upset her, and why should they both be agitated tonight?

"I'm fine," she replied, though she could see her aunt did not believe her. Instead of the truth, she gave her a fib. "I suppose I am feeling a little pensive tonight. My costume has me thinking about my mother. Do you think she would have liked it?"

"Of course she would," Aunt Augusta said without hesitation. "She would have loved it."

Olivia nodded, her gaze lowering to the mask again. Her inspiration for the costume had come from a collection of children's stories which had belonged to her mother, a gift she had apparently received from her own mother when she was a little girl.

The book was stained and well-worn, and one of Olivia's most prized possessions, a rare remembrance of her mother, and one she could actually hold in her hands.

"She would be proud of you, you know," Aunt Augusta said softly, reaching over to give her hand a squeeze. "Very proud."

Olivia met her gaze. "Do you think so?"

How nice it would have been to have a parent who was proud of her.

"I know so," Aunt Augusta said firmly, drawing a smile from Olivia's lips. "I only saw your mother once or twice during her confinement, but her excitement was obvious. She couldn't wait to meet you." Her eyes gentled with the memory. "She was an excellent woman. I wish you had known her."

Olivia's smile turned regretful. "So do I."

She thought of her mother often, of the memorable moments in her own life and what they might have been like had her mother been there to share them with her. She spoke to her sometimes, too, hoping the words would somehow find their way to her.

Her father had never wished to discuss her mother with her, so she'd had to rely on Aunt Augusta's meager memories to form an image of her in her mind. Lady Melissande Blakely—she was Melissande Simonnet before she married Olivia's father—was not related to Aunt Augusta by blood, but she knew the young lady from the time she made her come-out at the age of seventeen.

According to Aunt Augusta, Melissande had been shy and sweet and very pretty, and the young Earl Blakely was instantly smitten with her. The two married after a whirlwind courtship and, by all accounts, were very happy together.

It was difficult to reconcile the father she knew—distant, disinterested—with the image of a besotted swain wooing his lady love. Did her mother share his feelings? Was she smitten, too? Or was she tempted by other men? She wished she could ask her.

If only she hadn't died. If only she was here.

How different would her life have been if her mother had never gone?

Shoving the maudlin thoughts from her mind, Olivia secured her demi-mask over her eyes as their carriage rolled to a stop at the front of the Henleys' home. The carriage door swung open, and a footman secured the steps before handing Aunt Augusta down to the gravel path.

Olivia followed and the two ladies made their way into the entrance hall where they handed over their wraps before heading for the ballroom, the sounds of laughter and music signaling the way.

Lady Henley's ballroom was enormous and sparsely decorated, its only ornamentation the sweeping panels of burgundy and gold silk that sparkled beneath the candlelight. The guests were garniture enough, in truth; colorfully costumed to resemble their favorite character of the written word. Not a terribly original theme, but it was a favorite for a reason.

A quartet of musicians played Handel at the rear of the room while liveried servants in burgundy and gold circled the room with trays bearing drinks.

Olivia swept her gaze across the packed ballroom, spotting a Robinson Crusoe, a Little Bo-Peep, at least three Apollos and even a Bottom, arse's head and all. She pointed the costume out to her aunt, and they shared a smile.

Venturing further into the crowd gathered around the dance floor, Olivia searched for her would-be betrothed among the sea of faces. She smiled when she spotted him at the other end of the room, a dapper Romeo in knee breeches and a ruffled shirt. His mother was with him, *sans* costume, and a third party was there, as well, a pretty brunette Olivia did not recognize.

The young lady was dressed in a beautiful gown of emerald-green velvet with a full skirt and the trumpet sleeves that were so popular during the Renaissance.

Olivia's brow knit. Was the girl Juliet to Paxton's Romeo?

"Do you know the lady with Paxton?" she whispered to her aunt as the duke led the unknown young woman onto the dance floor.

Aunt Augusta studied the lady and shook her head. "I've never seen her before. Perhaps she is his sister?"

Olivia frowned. "He doesn't have a sister."

"A cousin, then?"

But she knew of no such cousin. The sudden appearance of this pretty young lady she did not know filled her with unease, though she couldn't explain why.

She was probably worrying over nothing.

"Ah, Keswick! Good evening, my boy," Aunt Augusta called out, and Olivia's shoulders stiffened.

With her heart pounding in her throat, she turned to greet him, steeling herself as she pasted a polite smile on her face. She tried not to think of their last encounter when he'd kissed her in Lady Chavel's rose gardens and then told her it was nothing but a consolation prize. Still, she could feel her cheeks warming as he approached.

"But where is your costume?" Aunt Augusta asked, her tone affronted. "Did you forget this ball was fancy dress?"

A regretful smile curved his lips. "I'm afraid I'm not much of a costume man, Lady Augusta. I'm only here to act as Emmy's chaperone. Therefore, I am exempt."

"Nonsense," Aunt Augusta said with a wave of her walking stick. "I am a chaperone and I have dressed up."

"And you look wonderful, my lady." Griffin bowed deeply, humor lighting his eyes. "You wear that dress far better than I ever could."

Olivia forced her gaze to the parquet floor, battling the urge to drink in every last inch of him. He wore no costume tonight, but he was breathtaking all the same. Dressed in black from his hat to his boots, he exuded confidence and strength, a seductive devil sent to tease and torment her.

"And what of Olivia?" Aunt Augusta asked. "Doesn't she look wonderful, as well?"

Olivia stiffened and her gaze shot to Griffin's of its own accord. His eyes swept over her costume then back up to her face, and whatever it was she saw in those dark gray depths made her want to squirm in her slippers. And not in a bad way.

"She certainly does," he said, his voice soft.

Olivia's blush deepened. "Thank you, my lord."

Why was she blushing? The compliment was coerced, for heaven's sake. *You are behaving like a ninny.*

"Oh, there's Delia!" Aunt Augusta blurted out, referring to her good friend, Mrs. Prewitt. She squeezed Olivia's arm. "She's just returned from her trip to Scotland, and I haven't seen her since she got back. Excuse me, my dear. Keswick."

And with that, she was off, charging through the crowd in her multi-colored gown, making Olivia smile when she used her walking stick to herd a bewigged Rob Roy out of her path.

"Your costume is magnificent," Griffin said, coming up beside her. "I cannot recall a peacock from any stories I've ever read. What is it from?"

Lacing her fingers behind her back, she turned to him, both relieved and annoyed by his casual attitude. Evidently their kiss had already left his memory.

She was not so lucky.

"It is from a story titled *Princess Rosette*," she said, snagging a glass of ratafia from a passing servant's tray. "She marries the King of the Peacocks."

Feeling abysmally out of her depths, she took a long drink from her glass, savoring the balm to her suddenly dry throat. Making small talk wasn't usually so difficult, but then she'd never attempted it with a man who, only two days ago, had put his tongue in her mouth.

"I don't remember that tale," he said, moving aside to let a pair of Roman goddesses pass by.

"There is no reason you should," she said with a polite smile. "It is one of Madame d'Aulnoy's creations. From her collection of stories called *Les Contes des Fées*."

His brows rose. "A French children's book?"

"My maternal grandmother was French," she explained. "The book belonged to my mother."

"I see. And this Princess Rosette, she is your favorite character from these stories?"

"Oh, no," Olivia answered, gazing into her empty glass. "That would be Belle-Belle. From *Belle-Belle ou Le Chevalier Fortune*." She slanted him an arch look. "Belle-Belle slays a dragon."

There. She could pretend nothing had happened, too.

"A dragon slayer? Impressive," Griff said before casting a pointed glance at her costume. "But why did you not come dressed as Belle-Belle, if she is your favorite?"

"Because Belle-Belle spends most of her story disguised as a boy." She curved her lips into an impish smile. "I could hardly attend Lady Henley's costume ball dressed in trousers, now could I?"

"More's the pity," he said, amusement creasing the corners of his eyes. "I would have liked to have seen that."

She shrugged. "I'm afraid you'll have to rely on your imagination instead."

His eyes glinted, all amusement gone, and she stilled as his gaze flicked to her lips, her breasts, her hips, scorching a path down her body all the way to her toes. His eyes snapped to her face and locked on hers, and the desire burning there, the *want*, shocked her to her very core.

She swallowed, scrambling for something to say, something sophisticated and coolly unaffected, but her mouth seemed incapable of forming words.

Was it true? Did he want her? Or was that look in his eyes the workings of her hopelessly hopeful imagination?

"Here you are, Livvy!" Emmy materialized out of nowhere, her color high, her breathing labored as if she'd sprinted across the ballroom. "I've been looking everywhere for you."

Olivia grinned, taking in Emmy's Lincoln green skirt and fitted coat, the jaunty bycocket perched on her head, the quiver and bow she'd strapped to her back.

It was a Robin Hood costume that would not scandalize the *ton*.

"You look glorious, Em," she said with a grin. "And your hat is simply div—"

"Please, Livvy." Emmy held up her hands. "I have something I must tell you. Something important." Her voice was low and urgent, and Olivia's smile slowly faded.

"What is it?" she asked, unease knotting her belly. "Is something the matter?"

Emmy nodded, her eyes pained. "It's the duke," she said. "He is betrothed."

Chapter Twelve

The duke is betrothed.

The words clanged through Olivia's mind like raucous, discordant bells. She gave her head a shake as if to clear them away, certain she must have misheard.

"Betrothed?" she echoed. "But...that is impossible. There must be some mistake."

Emmy shook her head, anger simmering in her eyes. "The young lady's name is Jane Withers. She is the daughter of one of the duchess's closest friends, and apparently the two mothers have long wished their children would marry..."

Olivia searched the room for Paxton, but he was no longer on the dance floor, and she could not find him in the crowd. She needed to see him, to meet his gaze and see for herself, in his eyes, that it wasn't true. *It cannot be true.*

"I don't understand," she whispered. "Why did he never mention her to me? Why did he let me believe he was mine? He said he cared for me. He said he would marry me—" Her throat caught, and her eyes fell closed as a wave of dizziness came over her. She longed to yank off her mask and toss it to the floor. "I have to leave. I can't stay here. I can't—"

She turned, preparing to flee, when a hand closed around her wrist, gentle but firm. Surprise parted her lips and her gaze shot up, straight into Griffin's fierce gray eyes.

"Don't," he said, his voice low and gruff. "Don't run away. Don't let him see your pain." He gave her wrist a gentle squeeze. "Dance with me, Olivia."

The quiet calm in his voice washed over her, soothing her nerves and easing the knot of panic in her chest. She nodded.

Griffin tucked her hand in the crook of his elbow and led her onto the crowded dance floor as the strains of Mozart's Sussex Waltz began to fill the room.

Olivia did her best to hold her head high, to show everyone in the ballroom that she was fine, that she would *always* be fine, but her heart thudded in her ears and her lips refused to keep a smile.

Her skin prickled, as if every pair of eyes in the room was watching her, though she couldn't bring herself to look, afraid of what she would find in their faces.

Pity. Derision. Smug satisfaction.

Paxton is betrothed.

How could it be true? After everything they'd been through, after weeks and weeks of patient waiting, he had betrothed himself to another woman.

She was too stunned to be angry with him. Her mind was hazy, sluggish, her body curiously numb, as if she'd received the news in a dream. Only she was awake, and this nightmare was all too real.

Numbly, she joined hands with Griffin, and they began to move around the dance floor in the opening steps of the waltz. Her limbs were stiff, but she did not stumble, steadied by the familiarity of the steps and the oddly comforting press of Griffin's hands in hers.

"Olivia." His soft voice drew her gaze to his. "*Smile.*"

"I am smiling," she muttered, not at all certain it was true.

"You're not," he said, with a pointed look at her mouth.

He slipped a hand around her waist and pulled her in close, his fingers pressing into her flesh, warm and strong, and despite the circumstances—despite *herself*—a tiny shiver ghosted across her skin.

She placed her hand on his shoulder and stretched her lips into a toothy grin, the muscles in her cheeks aching with the effort.

"You look like a rabid dog," he said, laughter shining in his eyes as he guided her around a passing couple. "Try again. With fewer teeth this time."

The urge to roll her eyes was strong, but she batted her lashes instead and softened her smile to demure. "How is this?"

He nodded approvingly. "Better. I could almost believe you like dancing with me."

Olivia snorted a soft laugh. "Clearly I missed my calling on the stage."

His smile deepened. "Clearly."

She studied him openly from behind her demi-mask, drinking in the strong planes of his face, the little lines creasing the corners of his eyes. Gratitude washed over her, warming her chest and she dropped her gaze to his evening coat.

He was a puzzle to her, this man. He did not like her and yet, here he was, dancing with her when he did not dance, all so she could salvage her pride.

"Griffin?"

His eyes met hers. "Yes?"

She parted her lips, intending to thank him, but the words slipped away as an older woman and her partner passed by, their gawking eyes pricking her skin like needles.

"...it is no less than she deserves..."

"...she brought this upon herself..."

Olivia stiffened, shame scorching the tips of her ears. She sucked in a soundless breath of air and fought to keep her smile.

"Ignore them," Griffin murmured, giving her hand a staying squeeze. "They are nothing to you."

She huffed out a humorless laugh. "They are right, though. I do deserve this."

"You don't believe that."

Her gaze fell to his cravat and snagged on the simple diamond pin tucked in the folds of ebony silk. Candlelight caught in the diamond and flashed, as if winking at her. Mocking her.

"The duke proposed to me last Season," she said, the words acrid on her tongue. "I turned him down. His mother has never forgiven me for it, but I thought Paxton had and that maybe, with a little time, he might ask me again." She swallowed. "Obviously I was wrong."

And now it was too late. She'd bungled everything, and the damage had been too great to repair.

Disappointment speared her but she fixed another smile to her lips and kept her gaze on Griffin's cravat. She would not look for Paxton again. She would not give him the satisfaction.

"Why did you turn him down?" Griffin asked, his tone oddly flat. "I should have thought you'd snap up the first duke to offer for you."

Silly. Spoiled. Title-chaser.

The words he'd slung at her all those months ago struck her like arrows, poison-tipped, straight through the heart, and her breath caught in her throat. Reality returned, abrupt, unmerciful, an unflinching reminder of his true feelings. His poor opinion.

He is not your friend.

Cloaking herself in pride, she threw him a teasing half-grin. "Isn't it obvious?" she said airily. "I was holding out for a prince."

His lips quirked as if torn between a smirk and a smile.

The final strains of the waltz faded to an end, bringing cold reality with it. Olivia fixed her smile and notched her chin up with queenly composure as she laid her hand on Griffin's proffered forearm.

"Thank you for the waltz, my lord." She kept her voice light and breezy as they exited the dance floor. "I realize how difficult it must have been for you, dancing with someone you hate. But I am grateful to you."

She looked at him, and his eyes shuttered. A muscle ticked in his jaw. "I don't hate you, Olivia."

She arched a brow. "But you don't like me, either."

He was silent, no words, not a single gesture to refute her words. Her heart gave a painful thud, and she widened her smile, her *armor*, before turning and walking away, the echo of his words nipping at her slippered heels.

I don't hate you, Olivia.

She swallowed past the lump in her throat, her cheeks flaming with embarrassment. With shame.

Because despite his ambivalence toward her, despite all her attempts at pushing him away, she still cared what he thought of her.

She suspected she always would.

SEVERAL HOURS AND ONE interminably long costume ball later, Olivia flopped onto her back on Emmy's bed and released a slow, exhausted sigh.

"Well," she said to the ceiling, "I think this evening qualifies as a complete and utter disaster, don't you?"

The mattress sank as Emmy sat down beside her. "I'm so sorry, Livvy. I know you had high hopes for tonight."

Olivia huffed out a humorless laugh. High hopes? Yes, she'd had high hopes for the evening. The higher the hopes, the greater the fall, apparently.

"I wanted a betrothal, and I got one," Olivia said dryly. "Pity it wasn't mine."

The evening should have been magical. She'd spent countless hours assembling her costume, and took such care with her appearance tonight, certain the romance of the evening would inspire her duke to finally ask for her hand.

Her duke. She scoffed. He'd never been her duke, had he? She'd wanted his name so badly she'd convinced herself their marriage was inevitable, a foregone conclusion, and she'd left no space for the possibility of an alternate outcome.

What a fool she'd been.

"You tried to warn me, didn't you?" She crossed her arms beneath her head and sighed. "You asked me what I would do if the duke should fall ill and die. I thought you were being morbid, but you knew something might happen, didn't you? You knew the duke would not be mine." She shook her head. "I should have listened to you."

"Paxton is a fool," Emmy said. "And if you would like for him to suddenly fall ill and die, I would be more than happy to look into it for you."

The glint in her eyes was almost frightening, and Olivia couldn't help but smile a little. "I almost wish he were dead," she said. "At least then I could tell myself he would have married me if we'd only had more time."

She didn't mean it, of course. No matter how angry she was with him, she would never wish him harm. He was as much a victim of his mother's overbearing personality as she was.

"Did you have no idea he was considering marrying this Miss Withers?" Emmy asked.

Olivia made room on the bed so Emmy could stretch out beside her. "I've never even heard of Miss Withers," she said, her exasperation showing in her voice. "He's never once mentioned her to me."

"It is obviously the match his mother wants. Paxton would rather marry you. Everyone knows that."

"I thought so, too," Olivia said, fussing with the sleeve of her nightrail. "I thought if I was patient, his regard for me would eventually eclipse his desire to please his mother. I thought I was making progress."

Her father's letter flashed in her mind, and she grimaced, her pride recoiling at the thought of conceding defeat. "I don't know what I'll do now."

"Well, I do," Emmy said with characteristic confidence. "You will compile a list of your many admirers, cross out the ones you don't like and let the rest fight for the honor of your hand."

Olivia wrinkled her nose. "Paxton was the only duke amongst them."

"Hang Paxton." Emmy slashed a hand through the air. "And hang dukes, for that matter. I never thought he was good enough for you, and he's just proved me right."

Olivia turned her head to look at her. "You've never liked him very much, have you?"

Emmy shrugged. "He's a nice man, but I never felt he was the right one for you." Her brows drew together, concern lighting her eyes. "Are you very disappointed?"

Olivia draped her hands across her belly and nibbled her bottom lip as she assessed her feelings. "My heart isn't broken, if that's what you are asking," she said slowly. "I am disappointed, of course, but honestly I feel more lost than anything else."

For weeks she'd thought of little else but catching herself a duke, putting her need to please her father above everything else. Now that it was over, she had no idea what to do with herself.

"I did want to marry him," she said, her gaze on the ceiling again. "Yes, because it would make me a duchess, but also because I genuinely liked him, and I believed we would be happy together. I still do." She shook her head and tried to smile. "But none of that matters now, does it? It is over."

Emmy gave Olivia's arm a gentle squeeze, but she made no reply. What else was there to say? Words would change nothing. What was done was done.

Paxton was betrothed to another, and Olivia had no choice but to let him go.

CHAPTER THIRTEEN

Griff rolled onto his back on the mattress and slung an arm over his eyes, his frustrated sigh rumbling through the quiet of his bedchamber.

Sleep eluded him.

The events of the evening tossed and turned in his head, his sister's news, his dance with Olivia, the look on her face, so small and pale, as she learned of that coward Paxton's betrothal.

His *betrayal*.

Anger stabbed at him. He'd held very little respect for the Duke of Paxton before tonight, but now, after seeing the hurt he'd wrought, he wanted nothing more than to watch the man pay for his cowardice.

And that surprised him.

The *intensity* of his reaction surprised him. He shouldn't care this much. She was his sister's friend, yes, and someone he'd known for years, so it stood to reason he would feel at least some concern for her well-being.

But to want to exact revenge on her behalf? Or do bodily harm to the man responsible for hurting her? He could not explain that. It wasn't like him at all.

He blew out another sigh and scrubbed his hand down his face.

"*Meow.*"

Artemis climbed onto his chest and sat, peering down at him with sleepy yellow eyes.

"I'm sorry, little one," he said, giving the kitten's chin a scratch. "Is my tossing and turning disturbing your slumber?"

Her answer was a swift chomp on the tip of his index finger.

He laughed through his wince and tugged free of her nettles for teeth. "I suppose that can only mean one thing," he said, inspecting his chewed finger. "You must be hungry."

"*Meow.*"

He nodded. "So am I. How about I see if I can scrounge up something for us to eat, hm?"

Transferring Artemis to the dark blue counterpane, he climbed out of bed and lit a candle on his chest of drawers. He crossed to the armchair where he'd discarded his evening clothes and tugged on the black shirt and trousers before donning his house slippers.

"I'll be back soon," he said to Artemis on his way to the door.

She plopped her rump on the bed and began washing her face, as if preparing for the meal ahead.

117

Chuckling softly to himself, Griff stepped into the hall with his lone candlestick and shut the door behind him before heading up the dark corridor toward the stairs.

He wasn't sure what he would find in the kitchens at this hour, but he would be happy with a crust of bread and a small wedge of cheese. Artemis liked cheese.

As he neared the stairs, his gaze caught on a faint sliver of light peeking through the cracked door of the drawing room. He frowned. Had Sally left a fire burning in the hearth?

He nudged the door open with his knuckles and peered inside.

The hearth was cold, but a candelabra sat perched on the mantel with all five candles lit. He flicked his gaze over the room, searching the chairs, the shadowed spaces, until finally he spotted her, a lone figure tucked away in the corner.

Olivia.

Of course it was Olivia.

She sat cross-legged on the sofa, her face in profile, and she looked pensive, her gaze fixed on the window beside her. She wore a white nightrail and a knitted shawl wrapped snugly around her shoulders. Her hair was down, glinting like gold beneath the soft candlelight.

"Can't sleep?" he asked from the doorway.

She turned and her mouth hitched up at one side, as if she was pleased to see him but didn't want to be.

"No," she said softly. "I thought reading might help, but I couldn't quiet my mind enough to concentrate on the words. So, I decided to give whisky a try instead." She raised a glass he hadn't noticed and gave it an unpracticed swirl.

"Whisky?" Griffin leaned his shoulder against the door jamb. "That's pretty potent stuff."

Especially for young ladies who had never had anything stronger than sherry.

"It seems to be what you men turn to when you've suffered a disappointment, so I thought it might work for me." She peered into her glass. "I don't know what you lot see in it. It's dreadful."

Griffin smiled. "One develops a taste for it."

She wrinkled her nose, clearly dubious, but made no reply. Her eyes, he noted, seemed weary, almost slumberous, as if she'd been crying. Now did not seem the time to mention it, though. She'd been hurt, and he had no desire to make her feel worse.

"May I join you?" he asked, against his better judgment.

"By all means, do." She raised her glass at him. "It's your drawing room, after all."

Quietly he closed the door behind him then crossed to the sideboard where he served himself a generous pour of whisky. He sat beside her on the sofa, careful not to get too close, and settled into the well-worn cushions, crossing one leg over the other.

He sipped his whisky and watched the candles burn. The silence was mostly comfortable, though he was keenly aware that she wore nothing but a thin cotton nightrail under her shawl.

He cleared his throat. "Paxton isn't worth all this fuss, you know." He looked at her. "There are plenty of other single men for you to marry."

She nodded, her gaze on her glass. "I know. But there was only one duke."

Griffin worked his jaw, annoyance prickling at his nape. Why was it that every time he felt himself softening toward her, she had to say something to ruin it?

"Is it really so important to you?" he asked. "Being a duchess?" He could not keep the censure from his voice, though, truth be told, he didn't try very hard.

"Yes," she said quietly. "But not for the reasons you think."

Curiosity and something else drew his gaze to her face; something in her voice, a faint thread of sadness. Or, perhaps, self-recrimination. "What do you mean?"

She sipped her whisky, cradling the crystal glass in both hands as she drank, and then she tipped her head back to rest against the sofa. He watched her throat work as she swallowed, her skin like silk beneath the candle's flame, and then it was his turn to swallow. He looked away.

"My father hates me," she finally said, the words a hollow whisper. "He always has. Ever since the day I was born."

Griffin's gaze flicked to her face, surprise knotting his brow. "He...what?"

"He hates me." Her tone was sure, almost nonchalant, as if fathers hating their daughters was commonplace. Her gaze met his. "I killed my mother, you see. My first day on this earth was her last, and I'm afraid my father has never forgiven me for it."

Shock froze him. He opened his mouth to reply, but no words came. He had none.

"I suppose it wouldn't have been so bad if I'd been born a boy," she went on. "But, alas, here I am. A daughter." She huffed out a derisive laugh. "My father lost his beloved wife, and then found himself saddled with the worthless child who'd killed her. Is it any wonder he hates me?"

Griffin's shock began to fade as anger took its place. What kind of father would hate his child for something she could not control? What kind of man could be so heartless? His hands clenched around his glass, the crystal biting into his flesh.

"Has your father...told you he hates you?" he asked gruffly, almost afraid to hear the answer.

"He's never said the words, no, but his disinterest speaks for itself." She drew in a deep breath, and wrapped her arms around her knees, her slippered toes peeking out from beneath the hem of her nightrail. "I remember trying so hard to please him when I was a little girl. I was so certain that if I could master languages and embroidery and music and riding, he would finally be proud of me. And then maybe he wouldn't despise me anymore. Maybe he could even come to love—"

She broke off, her voice wavering. "It didn't work, of course. He never once praised me for my accomplishments. He's never even reprimanded me for my transgressions, and there have been many, I assure you."

"I can believe it," he said, a smile tugging at his lips.

Olivia rested her cheek on her knees, her brow furrowing. "Nothing I ever did seemed to please him," she said, her voice softer now and limned in hurt. "None of it was ever enough. *I* am never enough. I know this, and yet, I continue to try." A rueful smile touched her lips. "I don't know why, but I can't seem to help myself."

"Is that why you wanted to marry Paxton?" Griffin guessed. "To make your father proud of you?"

He could understand the compulsion. He often wondered if his own father would be proud of him.

She lifted her head and breathed out a weary sigh. "In part, yes," she admitted. "But I messed it all up. I lost my duke. And now I don't know what to do."

Griffin studied her profile, thinking of all he'd learned, of his erroneous impression of the woman sitting beside him. Everywhere she went, men admired and adored her, and yet the only man she wanted to impress was her father. A man who refused to give her what she yearned for.

How wrong he'd been about her.

"You asked me earlier tonight why I turned the duke down last Season," Olivia said, the words quiet, almost tentative.

Her gaze met his, her blue eyes nearly black in the candlelight. Griffin's heart gave a disquieting thump.

"It was because of you," she said. "I wanted to marry you."

Devil's brew.

Olivia gazed down at the near-empty glass of whisky in her hands and frowned. *Whisky.* The name was far too tame for a spirit that could so easily loosen a lady's tongue.

The room was quiet, with only the ticking clock on the mantel to stand in the way of total silence. Griffin had gone mute, his mouth grim, brow puckered, apparently displeased by her confession, which she never would have made without the whisky's help.

Still, she couldn't bring herself to regret it. There was something freeing in telling the truth, even if this particular truth was more than a little embarrassing.

"You needn't look so worried," she said, stretching her legs out until her feet touched the rug. "I exorcized my infatuation for you months ago. Right after Christmas, to be exact. And I have no intention of renewing my regard."

She set her glass on the small table beside her and drew in a deep breath. "Perhaps I should concede defeat now and let my father choose a husband for me. I doubt he could do worse than I've done so far. I seem to have a weakness for men who don't want me."

Sinking a little lower into the sofa, she let her eyes fall closed, regret and melancholy washing over her in waves. She was feeling sorry for herself, and she hated the weakness. She tried so hard to be cheerful and positive, but she had to admit, it was exhausting sometimes.

A tear slid down her cheek, surprising her, and she brushed it away with an embarrassed laugh. "I'm sorry," she said. "It seems the whisky has made me maudlin."

Griffin's hand found hers, and Olivia stilled at the unexpected press of his palm, his long fingers lacing with hers, solid and warm. Bewildered, she looked at him, and found him watching her with serious eyes.

"You're enough, Olivia," he said, his voice husky. "You're more than enough."

The sincerity in his gaze, the gentle stroke of his thumb across her knuckles, held her mesmerized and she swallowed, her heart beating a frantic tattoo.

His throat was bare, his shirt collar loose, teasing at naked collarbones and a dusting of dark hair. Lord, but he was a handsome man, even with his hair mussed and his shirt rumpled.

More so, probably.

Her gaze dipped to his mouth, only inches from hers, and she wondered if he would kiss her again. Anticipation pricked her skin.

Stop it, she ordered herself. *Stop it now. There is nothing to anticipate.*

She pulled her gaze away and looked down at her lap, smoothing her fingers over the fringe edging her shawl. "I thought I was nearly done with all this," she said, her tone casual, as if she often held Griffin's hand in the dark. "The balls and parties and musicales..." She shook her head. "I'd hoped I was finished with them."

"But I thought you liked the whirl of the Season," Griffin said, a question in his voice.

"I do," she said. "I *did*. At least, I thought I did. I suppose I'm simply bored with it all now."

He nodded. "I know how you feel."

"I would love to travel," she said, wistfulness in the words. "Explore far off places, see parts of the world I've never seen before. Even parts of *England* I've never seen before would suffice. I just want to experience something outside of my everyday life."

Griffin sipped his whisky. "I've always wanted to visit Greece," he said. "Macedonia, Crete. Athens and its Acropolis."

Olivia rolled her head to the side to look at him. "So why haven't you?" she asked. "You're a single gentleman of means. You may come and go as you please."

He smiled and shook his head. "I've never felt I could come and go as I please."

"Why not?"

He shrugged. "The responsibilities of the marquessate keep me busy."

"Surely there are people you can hire to take care of things for a month or two."

"And then there's Emmy and my mother, of course."

Olivia gave him a wry look. "Both of whom would miss you terribly but would undoubtedly survive without you."

"Perhaps. But ever since my father died..." His brow creased. "It never felt right, leaving them. I can't explain it."

Olivia fell silent as she considered his words, his responsibilities as not only the marquess, but also as a brother and son, the head of the family. He was so young when his father died. He'd taken on so much. It was strange how she'd never considered that before, the responsibility, the burden he carried with him.

"Were you close with your father?" she asked.

Griffin's thumb stilled on her knuckles, and she held her breath, waiting to see if he would pull his hand from hers.

"Yes," he said finally. "We were very close. I wish I'd had more time with him."

Olivia nodded, the motion stilted against the sofa cushion. Emmy was barely three years old when she and Griffin lost their father, and she had no memories of the man, but Griffin must have many.

"What was he like?" she asked, already picturing the attentive, loving father she'd always heard him to be.

"He was tall. Broad-shouldered. Kind." He paused, as if lost in a memory. "I remember he always seemed to be laughing. We all did."

She could hear the smile in his voice, the affection, and it made her smile in turn, even as envy snaked around her heart.

"He sounds wonderful," she said softly, turning her head to look at him. "I'm sorry you lost him so young. It isn't fair."

"No. It isn't." His gaze met hers. "But neither is having a father who doesn't love you as he should."

Longing, keen and poignant, pulled at her heart and she shook her head at her own foolishness. "I wish I didn't care what he thinks of me. I wish I could let go of this need to please him, but..." Her words trailed off on a sigh.

"But he's your father," he said, squeezing her hand, and the understanding in his voice eased the ache in her chest.

"But he's my father."

And for better or worse, she would never stop wanting him to be proud of her.

She tipped her head back and gazed up at the ceiling, watching the candlelight flicker and play. "My stepmother is going to have a baby," she said, the words tumbling from her lips, still strange in their newness. Her brows drew together. "I used to dream of having a sibling when I was a little girl, a little brother or sister to play with and talk to. But now that it is finally happening, I don't know how I feel about it. I'm happy for Caroline, of course. She has yearned for a baby for many years, and I know she will be a wonderful mother, but—" She broke off and pressed her lips together, trapping the loathsome words inside.

Griffin turned to look at her. "But?"

"But I'm jealous, too," she whispered.

"Of Caroline?"

She shook her head. "Of the baby."

Her eyes fell closed, guilt and shame sitting on her chest like scorching hot bricks, and she swallowed. The admission had left a sour taste on her tongue. "I'm jealous of a child—my own sibling—who hasn't even been born yet," she muttered. "What is the matter with me?"

"Nothing."

"But—"

"There is nothing the matter with you, Olivia," he said firmly, brooking no argument. "Your feelings for your father are complicated. It stands to reason that your feelings for this child would be complicated, too."

Her eyes met his and she saw in them the sincere belief in his words. She gave him a small, grateful smile. "Thank you."

She'd never shared these feelings with anyone before, and it probably should have felt strange, sharing them now, here in the dark with Griffin. Instead, it felt...*right*.

Despite all their bickering, everything they'd been through, she trusted him with her secrets. He made her feel safe. And that unnerved her.

She could not afford to give him any more of herself than she already had. She could not allow her heart to reach for him the way it used to. The way it wanted to, even now.

"I should go," she said, slipping her hand from his. She felt the loss acutely, the absence of his touch, the comfort she'd found there, but she knew it was unwise to linger.

She rose to her feet, clutching the ends of her shawl with one hand.

Ever the gentleman, he stood, too.

She tipped her chin up to look at him, an awkward smile curving her lips. "Thank you, Griffin," she said. "For everything you've done for me tonight. I...I'll never forget it."

He smiled, his gray eyes glowing silver in the candlelight. "It's 'Griffin' tonight, is it?"

She shrugged. "We're friends. For tonight, at least."

His smile widened, amusement playing across his features, but she took no offense. He did not seem to be laughing at her. Indeed, she had the distinct impression she'd pleased him.

Oh, he was a puzzle. Fascinating, perplexing. Hopelessly unsolvable.

She brushed past him and made for the door, tucking her shawl around her as cold air breezed through her nightrail. She shivered and reached for the doorknob, her fingers grazing the cool brass just as a warm hand settled on her shoulder.

She turned, a question on her tongue, but the look in Griffin's eyes obliterated her every thought. He dipped his head and his mouth met hers, his kiss so soft, so tender, it buckled her knees.

He caught her to him, severing the kiss, his breath uneven and warm on her cheek. "I'm sorry," he said. "I shouldn't have done that. It was—"

"A mistake?" she chirped. "Another consolation prize, perhaps? Poor, pitiful Olivia, here's another kiss to make her feel better." Hurt speared her chest and sharpened her tongue. She could not take another rejection. Not tonight.

"I don't pity you, damn it," he growled. "You're the strongest person I've ever met. You're *remarkable*. And so damned beautiful you make me forget my own—"

She rose up on tiptoe and kissed him hard, snatching the words from his silver tongue. She did not want to hear them, afraid of what they might lead to, afraid they would make her fall again, so hard and so deep she would never find her way out again.

She curled her fingers into his shirt and tugged him close, seizing control as she molded her lips to his. She swept her tongue into his mouth, heady with desire, with her own brazenness, and the low groan rumbling from Griffin's throat.

His hands found her hips, his fingers dipping, his tongue tangling as he eased her against the door. The hard press of cold oak at her back made her shiver, even through her shawl and nightrail, the contrast stark against the heat of Griffin's chest and thighs.

She kissed him without reserve, letting her hands wander, her eager fingers slipping beneath the open collar of his shirt to explore whatever she could reach. His skin was hot and smooth to the touch, his chest firm and strong and sprinkled with crisp hair.

She wanted his shirt gone, out of the way so she could feast her eyes and hands on him, but she wasn't brave enough to ask for it. Not tonight. This moment was tenuous, the kiss fleeting, and she knew better than to press her luck.

Griffin eased his lips from hers, dipping his head to nuzzle her throat. "God, you smell good," he said, his voice ragged. "You always smell so bloody good."

His breath was warm against her skin, his tongue wet, tasting her, and her nipples pebbled, her belly clenching with need. She whimpered, shifting on her feet, trying desperately to ease the ache between her thighs, but movement only seemed to heighten it.

As if sensing her torment, Griffin eased his thigh between her legs, pressing into her core, and a moan escaped her lips, needy and frustrated. The contact was exquisite, his thigh hard as stone, the brush of her nightrail cool and deliciously rough against her wet, aching flesh.

She braced her hands on his shoulders then gave a slow, experimental roll of her hips, and it felt so good her toes curled into her slippers.

"Yes," Griffin rasped, his hot eyes locked on her face. "Chase it, petal. Take your pleasure."

His hands stroked up her calves, gathering her nightrail until her legs were bare, and she gasped at the first brush of his hands on her skin. His fingers flexed around her hips, his grip biting, coaxing, and a heated shiver skated along her skin.

She'd dreamed of these hands, of the warm, rough slide of his palms on her naked flesh, reverent and possessive and oh-so-desirous. Her dreams paled to the reality of his touch, and she was greedy for it now.

"You're so bloody beautiful," he whispered, his gaze on her face, watching her as she rode his thigh.

The words caressed, spiking her pleasure. She chased it, grinding against him, her hands gripping the hard ridge of his shoulders. She was sinfully wet, soaking her nightrail, her bud plump and throbbing, and her toes curled with every exquisite thrust.

"Give into it, petal," he urged. "Let me make you feel good." His voice was like sin, his hands pleasure itself as they slid like silk to the tops of her thighs.

Her head fell back at the first rasp of his thumb, thudding softly against the door, her lips parting on a silent moan. He stroked again, circling his thumb over the aching peak of her sex, his touch like fire, setting her ablaze.

"Come for me," he whispered as his fingers stroked and teased. Unrelenting. Driving her mad. "Give me your honey, petal."

She panted, arching into his hand, and with one final stroke of his wicked thumb, she shattered. Her limbs stiffened, stars bursting behind her eyes as a wave of pleasure arced through her, unlike any she'd ever known.

Boneless, she sagged against the door, her limbs quivering, her skin flushed hot.

Never had such intense desire awakened within her; never was it so pleasurable to sate it. Would it ever be so good again? Or was it only Griffin's touch that made her come alive?

Dense silence permeated the room, the only sound the beating of her still racing heart.

131

Tentatively, she opened her eyes.

Griffin had leaned his forearm on the door above her, and his head was bowed, his gaze lowered. He stood motionless, and yet, seemed to vibrate with energy.

"Goodness," she chirped. Or, tried to. Her throat was dry as dust, and the word came out more croak than chirp.

Amused gray eyes met hers. "Are you all right?"

Her face warmed and she straightened off the door, fussing with the folds of her shawl. "I'm marvelous, thank you. And you?"

The moment the question left her lips, she longed to take it back. Of course he wasn't all right. He had not...taken his pleasure.

At least, she assumed that was the reason for his...tenseness. Should she offer to—no, her mind shied from the notion. She would not know how to ask or what to do, and she had reached her limits on feeling foolish for one day.

"I'm marvelous, too," he said. His tone was mild, though she could see the ghost of a smile tugging at his lips. "Tonight was—" He broke off with a huffed laugh, his breath rustling her hair. "Tonight was..."

Tonight was *what?* Glorious? Surprising? A mistake?

Her chest grew tight, the moment vulnerable, *assailable*, and she knew she could not remain even a second longer.

"Tonight was interesting," she said, donning her breeziest smile, "but it should not have happened. And, of course, it absolutely cannot happen again."

There. She'd said it before he could.

Grappling for the door handle, she eased the door open, shuffling Griffin out of the way with sheer force of will and slipped from the room without another word.

What was there to say?

If she had stayed, she might have revealed more than she should, and Griffin did not need to know just how much tonight had meant to her. Not when there was every chance it had meant nothing to him.

She couldn't bear to stay and listen to him say it was all a mistake. Not tonight. Not after the way he'd made her feel, the way his arms had held her, the way his mouth had worshipped hers, as if she meant something to him. As if she mattered.

She wanted to hold onto that feeling just a little while longer.

But only for tonight.

Chapter Fourteen

Griffin leaned forward in his chair and propped his elbows on the well-polished mahogany table tucked in one corner of the room, an untouched glass of brandy his only companion.

It was early, not yet noon, and the club was nearly empty, a fact which pleased him well. He was in no mood for company today. He'd come only for the comfort and quiet, both of which could be found in spades here. The gentlemen's club was designed with comfort in mind with its low lighting, dark wood furnishings and ample seating to choose from, all upholstered in the finest of leather.

Even with these comforts, though, he could not seem to quiet his mind. Or his conscience.

With a frustrated groan, he fell back against his chair and scrubbed a hand down his face, regret slicing through him, a sharp blade to his gut.

For God's sake, he'd brought Olivia-bloody-Blakely to climax against his bloody drawing room door last night.

And now he couldn't get her out of his bloody mind.

Her flushed cheeks, her lush mouth ripened from his kisses, the way her lips had parted on a gasp as she found her release against his hand. He'd found his own release later, stroking himself to completion as he imagined those plump red lips around his cock.

With a curse, he reached for his glass and drank deeply, barely tasting it, though it was a superior blend. He set the glass on the table and cradled the cool crystal between his palms.

It was inevitable, he supposed, what had happened last night. For two years he'd tried to stay away from Olivia, keeping her at arm's length any way he could, but he always knew he was no match for her. He'd wanted her long before last night, and today he wanted her still.

Hell, he wanted her *more*.

And it wasn't because of the intimacies they'd shared—though, of course, that was reason enough.

It was because of her, because of everything he'd learned about her these past few days. Things he never knew before, things he'd never bothered to find out for himself.

His chest tightened as he thought of everything she'd told him last night, her admission that her father blamed her for her mother's death. He still had trouble believing that Earl Blakely—a gentleman—could treat his own daughter, his flesh and blood, so cruelly.

And, still, Olivia strove to please him, to make him proud of her, as if he deserved such attention.

It made sense now, her single-minded pursuit of the Duke of Paxton, a man who was inferior to her in nearly every way imaginable. She wanted him because he was a duke, because a duke was the best, second only to royalty, and she wanted to marry the best for her father's sake. Because she thought marrying the best would make him proud of her.

And, whether she realized it or not, she had hoped Paxton would give her the love and affection she'd always sought. Instead, the blackguard had thrown her over for another woman, a woman of his mother's choosing.

Bloody idiot.

Raised voices sounded from the door and Griff's head came up as—*speak of the devil*—the Duke of Paxton walked in, looking ridiculous in a mulberry suit with yellow cravat, and two other dandified gentlemen he did not know.

Griff's hands clenched around his glass, but it was the only outward reaction he would allow. Idly, he sipped his brandy, his gaze trained on the table as if deep in thought, though he watched the duke from the corner of his eye.

He considered what he should do, if anything. The man's actions had done nothing to improve Griff's opinion of him, but he wasn't Olivia's keeper, or even a blood relation, and he wasn't certain it was his place to come to her defense. Or even if his defense would be welcome.

In the end, Paxton made the decision for him.

"Ah, Keswick. Just the man I was hoping to see. May I join you?" Paxton hovered behind an empty chair at Griffin's table, his mouth turned up in a stupid smile.

"By all means." Griff motioned to the chair with his glass and watched the man as he settled stiffly into his seat.

Crossing one leg over the other, Paxton fussed with his cravat then his coat sleeves, and a full minute had passed until finally Griffin could take no more of it.

"So," he said, mahogany creaking as he sat back in his chair. "I understand congratulations are in order."

Paxton stiffened then slowly lowered his forearms to the padded leather armrests and gave a weak smile. "Yes, well...nothing has been finalized as yet, but thank you all the same."

Griffin arched a brow. "Don't you want to marry the young lady?"

An image of the duke's almost-betrothed flashed in his mind, a petite girl with light brown hair and pale, pale skin. She was a pretty thing, but she was no Olivia.

The duke shifted in his seat, a flash of discomfort lighting his eyes. "She is the daughter of my mother's dearest friend."

"Ah." Griffin nodded. "Your mothers are pushing for the match, eh?"

Paxton blew out a breath. "They're ravenous for it."

"And you hate to disappoint them."

The duke shrugged. "You have a mother. You know what it's like."

Griff almost smiled at that, the man's assumption that all relationships between mothers and sons must be like his. Griffin loved his mother, but he would never allow her to dictate whom he married. Not that his mother would try, or even wish to.

"I saw you dancing with Lady Olivia last night," Paxton said, making a great effort to keep his tone casual. "I don't believe I've ever seen you dance with anyone besides your mother and sister."

Griffin lifted one shoulder. "I made an exception," he said. "Lady Olivia is worth it."

He allowed a little smile to curve his lips, as if just the thought of her made him happy and noted with satisfaction when Paxton's mouth pinched in consternation.

"I see."

Griff arched a brow. "You disagree?"

"What? No!" The duke's eyes had gone wide. "No, of course not. Lady Olivia is a wonderful girl. It's only that I wondered—" He cleared his throat, his gaze on the table. "That is...do you intend to court her?"

Griff took his time with his answer, letting the silence stretch into uncomfortable territory as he slowly circled the rim of his glass with his forefinger. Only the crackle and pop of the fire burning in the nearby hearth filled the quiet.

"I might," he finally replied, infusing his tone with thoughtfulness. "I am in no rush to marry, but now that Olivia has been...set free, so to speak..." He trailed off, forcing the duke's imagination to fill in the rest. He felt not one iota of sympathy for the man beside him squirming in his chair.

"Right. Right." Paxton nodded, visibly agitated as his throat worked. "Well, I will leave you to your solitude now, Keswick. I'd best be off. Business to attend to, you know. Good day."

He shot to his feet, so abruptly he nearly knocked his chair to the floor, and then he was off, dashing for the door as if the hounds of hell were nipping at his heels.

A moment later, the two fops he'd come in with went after him, clearly confused. Griff chuckled to himself. The duke was so agitated he'd forgotten about his friends.

Let him suffer, he thought, inhaling deeply the faint scents of cheroot smoke and cologne. It was no less than he deserved after what he'd done to Olivia. And what he'd done to himself.

The idiot obviously wanted her, but as far as Griff was concerned, any man who so willingly sacrificed his own wants over the desires of his mother deserved to be unhappy.

CHAPTER FIFTEEN

HUNCHED OVER THE ESCRITOIRE in the drawing room, Olivia touched the tip of her quill pen to her cheek and studied the list of names before her. "No," she muttered, slashing a line through Viscount Amberson's name. "Far too fond of horses."

With a weary sigh, she leaned back in her chair and rolled her shoulders to loosen the knots. She'd been at this for hours, laboring over her list of potential husbands, and the exercise had left her far from optimistic. She knew she was probably being too choosy for someone racing against the clock as she was, but then, it was hard not to be, considering she was selecting the man she would spend the rest of her life with.

Her gaze wandered to the window, and she scowled at the bright blue sky, the cheerful sun, which seemed to be mocking her. A lovely spring day awaited her outside and she was in here, trapped at her desk like a schoolgirl with makeup work to do.

That was what this list felt like. Makeup work. Making up for wasted time.

Her shoulders slumped. How had her life come to this? How had her future gone from happy and hopeful to frighteningly unclear?

In her first Season, she'd been peppered with offers, turning down viscounts and earls and rich pillars of the community as if it were nothing, as if they would never stop coming. She'd been flattered by the offers, of course, but not one of them had actually tempted her to accept.

She'd told herself it was because she wasn't ready to settle down yet, that she'd wanted to enjoy herself before starting a family. And this had been true, at least in part. But what she hadn't realized—or perhaps, hadn't *wanted* to realize—was that she was waiting for an offer that hadn't yet come.

An offer that never would come.

She'd been waiting for Griffin, whether she realized it then or not, and had foolishly tossed aside those offers that had come—good offers, like Paxton's.

"What a ninny I was," she whispered to herself.

It would be so easy to be angry with Griffin, to blame him for her predicament, but she couldn't do it. It wasn't his fault he didn't feel for her what she felt for him. *What she* used *to feel for him, that is.*

It was her own doing, laying all her hopes at his feet, waiting for him to love her. He'd never given her any reason to hope, had never encouraged her or made her think he thought of her as anything more than his sister's friend.

Yes, he teased her, and some might be tempted to read something in this behavior. But he'd also called her a silly, shallow flirt, so perhaps he'd always poked at her because she annoyed him. It made more sense than the alternative.

Olivia set her pen down and rubbed at her tired eyes. Why was she thinking of Griffin again? She was supposed to be thinking of her future husband, and the Marquess of Keswick certainly did not fit the bill.

He seemed wholly disinterested in taking a bride, and even if he was looking to marry, he wouldn't marry her. He'd kissed her, yes, and seemed to find her attractive, in a begrudging sort of way, but none of this meant his opinion of her had changed.

You're the strongest person I know. You're remarkable.

His words ghosted through her mind, but she shoved them away, ignoring the frisson of pleasure skating up her spine. Perhaps his opinion of her had improved in these last few days, but nothing had changed because of it. He wasn't in love with her, he wasn't going to marry her, and she would do well to remember that and shove him from her mind.

Resolutely, she picked up her pen again and turned back to her list of names, determined to finish the task today. There was no time to waste.

"What are you doing?"

Olivia jumped in her seat then threw Emmy a glare over her shoulder. "You nearly scared me half to death!"

Emmy smiled as she perched on the edge of the klismoi chair situated beside the escritoire. "Apologies. I did say your name, but apparently you did not hear me." Her curious gaze dropped to the sheet of paper on the desk. "What are you working on with such concentration? A love letter?"

Olivia snorted. "Hardly. I'm compiling a list of potential husbands." She pursed her lips. "It isn't going very well."

"Oh." Emmy's brow knit. "But I thought—" She broke off, her frown deepening.

"You thought what?" Olivia asked, notching her head to one side.

"Well..." Emmy hesitated. "You know how much I hate to pry—"

"Oh? Since when?"

"*However...*" She flicked Olivia an unamused glance. "After last night, I'd hoped you would no longer have need for a list of potential husbands." She speared Olivia with expectant eyes.

"After last night?" Olivia frowned, even as her cheeks grew warm. Did Emmy know what had happened in the drawing room? *No. She couldn't.* "What on earth are you talking about?"

Emmy's brows darted up. "I know you were with Griffin last night. I smelled his soap on you when you finally came back to bed. *At two o'clock in the morning.* Naturally, I assumed something...interesting had happened between you."

Flashes of wet kisses and skilled fingers and whispered demands rolled through her mind, heating her cheeks anew, but she pushed them away. Something interesting had happened last night, but it wasn't what Emmy hoped.

"We talked, that's all," she said. *Well, mostly all.* "I couldn't sleep, and neither could he. We discussed the duke, and I thanked him for the waltz and that was it." She shrugged. "I'm sorry to disappoint you, Em, but there was no marriage proposal."

As much as she loathed keeping secrets from one of her dearest friends, telling Emmy of the kiss—*kisses*—would only encourage her to play matchmaker, and that was the last thing Olivia wanted.

"Rats." Emmy huffed a frustrated sigh. "I'd hoped my idiot brother had finally come to his senses."

"I know you did," Olivia said, a smile curling her lips. Emmy drove her mad at times, but her loyalty was second to none. "It is never going to happen, though. Your brother does not see me that way, and he never will."

"I disagree, Livvy. I think he does—"

"Now," Olivia interrupted, turning back to her list of names, "since you are here, you may help me with my husband list. What do you know of Earl Latimer?"

The message in Emmy's sigh was obvious, but Olivia ignored it, determined to continue on with her task and forget all about a certain bothersome marquess.

Before she had even picked up her pen, however, there was a soft scratch at the door. She turned to find their diminutive butler, Jessup, standing in the doorway.

"Yes, Jessup?"

"A caller has arrived, my lady. It is His Grace, the Duke of Paxton."

Olivia's heart sank. *Drat.* She was in no mood for a confrontation or an apology or whatever it was he'd come for today.

"You don't have to see him, Livvy," Emmy said, her astute gray eyes sympathetic. "Jessup can tell him you are not at home."

"I know," Olivia said with an appreciative smile. "But this conversation must happen sooner or later. I might as well get it over with now."

Emmy nodded. "As you wish. But if you should want me, I will be on the chaise in the corner, trying to control my temper. Call out to me if you need me to punch him for you."

A small smile curved her lips as she watched Emmy head for the chaise. She turned back to the waiting butler and said, "Thank you, Jessup. You may show His Grace in now."

"Very well, my lady."

Olivia rose and made her way to the sofa, standing before it with her hands clasped at her front, her lips stretched into a polite smile.

"Lady Olivia." Paxton's voice reached her ears before he'd even entered the room. "Thank you for agreeing to see me."

"Your Grace." She bobbed a curtsy as he approached, her greeting punctuating the new formality between them. "This is an unexpected visit."

"Do forgive me for calling so late," he said, his gaze flicking to Emmy before skittering back to Olivia. "I simply had to speak with you. Will you not sit with me?"

"Of course, Your Grace," Olivia said coolly. "But would you not care for a cup of tea first?"

"Thank you, no." His hands clenched at his sides, and he swallowed, visibly nervous.

Good. Let him suffer a little.

Olivia sank onto the sofa and clasped her hands on her knees, the picture of patient calm.

"I suppose by now you have learned about me and Miss Withers," he said as he claimed the seat beside her. His gaze was on his lap, as if he could not bring himself to look at her.

"Yes," she said simply. "I understand the lady's mother and yours are good friends."

His nod was glum. "They've known each other since they were girls, and have long desired a match between myself and Miss Withers. To join our families together."

"I see." Olivia cleared her throat, disappointment settling over her. Paxton had come to explain, to apologize, probably. It truly was over. "I know how important your mother's happiness is to you," she said. "And I wish you and Miss Withers a long and joyful life together."

Paxton swallowed again, his brown eyes beseeching as they rose to meet hers. "I don't want to marry her, Olivia. I want to marry you. You know how I feel about you, how I've always felt about you. I...admire you so much and I—I'm sorry to have hurt you like this."

Olivia's small smile was tight. "I know. I'm sorry, too. If I had accepted your offer last Season, maybe things would be different."

"I wish you had."

"So do I."

Paxton's gaze flicked nervously to the corner where Emmy sat, and then he reached out and gripped Olivia's hands in his. "It isn't too late. I'm not married yet, and no marriage contract has been signed." His brown eyes were fervent, more fervent than she'd ever seen them. "Please, Olivia. Give me time. That's all I need, a little more time to bring my mother around to my way of thinking."

She dropped her gaze to her lap and shook her head. "I don't think—"

"*Please,*" he repeated. "I know I have no right to ask this of you, but my heart does not care. My heart wants only you. Will you wait for me? Will you wait just a little while longer before you accept another man? Lord Keswick is a good prospect, I know, but—"

"Lord Keswick?" Olivia's head came up, her brows drawn together. "What does he have to do with this?"

Paxton's smile was sheepish. "He is the reason I am here. I saw him earlier at the club and he spoke of you. He was rather tight-lipped with his intentions, but I read between the lines and came straight here." His cheeks flushed. "I had to see you. I had to ensure you were not lost to me."

Olivia's lips parted, confusion fluttering in her chest. Griffin had discussed her with Paxton? But *why?*

She dropped her gaze to her lap and plucked an imaginary piece of fluff from her gown. "What did the marquess say to you?"

"Not much. I asked him if he intended to court you and he said he hadn't decided yet. But he left no doubt as to admiration for you."

Now she was more confused than ever. It was difficult to imagine Griffin, her severest critic, singing her praises to anyone, let alone to Paxton. So why had he done it? Why had he—*oh.*

Of course. That explained it.

Griffin's snide remarks and veiled insults had made his opinion of the duke more than obvious, specifically his relationship with his mother. Any compliment Griffin might have paid her earlier was simply his way of pranking Paxton for giving in to his mother's demands.

Olivia parted her lips, intending to set the duke straight and assure him Griffin had only been teasing him. But the words stalled as a thought occurred to her.

Paxton was *jealous*. The possibility that Griffin might court her, that she might *welcome* his courtship, had upset the duke so much he'd appeared in her drawing room unannounced and declared his intentions.

What possible benefit was there to setting him straight now?

It was only a small deception, after all. A little white lie, really. Where was the harm in letting him think it was true? Why shouldn't she use Griffin's prank to her advantage?

The marriage mart was not an even playing field, not for women. Only a fool would throw away an opportunity like this one, and she could not afford to be foolish.

She still wanted her duke.

"Lord Keswick is a fine gentleman," Olivia said lightly, her fingers toying with a loose thread on the sofa. "His good opinion is of great importance to me."

A long beat of silence passed before Paxton spoke again, his tone hesitant. "Are you...considering welcoming his suit?"

She met his gaze. "I think I should, don't you? He is a wealthy marquess, and you might marry another. I think it would be foolish not to consider him."

Paxton nodded, though his lips were set in a grim line. "I understand," he said quietly. "But please, promise me one thing? Promise me you will not rush to accept him. Please, give me a little more time before you do."

She dropped her gaze to her lap, as if considering his words, and then she nodded. "I will be patient, Your Grace. For as long as I can."

He excused himself then, determination shining in his eyes as he bowed to her and then quit the room.

Olivia listened for the sound of the front door closing then she slumped against the sofa with a sigh.

"There, you see?" she said to Emmy as she sat down beside her. "Your brother is helping me with the duke. He's hardly likely to do that if he hoped to marry me himself, is he?"

Confusion creased Emmy's dark brow. "No," she said slowly. "I suppose not." Her voice was thoughtful, but there was a distinct note of disappointment there, as well.

Olivia sighed. *Welcome to my life.*

Chapter Sixteen

OLIVIA WAS IN A cheerful mood when she arrived at the Keswick townhouse the following evening. The duke had not called on her like she'd hoped, but she knew she was in his thoughts.

At least, that was what his note had said, the one he'd sent to her this morning along with an enormous bouquet of dewy red roses which now graced the sofa table in the drawing room.

It was the largest bouquet she had ever received, and his choice of flower was not lost on her.

Perhaps there was hope for him yet.

Pushing aside thoughts of roses and the duke, Olivia leaned against the foot of Lady Keswick's bed and tried to look cheerful but not *too* cheerful.

The poor woman had been laid up for more than a week, and the inactivity seemed to have taken a toll on her spirits.

A crackling fire blazed in the hearth behind Aunt Augusta, who sat in a wingback chair beside the bed shuffling a deck of cards. Artemis snoozed at Lady Keswick's feet.

"And what is on tonight's agenda, girls?" Lady Keswick barked. "Is it Mrs. Lubbock's soirée? Or is that tomorrow evening?" Her mummified ankle was propped up on a pillow and a plate of biscuits sat in her lap, crumbs dotting the bed linens.

"No, it is tonight, Mama," Emmy said from Olivia's side. "And it is sure to be a dull evening. Isn't that right, Livvy?" She turned to her with beseeching gray eyes.

"Oh, yes. Dreadfully dull." Olivia nodded for emphasis.

Lady Keswick puffed out a wistful sigh. "I think a dull soirée sounds absolutely wonderful. I *miss* dull soirées."

Aunt Augusta laughed. "You've been confined to your bed too long, Lavinia. You *hate* Mrs. Lubbock, almost as much as you hate her soirées."

Lady Keswick harrumphed, waking Artemis, who rose with a mewl before clumsily climbing up the marchioness' legs to her lap, as if sensing her unhappiness.

Lady Keswick set her plate of biscuits aside and gave the kitten a smile. "At least I have this little one to keep me company tonight."

"And what have I been doing here for the past sennight but keeping you company?" Aunt Augusta said with a sniff. "*Excellent* company, I might add."

But Lady Keswick only waved the question away with her hand and kissed Artemis on the top of her head.

"I still don't understand what possessed Griffin to bring home a kitten," Emmy said, clearly trying to steer the conversation elsewhere. "He's never done such a thing before."

"Oh yes, he has," her mother said, a smile lighting her blue eyes. "He used to do it all the time when he was a boy."

"He did?" Emmy asked, surprise in her voice.

Olivia's ears perked up and she leaned a shoulder on the smooth oak bedpost, her gaze locked on the marchioness's face.

"Oh, yes," Lady Keswick said with a nod. "Kittens and rabbits and birds and squirrels, he showed no discrimination. He even brought home a baby badger once."

Emmy laughed. "A badger?"

"To this day, I have no idea where it came from." Lady Keswick chuckled. "I'll never forget the look on his face when he brought it home."

A miniature Griffin bringing orphaned animals home to his mother was just about the sweetest thing Olivia had ever heard. One had to wonder what he would say if he knew his mother was sharing stories about him as a boy. A smile curved her lips. She could almost hear his long-suffering sigh.

"I have no memory of him bringing any animals home," Emmy said, propping her hip against the mattress.

"No. You wouldn't have," her mother said, her eyes dimming. "He stopped doing it after your father died."

Olivia's heart squeezed. She knew how close Griffin was to his sire, how deeply the loss had affected him. How difficult it must have been to lose someone he'd loved so much.

"Of course, if Richard had lived," Lady Keswick said, her tone over-bright, "I have no doubt the two of them would eventually have turned our barn into a zoological garden. He was a lover of animals, too." She chuckled, though there was an unmistakable hint of melancholy in her voice. "I sometimes wonder if he loved his dogs more than he loved me."

Aunt Augusta snorted. "Nonsense. I remember how that man looked at you, Lavinia. Utter adoration."

The marchioness gave her a grateful smile. "Perhaps he did love me more than his dogs," she said. "A bit."

"Well, you *do* smell better," Aunt Augusta quipped.

The ladies all laughed and then, after saying their farewells, Olivia and Emmy quit the room.

"You go on ahead without me," Emmy said as they stepped into the corridor. "I left my shawl in my chamber. I'll meet you in the entrance hall in a few minutes."

Olivia nodded before heading up the corridor toward the stairs, her slippers a soft shush on the rug. Smiling to herself, she smoothed her gloved hands down the pink satin of her gown and a little thrill shot through her. She absolutely adored this gown, everything about it from its tiny puffed sleeves and fitted bodice, to its full skirt with the white beads adorning the hem.

Most of all, she adored how it made her feel, and she was glad she'd decided to wear it tonight.

She'd considered donning another blue dress for Paxton's sake, but in the end, she couldn't bring herself to do it. She was sick to death of blue in all its shades. She *needed* to wear pink tonight, to wear something she adored, something that made her feel good. Something just for herself.

If Paxton admired her as he claimed, he would admire her in pink, as well.

Descending the stairs, she chuckled softly, amused by the little rebellion. Paxton likely didn't care a jot what she wore tonight. In her experience, men were more interested in what a gown did for a lady's attributes than in the actual gown itself.

"Good evening, Olivia." Griffin's words greeted her as she stepped into the entrance hall, his voice, low and smooth, an instant, unwelcome reminder of all the sinful things he'd said the last time they were alone.

"Griffin. Good evening," she said, the words stilted as her gaze met his. "Emmy will be along shortly. She is collecting her shawl."

Her heart kicked up as she came to a stand before him, her fingers fussing nervously with the dance card tied to one wrist. She hadn't seen him since their...conversation in the drawing room two nights ago, when he'd kissed her senseless, and pleasured her with his hands against the door. Her cheeks warmed.

She'd promised herself she would behave as if that night hadn't happened, but standing here, gazing into his dark gray eyes, the task proved more difficult than she'd hoped.

"You look beautiful," Griffin said, the words gruff in their escape, as if he hadn't meant to free them.

Olivia swallowed, surprised by the compliment. She smoothed her palms down her skirts and thanked him, her voice surprisingly even given the tingles skating up her spine. *Had he ever paid her such a compliment before?*

"And you are looking very elegant this evening," she said, taking in his dark gray coat and black breeches. "Even with cat fur on your cravat."

Before she could second-guess herself, she reached out and brushed away the strands of black fur, so stark against the snowy white of his cravat.

"There. That's better." She looked up, and found him watching her with inscrutable eyes, his lips unsmiling and only inches from hers.

Desire sparked within her, heating her blood until her skin tingled with it. Hastily, she took a step back and clasped her hands behind her, lest they try to stray again.

Clearing her throat into the dense silence, she thrust all thoughts of kisses and drawing room doors to the back of her mind and conjured up Paxton's smiling face instead. *He* was who she should be thinking of tonight.

"So..." She cleared her throat again. "I understand you spoke with the Duke of Paxton yesterday."

Griffin's gaze met hers and he hooked a questioning brow. "I did."

A smile touched her lips. "He came to see me afterward," she explained. "I don't know what you said to him precisely, but whatever it was, he did not care for it."

Amusement lit his eyes. "Truthfully, I said very little."

Olivia raised her brows. "But?"

"But...when he asked if I was courting you—obviously unhappy with the idea—I couldn't resist letting him think I was considering it."

The mischief in his eyes made her want to laugh. "That wasn't very nice of you, Griff," she said, even as a smile pulled at her lips.

He shrugged. "Paxton wasn't very nice to you."

Her gaze went to the floor, her throat suddenly tight. What he'd said to Paxton...it had been more than just a prank. He'd done it for her. Because he didn't like what Paxton had done, because he cared for her. At least a little.

"Paxton was never betrothed to Miss Withers," she said quietly. "He is not going to marry her. He's going to marry me. He told me so."

The statement was met with a long silence.

Olivia raised her head and looked at him. Their gazes locked and her heart thudded at the probing intensity in his eyes.

"Your duke finally found the courage to stand up to his mother then?"

She pressed her lips together. "Well, no. Not yet. But he assures me it is only a matter of time."

Griffin's jaw clenched. "I see."

"He asked me to give him another chance, just a little more time, and I agreed. I believe we are meant to be married," she said. "And I am not ready to give up on him."

"Because he's a duke."

There was no recrimination in his voice, no judgment, only frustration and regret. As if he wanted better from her. Maybe even *for* her.

But Olivia could not permit herself to care about his opinion of her. She would do what she must and would make no apologies for it.

"Good things come to those who wait," she said with a little shrug.

"I hope you're right."

He studied her openly, as if trying to understand her, and she tipped her chin up as if she did not care.

"If you are truly so concerned for my future happiness, perhaps you would be willing to help me," she said.

His brow crooked. "What sort of help?"

She smiled. "As heartened as I am by Paxton's renewed promises, I think a bit of competition will be good for him. It will...keep him focused." She bit her lip. "I would like to use you, Griff. If I may."

He blinked, and his mouth took on a befuddled twist, if a mouth could look befuddled. "Use me?" he asked. His voice was strangely frayed.

She nodded. "To make Paxton jealous." She shook her head, a frown pulling at her lips. "I know it is devious to manipulate him so, perhaps even unscrupulous, but, well, I find I no longer care. Desperate times call for desperate measures, after all."

Griffin's jaw flexed. "You shouldn't have to manipulate him, Olivia. If I loved a woman the way he supposedly loves you, nothing would stand in my way."

She flicked a fingernail along the edge of her dance card. "Yes, well, Paxton is not like you." It was a gross understatement, and entirely irrelevant.

"So, will you help me?" she asked. "It will not require much of your time, only a waltz or two, perhaps a ride in the park. Just enough to make the lie believable."

The look on Griffin's face suggested he didn't entirely support the idea, but eventually he gave in. "Yes. I will help you."

She beamed. "Excellent. Then you will dance with me again tonight?"

"Of course."

He withdrew a pencil from his coat pocket then reached out and took hold of her wrist, turning her hand so he could lay the dance card in her palm. The heat from his hand seeped through her satin glove, searing her body as surely as if his hands were upon her.

She held very still, her breathing shallow as she watched him scrawl his name on the card, desperately trying not to think of the pleasure those hands had given her only two nights ago.

"There," he murmured, releasing her before taking a small step back.

She looked at him, his head bent, his face expressionless as he slipped the pencil into his pocket.

"Thank you, Griffin," she said, her voice slightly breathy. "I—"

"I'm so sorry for keeping you waiting!" Emmy breezed into the entrance hall and for the second time today, Olivia nearly jumped out of her skin.

"I couldn't find the shawl I wanted to bring," Emmy went on, "and had to ask Ivy where it had got to."

Settling said shawl around her shoulders, she glanced from Olivia to Griffin and back again. "Are you two ready to leave?"

"Yes," they replied in tandem.

Emmy grinned. "Excellent. Let's go."

THE JOURNEY TO WESTMINSTER was blessedly short, though not as short as Griffin's temper. He brooded the entire ride over, staring out the carriage window, his thoughts consumed by the maddening woman sitting on the bench across from him.

Damn it, how could Olivia even consider marrying the duke now? She meant to encourage his favors again, even after all he'd put her through, even though nothing had changed.

He didn't understand it.

But then, he didn't have to, did he? It was none of his business what Olivia Blakely did, or whom she married.

She wanted her duke and he had agreed to help her catch him. He would do what he could while his mother's ankle healed, and once she was back on her feet again, it would all be over, and everything would return to normal. That day couldn't come quickly enough.

"Here we are," Emmy said brightly as the carriage rolled to a stop.

The *finally* was left unsaid but greatly implied by the relief in her voice.

It had been an unusually quiet ride.

The trio filed out of the carriage and into Mrs. Lubbock's enormous entrance hall where they handed over their outer garments before being ushered into the lady's lively drawing room.

Music from the pianoforte filled the air with grating cheer, and all the chairs and sofas had been pushed against the walls to make space for dancing, leaving Griff to wonder if dancing was compulsory. Their hostess, a petite, ostentatious woman of middling years fluttered around the room, seeing to her guests' needs.

Griffin bit back a sigh as he followed Emmy and Olivia through the open doors, his gaze panning over the other guests' faces, all familiar, none welcome. *Another tedious affair with the same tedious crowd.*

He turned to his sister and tried for a pleasant expression. "I'm thirsty," he said. "Would you like a glass of—"

"Lady Olivia! Good evening!" An eager male voice broke in, and Griffin's gaze flicked to Gregory Sanford's youthful, pink-cheeked face. Smiling, the gentleman greeted Griffin and Emmy before turning back to Olivia.

"You look lovely this evening, my lady," Sanford said as his gaze crawled down her body. "May I request the next dance?"

The pup's eyes dipped to Olivia's cleavage again, lingering and lascivious, and Griffin squeezed his hands into fists as hostility surged, heating his blood.

"Thank you, my lord," Olivia said with a sweet smile. "I would be honored."

The baron bent his head to scrawl his name on her dance card and had barely finished uttering his thanks when another man—a Mr. Steffington—approached to request his own dance. Olivia acquiesced with another smile, just as genuine and lovely as the first, and Griffin felt its effects like a hard pinch to his already strained temper.

That was when—*God help him*—the Duke of Paxton appeared, out of nowhere, like an unwelcome surprise.

"Lady Olivia. At last, you've arrived." Paxton's voice was like the bleating of a randy goat and even as Sanford and Steffington departed, the duke had eyes only for Olivia. Bending his head, he brushed a kiss to her knuckles, his adoring gaze never leaving her face.

Griffin's nostrils flared.

"Good evening, Your Grace," Olivia murmured, dipping into a shallow curtsy.

"And Lady Emmaline, Lord Keswick," Paxton said with considerably less warmth. "Good evening to you."

Emmy curtsied while Griffin gave a cool nod.

"The ratafia this evening is surprisingly flavorful, Lady Olivia," Paxton said, turning to her with a smile. "Would you care to accompany me to the refreshments table for a glass?"

Olivia bowed her head prettily. "That would be lovely, Your Grace." She turned her most charming smile on Griffin, batting her lashes at him for good measure. "And I shall meet with you later, Lord Keswick, yes? For our waltz?"

Griff sketched a bow. "I will be counting down the minutes, my lady."

Her eyes flared with humor and then she was gone, walking away on the arm of the idiot duke as if she belonged there. Displeasure raked through him, scraping his nerves, and he thrust his hands into his pockets.

She was beautiful tonight, just as he'd told her. He tracked her progress as she and Paxton crossed the room toward the refreshments, drinking in her loveliness, those shining golden curls and elegant shoulders, the dip of her waist, those lush hips swaying beneath pale pink silk.

Who was he fooling? Olivia was always beautiful. Far too good for the likes of the numbskull she intended to marry. He only wished she knew it, too.

"They make a handsome couple, don't they?" Emmy said, startling him from his reverie.

Griffin shrugged. "I suppose so."

"It's nice of you to help her like this. I never thought of you as the matchmaking sort." She chuckled. "Mother will be so proud."

"I wasn't matchmaking," he grumbled.

"No? But Olivia told me you are the reason why His Grace went to see her yesterday, why he is pursuing her again."

"That wasn't my intention," Griff said, shifting on his feet. "I don't much like the duke, and I like even less what he did to Olivia. When he approached me yesterday to fish after my intentions, I decided to exact a little revenge on her behalf."

"I see."

Something in her tone drew his gaze, and he found her watching him—studying him, more like—as if searching his face for the answer to a riddle.

"What?" he asked, irrationally annoyed.

"You care for Olivia a great deal, don't you?" Her voice was soft but frank.

Griff's shoulders stiffened and his heart slowed to an uncomfortable thud. "She's your friend," he said, keeping his voice even. "I don't want to see any of my sister's friends harmed."

Emmy gave her head a slow shake, her gaze unrelenting. "No. It is more than that."

His jaw clenched. "It isn't."

"You two are obviously mad for each other," she said softly. "Why have you done nothing about it?"

"That's enough, Em." The urge to flee the room was growing by the minute.

"I am disappointed in you. Do you really mean to give her up? Do you really mean to let her marry a man she doesn't love? A man who does not deserve her?"

"Emmy." He shot his sister a warning look. "That is enough."

Her nostrils flared and she gave him a disapproving frown, but she said nothing more, simply heaved an exasperated sigh and walked away, shaking her head.

Griffin blew out an exasperated breath. Where in bloody blazes had that come from?

Emmy had never said anything like that before, had never even hinted at it, so what had possessed her to say something here, now?

And where had she got such a ridiculous idea in the first place?

Olivia might have fostered a *tendre* for him once, and there was no denying the attraction between them, but...*mad for each other?* God, no. She was too silly, too shallow, too...

He sighed. No. She was none of those things, was she? He used to think she was, partly because he'd grown used to thinking of her that way, and partly because that was the impression she gave, whether intentionally or not, he didn't know.

But he couldn't, in good conscience, continue to claim she was silly and shallow. Not after all he'd learned about her.

Still, no matter how much his opinion of her had changed, nothing else had. He could admit to being attracted to her—there was no denying it—but that was as far as it would go. Even if he were mad for her as Emmy claimed, he would not marry her. He wouldn't even consider it. He wasn't ready for marriage.

And whatever Olivia's feelings for him might be, he doubted she would have him, even if he offered. She wanted a duke, and while Griffin did not much care for the one she'd chosen, even he had to admit his objections amounted to very little. She could do worse than the Duke of Paxton, and if he was the man she wanted, who was he to stand in her way?

She was his sister's friend and she had asked for his assistance. He would do what he could to help her snag her duke and then he would let the chips fall where they may.

CHAPTER SEVENTEEN

Oh, how the tables had turned.

Olivia smiled to herself as she slipped into the night, her soft-soled slippers silent on the granite stone floor of the terrace.

Only days ago, it was she who had lured Paxton into the gardens for a kiss, and now, here she was, meeting him for a tryst at his invitation.

Stepping out onto the lawn, she made her way into Mrs. Lubbock's well-groomed garden and headed toward the decorative folly nestled within a tidy grove of cherry trees bursting with blooms.

Miss Winters was here tonight, as well, but Paxton had only danced with her once and only because his mother had asked him to. Otherwise, he'd barely left Olivia's side, and had claimed both a waltz and a quadrille from her. Yes, he was being most attentive tonight.

And it was all thanks to Griffin.

Odd, that. Never in a thousand years would she have guessed that Griffin, the Marquess of Keswick would one day help her catch her duke.

"Over here," came a whispered hiss from the folly, a miniature Chinese pagoda painted red and gold.

Squinting into the darkness, she spotted Paxton, tucked away in the shadows, beckoning to her with his hand. A smile touched her lips and she went to him, satisfaction warming her insides.

Here it is, she thought. *The moment has finally come.* Paxton would at last claim his kiss, the kiss of a man courting the woman he hoped to marry, one he should have claimed ages ago.

"Thank you for meeting me," Paxton said, making room for her on the wooden bench. "I know this is...unusual."

Olivia sat and settled her shawl around her shoulders against the bite in the night breeze. "I admit, I was surprised by the invitation," she said. "Considering what happened the last time we were alone in a garden together."

He had the grace to look mildly sheepish. "I know. I behaved like a nincompoop." He sighed. "I was...nervous, you see. And worried."

She shot him a quizzical look. "Worried?"

"Of disappointing you."

She shook her head, her smile gentle. "It is only a kiss, Paxton. It is not a test with only one chance at passing it."

He nodded, doubt still wrinkling his brow. "I know, but..." He swallowed, the workings of his throat audible in the quiet. "I...am not a man of experience, you see. I—I've never kissed a woman before."

Oh. Olivia's consternation eased as understanding—and surprise—came over her. It made sense now, his reluctance to kiss her. It was all down to his male pride. She should have guessed. If she'd learned one thing about men over the years, it was how much they hated to look foolish.

Taking Paxton's hands in hers, she smiled at him. "That is nothing to be ashamed of, Your Grace. On the contrary, I think it speaks well of your character. It shows you to be a gentleman of patience and restraint, and those are qualities any man would be glad to have."

Paxton puffed out his chest a bit, clearly pleased by her assessment. "Thank you, Lady Olivia."

His gaze roved over her face, and Olivia held on to her smile, hoping it conveyed her understanding, her patience. She would not press him this time. If he wanted this kiss, he would have to claim it.

"May I kiss you now?" he asked, his voice hesitant yet hopeful.

"You may."

He leaned in, slowly and somewhat awkwardly, and Olivia's eyes drifted closed. His warm, minty breath puffed against her lips and then his mouth touched hers, soft and cool and respectful.

And then it was over.

She opened her eyes and returned Paxton's smile, even as a tiny frisson of disappointment skittered down her spine. She squashed it.

So there had been no jolt of pleasure, no spark of desire. It was only one kiss, and it was his first. *Their* first.

It will get better, she told herself. It *will*.

"Thank you, Lady Olivia." Even beneath the shadows, she could see the pink in his cheeks, and he looked rather pleased with himself.

She dipped her head, hoping to look demure as she hid her smile. At least the duke had enjoyed their kiss.

"We should probably return to the ballroom," he said, clearing his throat. "We've been gone for quite some time."

Olivia nodded. "And your mother will certainly be looking for you."

"Yes. She certainly will." He rose and held out his hand. "Shall we?"

She shook her head. "You go on. I would like to stay here for another minute or two. I am still overwarm from all the dancing I've done tonight."

Paxton hesitated, as if he couldn't decide whether he should leave her there or stay. She made the decision for him.

"Go on, Paxton," she said with a smile. "I will be along shortly."

He wavered another beat and then sketched a bow before turning and heading for the house.

Olivia watched him cross the lawn and disappear from sight. Then she slumped against the bench and blew out a heavy sigh.

Well, Paxton had finally done it. After weeks and weeks of waiting, he'd finally kissed her. And it had been fine.

She wasn't sure what she'd been expecting exactly, but she had to admit, she'd expected better than *fine*. Still, it was a beginning, and a good sign that he meant what he said. He wanted to marry her, so much so that he'd given her his first kiss.

Rising from the bench, she strolled to the opposite end of the pagoda and rested her shoulder against the first pillar she reached.

Tucking her shawl around her chilled arms, she gazed out at the darkened garden beyond and drew in a breath of cool night air, faintly scented with new grass and cherry blossoms.

She smiled, still thinking of Paxton's blushing cheeks and the bashful way he'd asked her for a kiss. He really was the sweetest of men, so respectful and considerate. She would be fortunate to call him husband.

"Well? Was it magnificent?"

A sputtered gasp escaped her lips, and she whirled around, her hand at her throat. "Griffin?" She squinted at the figure reclining on a wooden bench. "What are you doing out here? Did you follow me?"

His lips curved into a smile, just visible in the dark. "I was here before you, Olivia."

"Hm." Her galloping heart slowed to a trot, and she leaned against the pillar again, folding her arms across her chest. "I haven't interrupted another tryst, have I?"

He chuckled. "No. There is no tryst. I came out here for a breath of fresh air, nothing more."

The tension in her shoulders eased a bit and she nodded, though she knew he likely could not see the motion in the dark. Her gaze dropped to her slippers, and she studied the pink satin bows on her toes. A little sigh escaped her lips. What an unusual evening this was turning out to be.

"Speaking of trysts..." Griffin said, his voice low and teasing. "Was it magnificent like you hoped?"

Her jaw clenched and she ignored the question for a moment, irritated by it, and by him for remembering those silly words she'd uttered that night at the opera.

Paxton will kiss me when the time is right, and when he does, it is sure to be magnificent.

"You know that is none of your business, Griffin," she said with a disapproving sniff.

He smiled. "That bad, was it?"

"It wasn't bad," she shot back with more venom than was warranted, but *really*, her first kiss with Paxton should have been private, dash it all.

Why had Griffin gone to the pagoda for fresh air? Why did he always seem to be there to witness her most vulnerable moments?

"But it wasn't magnificent, either," Griffin said, and it wasn't a question, as if he knew her thoughts.

She could feel his gaze on her, curious and encroaching. Why she chose to answer him truthfully was anyone's guess.

"It was pleasant," she said. "It wasn't the best kiss I've ever received, but it wasn't the worst, either. Far from it, actually."

Griffin shifted on the bench seat and crossed one leg over the other in a distracting display of graceful, unhurried strength. She swallowed. He moved like no other man she had ever known. It was frustrating how regularly she seemed to notice.

"Tell me about it," he said. "Your worst kiss. Who gave it to you?"

"You want the gentleman's name?" She shot him a reproachful look. "Would that not violate some centuries-old code of honor amongst men?"

He smiled at that. "Come. I won't tell anyone."

"Well..." She wrinkled her nose. "It was Roger Osterbrook, if you must know. He had fishy breath and presumptuous hands." The unpleasant memory sent a shudder up her spine.

"Did he harm you?" Griffin's voice was low but hard as iron, and a silly little thrill shot through her. She ignored it.

"No, but I did harm him," she said with no small amount of satisfaction. "I kneed him right in his delicate bits."

He chuckled. "Good."

A companionable silence settled between them and neither said a word for several moments as a gentle breeze rustled the trees around them. A lone nightingale trilled in the distance, its song soft and sweet.

Olivia shifted on her feet and let her head fall against the smooth pillar. She should probably return to the party soon. She would be missed.

Perhaps just a few minutes more.

"Does that happen often?" Griffin asked her, his tone quietly curious. "With men?"

She lifted her head. "What? Presumptuous hands?"

"Yes."

"Not terribly often, no." She threw him a reproachful look but kept her tone light. "I don't let just anyone kiss me, you know. Silly and shallow I may be, but I am not totally without scruples."

His chest rose and fell with his sigh. "I know you're not," he said. "I shouldn't have said those things. It was wrong, and I'm sorry."

She swallowed, surprise and pleasure warming her chest. She had not expected an apology from him.

"I admit to enjoying the company of gentlemen," she said with a shrug, "but I am not a flirt." A rueful smile tugged at her lips. "I can understand why you would draw such a conclusion, though, after my behavior that night in the Stevensons' library." Her gaze fell to the floorboards, and she toyed with the fringe on her shawl. "I am not usually so forward, but I had overindulged on mulled wine and I'm afraid it made me a bit...foolish."

She looked at him, saw his lips curl at the corners, but she could not decipher the message in his smile.

"Was that the only reason?" he asked. "The mulled wine?"

She lifted a shoulder. "I will admit to feeling some small measure of curiosity, as well. I did wonder a time or two what it would be like to kiss you."

This, it seemed, was a night for confessions.

"Only a time or two?" Griffin pressed a hand to his heart as if wounded.

She rolled her eyes, battling a smile. "Yes, during those rare moments when I wasn't fantasizing about strangling you instead."

He grinned, his teeth flashing white in the dark. "So?" he asked. "What was it like?"

He *would* ask that, the scoundrel.

She held silent for a long beat, chewing on her lip as if giving the question a great deal of thought. "You are...not unskilled," she finally said.

"A glowing endorsement."

The wry drawl brought a smile to her lips. "But surely the Marquess of Keswick, breaker of hearts, needs no endorsement from me. Your reputation is endorsement enough already."

He huffed out a sigh. "My *reputation* is greatly exaggerated."

She wondered at that remark, and nearly asked him what he meant by it, but something made her hesitate. His reputation was none of her business, true, but it was more than that. It was self-preservation.

She did not want to think better of him. Her defenses were shaky enough already.

"Well, I envy your exaggerated reputation," she said. "Men may do as they please, while us women must be good every day of our lives." She shook her head. "If the *ton* knew I had kissed fourteen different gentlemen, I would surely be tossed out of London like so much spoiled fruit."

"You're right," he said quietly. "It isn't fair."

"No, it isn't." She had long thought society's dictates were unjust, but what could she do about it? One must have power to effect change, and women were all but powerless. Perhaps one day that would not be so.

"Fourteen, eh?" Griffin said thoughtfully.

She folded her arms over her chest. "Too many for your delicate sensibilities?"

He smiled. "Certainly one too many from Roger Oster-brook."

"True."

He draped an arm along the back of the bench and cocked his head to one side, regarding her openly. "So, if Osterbrook gave you your worst kiss..."

Olivia froze.

"...who gave you your best?"

The question grated like an unwelcome surprise, and she turned her back on it, shifting to face the garden where his knowing gaze could not reach her.

"That is an impertinent question, as you well know." Her tone was light, but with a hint of warning, too; one she hoped he would heed.

The bench creaked and then Griffin was beside her, his hands in his pockets, his gaze on the sky. "I'd still like to hear the answer," he said.

Gripping the ends of her shawl, she stepped forward, away from him, his proximity a complication she could not afford. Not if she wanted to keep her wits about her.

"You first," she said, infusing the words with a teasing lilt. "Who gave you the best kiss you've ever had?"

"You."

She froze, warm tingles unfurling in her belly. She heard the shuffle of his footsteps as he drew near, felt the warmth of his body at her back, and she let out a breathless little laugh as she turned to face him.

"You're teasing me," she said faintly, searching his face for a smile, a glint of mockery and finding none.

He shook his head. "No."

"No?"

Her breath stuttered as his hands curved around her waist and gently pulled her in, his eyes ablaze.

"No," he whispered. And then he covered her lips with his.

CHAPTER EIGHTEEN

THEY SHOULDN'T BE DOING this. The thought snaked through Griffin's mind, but he ignored it and deepened the kiss instead, gripping Olivia's delectable hips as he swept his tongue into her mouth.

He'd hated watching her dance with other men tonight, hated even more hearing her with Paxton, knowing the fool had kissed her, *touched* her, and she had welcomed it. Even now he could still feel the knot of jealousy deep in his gut. It should be *his* mouth on hers, *his* hands on her body. He wanted to taste her everywhere, he wanted to own her, use her, surrender to her.

God, he must be losing his mind.

Olivia whimpered, her lips meeting his in desperate strokes, the eager slide of her tongue stiffening his cock until the ache was almost unbearable.

He widened his stance and slid his hands down to her arse, urging her closer until hips met hips and her breasts were flattened against his chest. *There.* He could feel her everywhere now, soft and warm and so bloody good he never wanted to let go.

Her arms looped around his neck, her fingers threading through his hair as she whispered his name.

Satisfaction flowed through him, a warm balm loosening the knot of jealousy in his belly. She'd allowed Paxton to kiss her, but she hadn't asked for more. She hadn't wanted more.

She wanted more from *him*, though, didn't she?

"Come," he whispered, easing her toward the bench. "Come with me."

Her eyes met his, nearly black and drenched in desire, and Griffin's breath caught in his throat. Olivia aroused was without a doubt the most beautiful sight he'd ever seen.

He pulled her down onto the bench until they were both sitting, with her straddling his lap. Their mouths met again, in hungry, wet kisses that seemed to heat the very air around them. Her scent invaded, an intoxicating blend of jasmine and lemonade and lust.

His hands found her hips and he tugged, a guttural groan rumbling in his throat as the heat of her settled directly, *deliciously* onto his straining cock. He kissed her harder, his lips ravenous as he filled his hands with her, squeezing her hips, shaping her waist, her back, her thighs.

Her breasts, plump and creamy, tantalized above the neckline of her gown, and he eased his mouth from hers so he could see her better.

"Christ, you're lovely," he said, brushing the pads of his thumbs along the swell of her breasts. "Your body..." He swallowed. "I hunger for it. I hunger for you."

Heart thudding in his chest, he held her gaze as he hooked his thumbs beneath the edge of her bodice and tugged. Her breasts beckoned, her nipples pebbling beneath the thin cotton chemise, and he bent his head to take one in his mouth.

She hissed in a breath, her fingers threading in his hair as she arched into him, unintentionally bearing down on the hard ridge of his erection. He thrust against her warmth, drawing her nipple deeper into his mouth, his hands gripping her arse.

"Yes," she whispered. "Yes, yes..." She began to move her hips, grinding her wet heat against his cock in slow, rhythmic circles, her buttocks clenching beneath his palms with every thrust.

Griffin eased his head back to watch her.

"Yes, petal," he urged, his gaze locked on her face, his hands gripping her hips. "Ride me. Ride my cock. Let me feel your pleasure."

Her head fell back, and her lips parted, and he pressed his lips to her throat, tasting her, nipping her skin with his teeth. A gasp caught on a groan and then she stiffened, her hands clutching his shoulders as tremors wracked her body.

Her eyelids fluttered open a moment later and she lowered her head, meeting his gaze.

"Oh, my," she whispered, her throat working as she swallowed. "That was...unexpected."

He smiled and brushed his mouth over her heated cheek. "Will you admit now that my kiss is your best?"

She pressed her lips together, considering her answer. "Would you believe me if I said it wasn't?"

"Not after that, no."

She huffed out a laugh. "No, I suppose you wouldn't." Her gaze dipped to his throat, and he could almost hear her thoughts, the self-recrimination, the doubt. She was only seconds away from regretting what she'd done.

"Don't," he said softly. "Don't be embarrassed." He reached out to tuck a loose strand of hair behind her ear, his body still thrumming, his erection still throbbing against her core. He ignored it.

"I can't help it," she said. "I seem to lose all sense of decorum with you. I...forget myself."

Griffin trailed his thumb along her jaw and over her lips, cresting the tiny cleft in her chin. He couldn't seem to stop touching her. "You make me forget myself, too," he said softly. "When I take myself in hand, it is you I think of."

Her gaze flew to his, wide with surprise.

"I imagine it's your hand around my cock instead of my own."

"You do?" Her voice was faint, incredulous, and her cheeks had flushed a gorgeous shade of pink.

"And sometimes," he said, "I imagine it's your mouth instead of your hand."

Her tongue darted out to wet her lips, and Griff couldn't tell if she was scandalized or aroused by his admission. He fervently hoped it was the latter.

"I had no idea you thought of me doing those things," she said softly. "Or at all."

God, if she only knew.

Her gaze fell to his trousers, and her hands went to his falls, her knuckles brushing against his erection. His breath caught in his throat, and pleasure, sweet and intense, shot through him, as if he were an untried lad in the throes of his first sexual experience.

"Touch me, Olivia." His voice was hoarse, pleading. He swallowed. "Let me feel your hands on me."

Her gaze met his, dark and unwavering, as she began to remove her gloves, her movements deliberate and unhurried.

She set her gloves on the bench and a moment later his falls slackened, and his cock sprang free. His breath hissed through his teeth as her fingers closed around his thick length. She stroked him gently, tentatively, her hand soft and warm, and Griffin's eyes fell closed.

"Like this?" she whispered. "Am I doing it right?"

"Yes, petal," he said roughly. "Just like that. Exactly like that."

God, her touch. The pleasure she wrought on his body...

It was unlike anything he'd ever experienced—*beyond* anything he'd ever experienced—and he was desperate for more. Insatiable. Ruined.

"You're so hot," she mused, her brow furrowed as she stroked him. "So soft yet so hard."

"That's you," he said through gritted teeth. "That is what your touch does to me."

His hips jerked, his body begging for release as she worked him over, the pleasure beginning to build, and he watched her face as she pumped her sweet little hand down his cock. Working so hard to please him. God, how she undid him.

He was moments away from spending in her hand. It was too late to stop it—he was too *weak* to stop it—and somehow he had the foresight to tug his handkerchief from his coat pocket.

He wrapped his hand around hers and stroked hard, once, twice, a third time, and with a rough, guttural groan, spent his seed into the handkerchief.

A long, fraught moment passed with only the sound of their labored breathing between them. Griffin's head tipped back, and he swallowed, his heart thudding in his throat.

"Christ above, Olivia," he muttered, his voice an uneven rasp. "I—"

He broke off and his head shot up, his shoulders tensing. *Voices.* They were no longer alone.

Olivia's breath caught and her eyes widened in alarm as she turned to look in the direction of the house. With frantic movements, she scrambled off his lap and brushed hurried hands over her dress. Griffin reached out to help, but she shied from his touch and before he could utter another word, she was gone, dashing toward the house.

He watched her leave, her retreating form barely visible beneath the moonlight, and only when she'd disappeared from sight did he relax. The voices he'd heard only moments ago were silent now, and he hoped that meant they'd returned to the ballroom. He did not wish to share the garden with anyone, not like this, with his breathing still ragged and his mind reeling in the aftermath of Olivia's touch.

"Bloody hell," he muttered, and went to rake his fingers through his hair, only then realizing he still held his soiled handkerchief. He thrust the linen into his trouser pocket then refastened his falls and tucked his shirt into his waistband.

With a sigh, he rose and ambled over to the nearest pillar, leaning his arm against the smooth wood. He turned his gaze up to the night sky and sighed again, seeing none of it. Pleasure still thrummed through him, his skin prickling with the memory of her soft hands, his body hungry for more of her. He wanted her, more than he had before, though how that was possible he did not know.

All he knew was every taste of her lips, every touch of her hands only seemed to intensify his yearning for her.

He muttered another curse and scrubbed a hand down his face. What was this effect she had on him? Why could he not stay away from her?

Olivia was not his to desire, and yet, desire her he did, even though he knew he shouldn't. Even though she was practically promised to another man.

What in bloody blazes was wrong with him?

Chapter Nineteen

Two nights later, Olivia stepped down from the carriage onto the pavement in front of Vauxhall Gardens and tipped her head back to gaze up at the night sky. *Not a cloud in sight,* she noted with a satisfied smile. It was the perfect canvas for fireworks.

"Thank you, John," Aunt Augusta said cheerfully as the footman handed her down from the carriage.

The two ladies set off toward the entrance to the pleasure gardens, joining the stream of fellow patrons with the same destination in mind. The clap of Aunt Augusta's walking stick on the pavement kept time as she hummed an offkey tune, her voluminous emerald-green skirts swishing with every step.

"You're certainly in a good mood this evening," Olivia said with amusement.

"I am," Aunt Augusta said. "It feels good to be *out.* I was beginning to grow weary of card games."

"And of Lady Keswick, I imagine." Olivia sent her aunt a knowing glance.

The lady's hazel eyes twinkled, but she only said, "I adore Lady Keswick."

"I know you do," Olivia said. "But two people can spend too much time together. Even the best of friends."

Aunt Augusta sighed. "I cannot disagree with that," she said. "Still, I have to wonder at the swiftness of Lavinia's recovery. I think, perhaps, it is more wishful thinking than anything else."

Olivia nodded. "You cannot blame her for it, though. I should hate to be cooped up in bed for two weeks."

"As would I," Aunt Augusta said. "I only hope her impatience does not lead to a setback in her ankle's healing. Regardless, my services are no longer needed, and I have been relieved of duty." She threw Olivia a sidelong glance. "I hope you are not too disappointed to have your old auntie as chaperone again."

"Nonsense," Olivia said, looping her arm through her aunt's. "You are always my first choice for chaperone."

"Good," Aunt Augusta said briskly. "Because you have no choice in the matter."

Olivia laughed. In truth, she was excited to spend a night out with her aunt. She'd seen very little of her these last two weeks, and Lady Keswick's mended ankle meant things would return to normal now, which meant she would see more of her aunt. And less of Griffin.

It was for the best, of course. Nothing good came of their spending time together, willingly or not. What had happened during their last encounter was testament to that.

Her cheeks flushed hot as she remembered what they'd done on that bench in Mrs. Lubbock's garden folly, the whispered words and heated confessions they'd shared. She'd thought of those moments many times these last two days, and still she could not understand how it had happened. Or why.

Why had he kissed her again? And why had she let him? Nothing would come of it—nothing good, at least—and she was nearly betrothed to another man, for heaven's sake. So why had she allowed herself to fall under his spell again?

What was this effect he had on her that made her lose her senses so?

It was a good thing Lady Keswick's ankle had healed. It was past time for things to return to how they'd been before, to the sanity and safety of normalcy.

Shoving thoughts of Griffin from her mind, Olivia and her aunt paid for their admittance before stepping through the doors and into the Proprietor's House, and after a brief walk down a short corridor, finally reached the pleasure gardens.

Hundreds of flickering lamps beckoned, the blue glass globes suspended from posts and obelisks, and even the trees. Twin rows of sturdy oaks framed the Grand Walk before them, casting the long path in a warm, romantic glow.

A large rotunda loomed on their left and from their right, music could be heard from the Orchestra, a tiered wooden building nestled between the Walk and a large grove of deciduous trees where patrons could gather to dance and enjoy the musicians' skillful play.

"I wish Sophie could be here tonight," Olivia said as they strolled up the gravel path, passing their fellow patrons with smiles of greeting. "It is odd going to Vauxhall without her. She loves it so much."

Aunt Augusta smiled. "That she does."

"Do you remember the first time you brought us here?" Olivia chuckled as memories of that night two years ago filled her mind. "Sophie was like a little girl, watching the tightrope walkers and the fire breathers, her eyes as big as saucers. She talked about it for weeks after." Her smile dimmed and a sigh escaped her lips.

Aunt Augusta patted her hand, still looped around her aunt's arm. "You will have many more chances to visit Vauxhall with Sophie, my dear."

Olivia nodded. "I know. But things will never be the same again, will they? It will never be the three of us, the way it used to be."

"No. It won't. But such is life. Nothing can remain the same forever."

The wistfulness in her aunt's voice, the bittersweet smile turning her lips, made Olivia pause, and it dawned on her then how much her aunt's life would change in the coming months. Sophie was already married, and once Olivia followed suit, Aunt Augusta would be alone.

Shame washed over her as she realized how focused she'd been on her own future, giving no thought whatsoever to her aunt's, or what her plans entailed.

"What will you do, Aunt? After I've married?"

She turned to look at her and watched as her aunt drew in a deep breath of air. "I haven't decided yet," she said. "I might reside in London, or I might go and stay with my cousin Mary in Bath." She smiled. "I suppose I'll go where the wind takes me."

"I shall miss you," Olivia said. "It will be strange not seeing you every day."

"I know, dearest. I know. But I will write to you every week, and I will visit you often. So often, in fact, that you will hardly have a chance to miss me."

Olivia gave her a small smile, though it was sad. *She* was sad. How would she get by without her aunt there with her, as she'd always been?

"And pretty soon," Aunt Augusta went on cheerfully, "you will start a family of your own, and you will be far too busy with your brood of children to even notice I'm not there."

Olivia nodded, unconvinced but heartened a bit by the mention of children. "I am looking forward to having a baby. I hope I will be a good mother."

"You will be," Aunt Augusta said, patting her hand again. "After all, you come from a long line of excellent mothers. You never met your mother's mother—your grandmother—but she was a wonderful woman, and she adored your mother. Just as your mother adored you."

Olivia smiled, hugging her aunt's arm as they followed the path, the colored lamps lighting their way.

What would she have done without this woman? What sort of person would she be now if not for the love and guidance she'd received from her all these years? Aunt Augusta had played such an important part in her life, had always been there for her, when she didn't have to be.

She was her great-aunt, her grandmother's sister, a grandmother Olivia never knew. Aunt Augusta had never owed her a thing, and yet, she'd taken her under her wing and provided the love and attention she'd so desperately craved.

Olivia would be forever grateful for that.

AN HOUR OR SO later, at Aunt Augusta's announcement that she was *beyond famished*, Olivia and her aunt made the short trek to the pavilion where they rented a supper box.

As they passed the colonnade of boxes on their way to their own, Olivia's name was called out.

"Lady Olivia!"

She turned and spotted the Duke of Paxton in one of the supper boxes, his face wreathed in smiles. His mother sat beside him, as rigid and unapproachable as ever in a high-necked gown of olive-green wool.

"Good evening, Your Graces," Olivia said as she approached, Aunt Augusta beside her. "What a delightful surprise to see you here."

She bobbed a curtsy in greeting to the duchess and received a regal nod in return.

"Are you enjoying your evening?" Paxton asked, setting his glass on the table and cupping both hands around it.

"Oh, yes. We are having a lovely time," Olivia said with a bright smile. "We have just rented a supper box. Aunt Augusta is hungry."

"Famished, in fact," her aunt said, the hint not subtle in the slightest.

"I suggest you avoid the ham, Lady Augusta," the duchess said, wrinkling her nose. "The fare tonight was less than satisfying, and the portions less than generous."

"But the arrack punch more than makes up for it," Paxton said, raising his glass. "I tried to convince Mother to order a glass of her own, but she wouldn't hear of it."

His easy smile suggested he might have had his fair share of said punch this evening.

"Rum punch is not a suitable drink for ladies," the duchess intoned. "Indeed, it is barely suitable for gentlemen." She peered down her nose at his glass and gave a disapproving sniff.

Olivia dipped her head to mask her amusement.

"Thank you for warning me on the ham, Your Grace," Aunt Augusta said to the duchess, clearly battling a smile of her own. "Olivia and I will leave you to your meal now. I do hope you enjoy the fireworks later."

Olivia bobbed a curtsy and turned to follow after her aunt, but the duchess's voice stopped her.

"Lady Olivia?"

She turned back, surprise surely showing in her eyes. The duchess rarely addressed her. "Yes, Your Grace?"

The lady's smile was not warm, but it was considerably less frosty than Olivia was accustomed to receiving from her. "I would like to invite you and your aunt to take tea with me," the duchess said. "Perhaps later in the week?"

Olivia blinked. "Oh. I—yes, of course, Your Grace. We should be delighted."

The duchess inclined her head. "Very good," she said. "You may expect an invitation from me soon."

A *summons*, more like. But Olivia was too stunned to be irritated by the duchess's queenly manner. Too stunned and too thrilled. She didn't dare look at Paxton, lest she break into a triumphant grin.

"Thank you, Your Grace."

She bobbed another farewell curtsy and then she and Aunt Augusta made their way to their rented supper box and sat down at the table.

Aunt Augusta propped her walking stick against the empty chair beside her and sent Olivia a speaking glance. "Tea with the duchess," she said. "That is certainly a good sign."

Fighting the urge to grin, Olivia glanced down at the menu and pretended to peruse the fare. "Paxton assured me he was chipping away at his mother's resistance, but I wasn't certain I believed him." She pursed her lips. "I hope our visit goes well."

"It will, dearest," Aunt Augusta said. "Simply be yourself and everything will be fine. Now"—she slipped the menu from Olivia's hands—"let's see what less-than-satisfying fare appeals to me tonight."

Olivia laughed. "I'm more interested in the punch."

"So am I, truth be told." Aunt Augusta's eyes twinkled with mirth. "But you heard the duchess. Rum punch is not a suitable drink for ladies of refinement."

Olivia sighed. "Honestly, I wouldn't mind being a little less refined on occasion."

"Well, that is an odd thing for a hopeful-duchess to say." Aunt Augusta flicked a pointed glance in the direction of Paxton and his mother. "If everything goes as you hope it will, you shall have a lifetime of refinement ahead of you."

Olivia's brows dipped and she parted her lips to reply, but she had none. Her aunt was right. Life as a duchess would be different from the life she knew now. Better in some ways, yes, but more restrictive, too, with greater responsibilities.

"Oh, dear. Have we interrupted an argument?"

Olivia's head came up as Lady Keswick approached, pausing at the edge of their supper box. Griffin was with her, his gaze trained on Olivia's face, and she flushed hot at the sight of him, memories of their last meeting flooding her mind.

"Lavinia!" Aunt Augusta blurted out. "What on earth are you doing here?"

Lady Keswick's brows rose. "Isn't it obvious, Augusta? I've come to ruin your evening."

Olivia bit back a grin.

"That isn't what I meant," Aunt Augusta said. "I am only surprised to see you—"

"I know, I know." Lady Keswick shooed her words away with a wave of her gloved hand. "I was only teasing you. It was an impulse, wanting to come here tonight, and my wonderful son agreed to escort me."

She turned to Griffin with a beaming smile, which he returned with a gallant bow of his head. Olivia's heart melted a little at the obvious affection in his eyes as he smiled at his mother, and she forced herself to look away.

"Well, now you're here, would you like to join us?" Aunt Augusta asked, motioning at the table.

"That would be lovely, thank you," Lady Keswick said, and then she entered the supper box and waited while Aunt Augusta moved her walking stick out of the way, eyeing the appendage with wary distrust as she claimed the chair beside her.

Griffin sat down in the empty chair at Olivia's other side as the two older ladies bent over the menu to discuss what they would order.

"How are you?" Griffin asked, his voice a low murmur. He leaned his elbows on the table and crossed his forearms, flouting etiquette, and Olivia caught a whiff of his soap, sweet and spicy and wholly him.

She cleared her throat. "I'm very well, thank you," she said with all the nonchalance she could manage. "No Emmy tonight?"

He shook his head. "She's at home with a headache, I'm afraid. But Mother wanted to visit Vauxhall, so..." He trailed off with a shrug, as if to say, *what else could I do?*

Olivia smiled. "You're a good son."

"I do try." He turned his head, his gaze flicking to the dance floor and then back to hers. "Will you dance with me?"

She hesitated, tempted to accept, even as the offer surprised her. She'd had no idea what to expect when she saw him again, no idea how he would behave with her after what they'd shared in Mrs. Lubbock's folly.

Evidently he was still willing to help her catch her duke.

But dancing with him, *touching* him, did not seem wise, not after all that had happened between them, even if it was solely for the duke's benefit.

"It is kind of you to offer, Griffin," she said, "but unnecessary. The duchess has—"

"Hang the duchess," he whispered, mischief sparking in his eyes. "Dance with me, Olivia."

It was the look in his eyes that convinced her. There was no resisting it, the warmth, the daring there in those dark gray depths, urging her to say yes.

She nodded once and Griffin rose to his feet, holding out a gloved hand. She placed her fingers on his palm, ignoring the shiver of warmth working its way up her arm as she stood and followed him onto the dance floor.

The orchestra plucked the beginning strands of a waltz as Griffin shifted her hand to his shoulder and settled his long, powerful fingers around her waist. Her skin burned beneath his touch. Oh, she loved the feel of his hands on her body.

Thoughts of their last encounter invaded her mind as he guided her around the dance floor in slow, sweeping circles, and her throat went dry at the memory of his hands on her flesh, his mouth hungry for hers, his whispered words in the dark.

She'd thought of little else since then, but it was clear Griffin did not suffer from the same malady. He was behaving as if nothing out of the ordinary had happened. But then, perhaps that was exactly what it had been for him. Perhaps it was something very ordinary to him, something that occurred as regularly as the sun rose.

It was silly of her to allow what had happened to go to her head. It had been an extraordinary occurrence, but it was over now, a fading memory, and it would do no good to dwell on it. Especially not here.

"You've gone awfully quiet," Griffin murmured, his voice low and keen with interest. "What are you thinking about?"

She would rather swim naked in a leech-infested lake than answer that question truthfully, so she looked up at him and blurted out the first thought that popped into her head.

"How many lovers have you had?"

Surprise flashed in his eyes, mirroring her own bemusement, but she did not take the question back. It was not what she'd meant to say, but it was out there now and, right or wrong, she wanted to hear the answer.

"Five," he said evenly.

She blinked. "Five?" Skepticism threaded her voice, and she nearly trod on his toes.

"Yes, five," he repeated, arching a single dark brow. "Shall I name them for you?"

"Of course not!"

A smile tugged at the corners of his lips, and she realized he was teasing her. Only their position on a public ballroom floor kept her from scowling at him.

"I told you before," he said softly, "my reputation is greatly exaggerated."

Olivia eyed him, searching his face for signs of deception but his expression was open, his gaze frank.

Even so...*five?* Surely that could not be right. His reputation as a rake and a rogue was well known amongst the *ton*, if not well documented. How could he have earned such a reputation without...*earning* it?

And was it five before her? Or five *including* her? Could she even count herself as one of his lovers? She had no idea if what they'd done in the folly qualified, but she would sooner die than ask.

Besides, it hardly mattered, did it?

"Are you disappointed?"

The amusement in his voice drew her gaze and she shook her head. "Surprised, that's all. I always thought of you as a great lover of women."

Like a handsome bird flitting from branch to branch, singing his songs of seduction. It was an odd feeling, reassessing an opinion she'd always thought to be an incontrovertible truth.

"You seemed happy enough two nights ago," Griffin said, his voice low, his eyes alight with mischief.

Warmth flooded her cheeks, and she gave him a scolding look. "You know that is not what I meant."

His smile deepened as he whirled her around the dance floor, and he fell silent for a long moment, his eyes thoughtful, as if examining a truth he'd never considered before.

A rare moment of uncertainty from the ever-confident Marquess of Keswick.

"I like women, of course," he said finally, the words slow and measured like a newly-born thought. "And I am well aware of my reputation as a prolific lover. I have done nothing to refute it because what I do is nobody's business but my own."

Olivia pressed her lips together. *If only women were afforded the same freedoms.*

"I enjoy lovemaking, but I am not some rutting beast." His voice was quiet, his eyes serious and steady on hers. "When I take a lover, it is because I want *her*. Because I like her and enjoy spending time with her."

She nodded her understanding, even as envy thickened her throat and tightened her chest. Her gaze fell to the simple folds of his white cravat and she briefly closed her eyes. What was it like, being Griffin's lover? Being desired by him? Chosen by him? What was it like to have more of him than she'd already had?

What was it like to have all of him?

She looked up at his face, a tangle of emotions tying her belly in knots. "Did you love them?" she asked, before she could stop herself.

His gaze met hers and he smiled. "No."

It was one of his enigmatic smiles, equally irresistible and irritating, and Olivia could not tell whether he was laughing at her or at himself. She fought to keep her expression clear, trying to sort through her emotions. Was it silly to feel relieved? Griffin did not love her, but neither did he love someone else. That shouldn't matter, but somehow it did.

Foolish girl.

Blessedly, the music drew to a close, signaling an end to the waltz. Olivia pasted a smile on her lips and exited the dance floor on Griffin's arm.

Her gaze collided with Paxton's on the way back to her supper box, and the unhappy look on his face filled her with guilt, but she shoved the feeling away. She had done nothing wrong. He was not her husband nor even her betrothed, and there was no reason she should not dance with other men.

"Thank you for the dance, my lord," she said to Griffin as they neared the supper box, tossing him an airy smile.

"The pleasure was all mine, petal."

His voice was a husky whisper, intended only for her ears, and Olivia's throat went dry as a desert. She tore her gaze from his and swallowed hard, struggling for composure as tingles skittered up and down her body.

Dratted man.

Were his intimate words and affectionate looks genuine? Or was it all for Paxton's benefit?

It all felt so real, so *thrilling*, but how could she trust her own senses where Griffin was concerned?

And if it was real, what did it even matter? What would it change?

Straightening her shoulders, she shoved the last remnants of their waltz from her mind and entered the supper box, her smile and her self-preservation firmly restored.

Griffin's behavior was baffling and intriguing, but she could not allow him to distract her from her goal. She could not afford to play the fool again. Not when she was so close to securing the future she'd worked so long and so hard for.

She'd come too far to squander her time on fantasies best left abandoned.

CHAPTER TWENTY

THREE NIGHTS LATER, GRIFFIN stood in his drawing room doorway with Artemis tucked in the crook of one arm, and watched as his mother scurried about the room, a bundle of agitated energy shuffling furniture and barking orders at the maids like a diminutive naval captain.

Smiling to himself, he shook his head. He'd suggested she postpone tonight's dinner party, citing her ankle's very recent recovery, but she would have none of it, insisting too much work had already gone into the event to put it off.

Confounding woman. His mother was so sweet-natured it was easy to forget how stubborn she could sometimes be.

Stepping into the room, he called out, "Can I be of any assistance?"

Lady Keswick pushed a leather chair up against the wall then stepped back to study her handiwork. "No, thank you, darling. You would only be in the way."

Griffin scratched Artemis behind the ear and prayed for patience. "Fine," he said, "but why don't you let Lucy and

Martha move the furniture? I doubt the doctor would approve of so much activity so soon after your injury."

"I told you, darling. It's all better now." Lady Keswick turned to him and pushed a curl off her face. "Besides, I think we're finished in here."

She crossed the room to him and gave his cheek an affectionate pat before doing the same to Artemis. "Martha," she called out, speaking to the dark-haired maid. "You may take Artemis now and retire to your room until the party is ended."

"Yes, my lady."

Artemis mewled as Griffin handed her to Martha, and he gave her head a scratch. "You be good, little one, and behave yourself for Martha."

The maid gave him a reassuring smile. "I'll take good care of her, my lord. We'll have a jolly good time together."

Griffin smiled. "Thank you, Martha."

She and Lucy left the drawing room to resume their duties, leaving Griff with his mother.

"Well?" she asked, plunking her hands on her hips. "What do you think of the room?"

He swept his gaze over the room and nodded. "It looks very nice."

"Good," she said. "Because I am exhausted." She sighed. "There are days I cannot wait to hand over my duties as hostess to the next Lady Keswick, and this is one of those days."

She shot him a pointed look and Griffin couldn't help but laugh. "Come, Mother. You love hosting dinner parties."

"Most of the time, yes. But not always. And not forever."

He'd never considered what life would be like when he married, how it would be his wife planning their dinner parties instead of his mother.

Olivia's image came to mind, and he envisioned her in the role of hostess, compiling guest lists, planning meals, ordering the servants about, her hair mussed from moving furniture but still the most beautiful woman he'd ever seen.

He pressed his lips together, discomfited by the image, and even more by how right it felt.

This wasn't the first time he'd had such thoughts. Olivia seemed to be on his mind more and more ever since Mrs. Lubbock's soirée. Of course, it made sense, didn't it?

Lust was a powerful thing, after all. His preoccupation with her this week was nothing more than a natural reaction to a jolly good orgasm.

It stood to reason he would want another one, that he would want *her*. He did want her. He liked her and liked being with her. The time he'd spent with her recently had opened his eyes and showed him how fine she was, how much there was to admire in her.

Yes, he liked her. Enough that she had him thinking of the future, of a future with *her,* which was absolute madness...

Wasn't it?

Of course it is. You're not ready for marriage, remember?

Still, he could not deny the thrill of anticipation that shot through him at the thought of seeing her again. He craved more of her company. He missed her.

When had he begun to miss her?

"Well, I suppose I had best get myself dressed," Lady Keswick said, interrupting his thoughts. "The guests will be arriving soon."

Griffin gave her a smile. "I'm ready for them."

His mother gave his evening attire the once-over and nodded her approval. "You look very well," she said. "And more like your father every day, it seems."

"I shall take that as a compliment," he said. "Though, I must admit, I hardly remember what he looks like anymore."

He hardly remembered his father at all anymore. Just a handful of memories remained, an ephemeral sense of what the man had been like. That was all he was left with now.

"You were so young when your father died," Lady Keswick said, her smile dimming. "Just a little boy, only ten years old. I often wonder if..." She trailed off, her brows knit with uncertainty.

"If what?"

She looked at him, her eyes brimming with sorrow. "You loved your father so much," she said softly. "You idolized him. And when we lost him..." She drew in a deep breath, her mouth grim. "I didn't know what to do with you, Griffin. You were so sad, so *lost*. The only thing I could think to do was send you to Eton. I hoped the change would distract you from your grief."

Griffin's chest tightened as memories and feelings from that time assailed him.

"It was one of the most difficult things I've ever had to do, sending you away like that," she said. "And I've often wondered if it was the right decision."

Her eyes searched his, and he could see regret there, and vulnerability, too.

He took her hands in his and squeezed. "It was, Mother. It was."

He hadn't thought so at the time, though. His mother's decision had confused him greatly and hurt him deeply. He realized many years ago, however, that it was the best thing she could have done for him. He'd found solace in the distraction of new surroundings, new friends, learning new things. And it had been good to leave his home for a time, the home where he'd spent so many happy years with his father, who was gone now, never to walk the corridors of Keswick Hall again.

He hadn't considered before now just how difficult it must have been for his mother after his father died, being alone with two small children, trying to help them with their grief when her own must have been nearly unbearable.

"That must have been a difficult time for you," he said, the words woefully insufficient. "Caring for me and Emmy while trying to cope with your own grief. How did you manage it?"

Lady Keswick shrugged. "I honestly don't know. That first year after his death..." She shook her head. "I did not think I would survive it. I couldn't understand how he was there one moment and gone the next, or why God had given him to me, only to take him away. I couldn't understand what I had done to deserve that. I almost wished I had never—"

She broke off, her voice wavering, and Griffin held his breath as he waited for the rest of those words to fall.

I almost wished I had never met him.

But Lady Keswick only shook her head again, as if clearing the memories from her mind and then she clapped her hands together with forced cheer and said, "But never mind all that. We have a dinner to host, and I still need to get dressed."

She gave him a bright smile that was a touch too tight to be believable, and then she turned and headed for the door.

Griffin watched her leave, absently following the muted clip of her footsteps in the corridor as his mind filled with memories of those months after his father died—the black wreath on the front door, the mirrors covered in crepe. The unnatural silence that seemed to smother every inch of the house.

With a curse, he raked his hand through his hair. His mother regretted knowing his father.

The realization soured his stomach, and he swallowed the knot of unease thickening his throat. Why was he so upset? He shouldn't be. Her words were hardly a surprise. He knew how much his father's death had hurt her, how much it haunted her now, even twenty years later.

Her admission only confirmed what he'd always known but had allowed himself to forget. Marriage was a risk. A necessary one, yes, but a risk all the same, and one best handled with care and caution. Of course, he wasn't ready for marriage, so he needn't worry about it now. Any thoughts he might have had on the subject were only that. Thoughts, nothing more.

Still, he thought, as he headed for the door, there was no sense in courting complications. He liked Olivia—liked her more than he would have thought possible—but it could go no further than that.

He must keep her at arm's length, at least until after she was married.

Better safe than sorry.

OLIVIA HAD ALWAYS LOVED Lady Keswick's dinner parties. The marchioness was a natural hostess, and spared no expense, spoiling her guests with decadent dishes and fine wines. Even her decorations were a delight for the senses, and this evening was no exception.

The drawing room, where the guests had gathered after dinner, was warm and cozy with a cheerful fire burning in the hearth and frothy swathes of green and blue lace draped across the doors and windows. Candles burned everywhere, bathing the room in a soft, dreamy glow.

It was lovely, and yet, Olivia had barely spared the room a glance.

Seated beside Emmy on a plush velvet sofa, she sipped her sherry and pretended to listen while Miss Highwater performed on the pianoforte. Her skill was exceptional, her voice a gift from the heavens, but Olivia was too distracted to pay the performance its due.

She'd been distracted all evening, almost from the moment she first arrived, and there was only one explanation for it.

Griffin.

It was all *his* fault.

Battling a frustrated frown, she stole another glance at the reason for her evening's discontentment. He was seated beside his mother nearer to the pianoforte, watching Miss Highwater as she played, his profile only partially visible. The sight of his strong jaw and broad shoulders made Olivia's belly flutter.

Foolish girl.

It was no secret that Lady Keswick had invited Miss Highwater tonight in the hopes she might catch her son's eye.

And maybe she would. She was a lovely young lady, and more than qualified to fill the role of marchioness. Griffin would be lucky indeed to catch her.

In fact, Olivia hoped he would. Then, perhaps, he would finally cease tormenting her.

Irritation prickled anew at the nape of her neck as she recalled the cool greeting she'd received from him when she arrived tonight. A distracted welcome and a half-hearted bow and that was that. Dismissed without so much as a smile.

It was the only attention she'd received from him all evening, and it was driving her mad.

What had happened to the man he'd been that night at Vauxhall Gardens? Where was the man with admiration in his smile, and warmth in his eyes?

She liked *that* Griffin, and she wanted him back.

And that was what frustrated her the most. Why did she care? So what if he ignored her? So what if his behavior had changed?

None of it mattered and, truth be told, she was more frustrated with herself than with him. She should be happy tonight. No, she should be *ecstatic* tonight.

She'd spent nearly an hour in the Duchess of Paxton's morning room today, making small talk and drinking tea. And it had gone *well*. Better, even, than she had hoped. After weeks and weeks of trying and waiting, she was finally making strides and still she allowed Griffin to distract her.

She sighed. *What a ninny you are.*

Miss Highwater's song ended with a flourish on the keys and her small audience erupted into enthusiastic applause. Olivia joined in, forcing a smile as she clapped her free hand against her glass and leisurely rose to her feet.

She needed another sherry.

Crossing the room to the refreshments table, she paused at the tray of sweets, eyeing the raspberry tartlets. *Oh, why not?* She deserved a little indulgence tonight.

Nibbling on the sweet, she poured herself another glass of sherry then turned to face the room just as Emmy approached her, a frown marring her heart-shaped face.

"What's wrong?" Olivia asked.

"What's wrong is that I was not born a man," Emmy said, her voice a low grumble.

With a huff, she began piling biscuits and tarts onto her plate, the plunk of pastry on porcelain an audible show of her agitation.

Fighting back a smile, Olivia asked, "What happened?"

"It's Griffin," Emmy muttered. "He's leaving the party early."

Olivia flicked a glance over her shoulder and watched as Griffin leaned down to press a kiss to his mother's cheek. A lock of thick, dark hair fell over his brow and a smile touched his lips. Longing struck her heart, sharp and sweet, and she tore her gaze away.

"Why is he leaving?" she asked.

"He told my mother he has work to do tonight in preparation for an important meeting tomorrow morning," Emmy groused. "I think she suspects he's fibbing, but what can she do? He is the marquess, after all." She sighed. "It isn't fair."

"You don't really want to be the marquess," Olivia said. "Do you?"

"Of course not," Emmy said. "Far too much paperwork. But I wouldn't mind being the second son."

Olivia's smile was tight as she gazed down at her glass of sherry, trying not to watch Griffin as he crossed the drawing room toward the door. She sucked in a short breath of air and waited for the tightness in her chest to ease.

"Is something wrong, Livvy?"

She looked up. "Of course not. Everything is fine."

Emmy eyed her with suspicion. "No. You've seemed out of sorts all evening. And you were even glowering at Miss Highwater during her performance."

"I was not," she said, though the argument lacked conviction.

"You were. Which means, either you loathe her for absolutely no reason, or something else is troubling you."

Olivia worried her lip between her teeth. Perhaps she should tell her. Perhaps sharing her troubles with a friend would make her feel better. Emmy could chatter a person's ear clean off, but she was a surprisingly good listener, too.

"Something is troubling me," she said quietly. "Or, rather, *someone*."

Emmy's brows rose with interest. "Who?"

Olivia's gaze fell to her glass of sherry. "Your brother."

"Ah." Emmy did not sound surprised. "What has the fool done now?"

Olivia blew out a frustrated breath and walked over to the hearth, away from the other guests. Emmy followed with her plate in hand, munching on a biscuit.

"I'm so confused, Em," Olivia said as she turned to face her.

Emmy's brow puckered. "Confused about what?"

"About him, about his feelings," she said. "About *my* feelings." She leaned her shoulder against the cool papered wall beside the hearth and sighed. "Things are finally beginning to look up for me. Paxton wants to marry me, and I think his mother is finally coming around to the idea. I should be thrilled, and yet...I can't stop thinking about Griffin."

Emmy regarded her in silence for a long, uncomfortable moment before she finally spoke. "Did something happen between the two of you? Has something changed?"

Olivia's gaze dropped to her sherry again and she pursed her lips, considering just how much she ought to share. "We...kissed."

She looked up to find Emmy watching her with wide gray eyes, the half-eaten biscuit in her hand hovering halfway to her mouth.

"You did *what?*" she hissed. "Where? *When?*"

"In Lady Chavel's rose garden," Olivia said, her cheeks warming. "And then again in your drawing room. And a third time in Mrs. Lubbock's folly."

Emmy's jaw dropped open. "You've shared *three* kisses and you're just now telling me?"

Olivia gave a sheepish half-shrug. "You're his sister. Talking about it with you felt...strange."

Emmy frowned. "I suppose that makes sense," she said, though she did not seem happy about it. If there was one thing Emmy hated above all else, it was being left out.

"So, you've shared three kisses," she said, dropping the unfinished biscuit onto her plate. "What are you going to do about it?"

Olivia shook her head. "I don't know. Nothing, probably."

"Nothing?" Her frown deepened. "He kissed you three times, Livvy. Don't you think that means something?"

Her gaze drifted to the pianoforte, where a new young lady had begun to perform. She honestly didn't know what to think. She wished it meant something. She wished it meant *everything*, but she was not naive. Two people could share physical intimacies without also sharing emotional ones.

"Perhaps it does mean something," she said quietly. "But I don't think it means enough to make him want to marry me."

"You could always ask him."

Olivia huffed out a laugh. "Ask him to marry me? Are you mad?"

"Ask him how he feels," Emmy corrected. "Talk to him. What do you have to lose?"

"Besides my pride?" She grimaced. The thought of humiliating herself before him again was insupportable.

"Well, it's better than spending the rest of your life wondering what might have been, isn't it?"

Olivia fell silent as Emmy's words knocked around in her head. Would she regret never knowing? If she married Paxton, would she still be wondering, years from now, if her life might have been different if she'd been braver?

"What if he rejects me?" she asked, the thought sending her heart thudding in her chest. "What if he turns me away? How will I ever face him again?"

He'd been so cool toward her tonight, so distant. Not remotely encouraging, and certainly not lovelorn.

"But what if he doesn't turn you away?" Emmy said. "What if he tells you he loves you? That he wants to marry you?"

Olivia's lips thinned. "If he wanted to marry me, surely he would have asked me by now."

"Would he?" Emmy said, her tone gentle but challenging. "You have spent these last two months doing everything you can to become a duchess. Perhaps he thinks you would turn down an offer from a marquess."

Emmy's words made Olivia pause and her brow furrowed. Could she be right? Was it possible he wanted to marry her but was afraid she would reject him?

And was she brave enough to find out?

"Go to him, Livvy," Emmy said softly. "Go to his study and talk to him."

"But what about your mother's party? I cannot just disappear."

"Leave that to me," Emmy said with a wave of her hand. "I'll tell everyone you were feeling unwell and retired to my chamber for a brief rest."

Olivia gripped Emmy's hand in hers and squeezed. "Thank you," she said. "You're a good friend."

"I'm the best," Emmy said, her gray eyes twinkling. "Now, *go*."

Chapter Twenty-One

Ten minutes later, Olivia stood outside Griffin's study, her heart racing as she stared at the closed door in front of her. *Oh, God.* She wasn't sure she could go through with it.

She licked her lips and tried to swallow past the knot in her very dry throat, her thoughts a tangle of worries and fears and flagging courage. Was she really going to do this? Was she really about to walk through that door and ask the man inside if he would like to marry her?

She must have lost her mind. Only a simpleton would do what she was about to do.

Emmy was right, though. She would regret it if she didn't ask, if she didn't know, once and for all. She had to do this. Even if the likelihood of a good outcome was abysmally low.

Raising her knuckles to the door, she rapped them lightly on the hard wood and waited, her heart knocking against her ribcage like a thing possessed.

The soft snick of the latch punctuated the cloying silence, and time seemed to slow as the door swung open on silent hinges.

She looked up, and there was Griffin, staring at her from the open doorway.

"Olivia?" Surprise sparked in his eyes. "What are you—shouldn't you be with the other guests?"

Somehow she managed a smile even as her legs itched to carry her far, far away.

Only minutes ago, this had all made sense, but now, standing before him in the darkened corridor, she felt exposed and vulnerable.

That he was so tall and broad, so *imposing*, did not help matters in the slightest.

"Yes, I should, but—" She swallowed, and smoothed trembling hands down the front of her dress. "May I...speak with you for a moment?"

His brows rose at the unusual request, but he stepped back without protest, clearing the way for her. "Of course. Come in."

Heart pounding and fingers fidgeting, Olivia stepped into his study, and turned to watch him as he closed the door, shutting them inside.

No turning back now.

She swallowed.

"Please, have a seat," Griffin said, gesturing to his desk.

He'd removed his coat and cravat and wore only a green silk waistcoat over a white linen shirt and black trousers. His shirtsleeves were rolled up to his elbows, and as she sat, she tried not to stare at his bare forearms.

Clearing her throat, she glanced around the room, stalling for time as she took in the blazing fire, the mahogany furnishings and leather-bound books, as if this was the first time she'd been here, though, of course, she'd seen the room dozens of times. At least it gave her something to do while she tried to think of what on earth she meant to say to the man sitting across from her.

"Olivia?"

Griffin's voice drew her gaze to his.

"Am I in trouble?" he asked with a teasing half-smile. "Perhaps I should be sitting in your seat instead."

She smiled weakly and shook her head. "You're not in trouble." *But I certainly am.*

"Are you unwell?" he asked, his smile fading. He leaned forward on his forearms, his eyes flicking over her face, both curious and concerned.

"No, no. I am perfectly well, I assure you." She cleared her throat again. "I am here because I...because..." She ran her tongue over the crooked line of her teeth as her gaze dropped to her lap.

How in heaven's name did people do this? How did anyone muster up the courage to lay their heart bare before another human being?

She'd never thought about it before now, how harrowing it was to confess one's feelings to another, uncertain of their reaction, completely at their mercy. She'd never felt more vulnerable.

"What is it, Olivia?"

She could hear the alarm in his voice and when she looked at him, the patience in his steady gaze made her heart squeeze. He thought she was in trouble. He was prepared to help her in any way he could because he was an honorable man, and she was his sister's dearest friend.

He was not prepared for a marriage proposal. Her feelings for him—and his for her, whatever they may be—were the furthest thing from his mind right now.

This is madness.

Her resolve crumbled to dust.

"Forgive me," she said, pushing to her feet. "This was a mistake. I—pardon me for disturbing you."

"Olivia—"

But she was already on her way to the door, her desperation to leave quickening her steps. *Stupid, stupid girl.* Had she really come here to ask him to marry her? To ask him if he loved her? God, how pathetic. How foolish.

"Olivia, wait." Griffin's hand closed around her wrist as she reached for the door, and he tugged gently until she turned to face him.

"Why did you come?" he asked, his eyes searching hers. "Why did you want to see me?"

She shook her head and forced a smile. "It was nothing, Griffin. Please, forget about it."

His lips formed a stubborn line, the way they always did when he wasn't willing to give up just yet. "What is it?" he asked. "Are you unwell? Whatever is wrong, you can tell me."

"I told you, I am fine," she said, widening her smile. "Indeed, I've never been happier. After all, I will be a duchess soon. What more could a girl possibly hope for?"

His gaze sharpened on hers, his hand still grasping her wrist, warm and solid through the cuff of her sleeve. "You don't look terribly happy to me," he said quietly.

Her heart clenched. *God, this man's eyes. They saw far too much.*

"Well, you're wrong," she said. "I am happy. Ecstatically happy. I am so happy I—" Her voice cracked and, to her horror, tears began to well in her eyes.

Frantically, she whirled toward the door, pulling her wrist free of his grasp, but his hands stayed her again, gripping her shoulders and gently urging her into the warm cradle of his arms.

Her eyes fell closed, and she swallowed as tears trickled down her cheeks. She sighed, pressing her face into his chest, inhaling his scent as his arms wrapped tightly around her.

It was strange, seeking comfort in the arms of the very man responsible for her heartache, but she didn't care. It felt too good, and she was too weak to pull away. She would scold herself for the failing tomorrow. For now, she would savor this moment.

"Don't marry Paxton, Olivia." Griffin's mouth brushed against her hair as he spoke. "He cannot make you happy. And you deserve a man who will make you happy."

Her heart dipped and she drew back so she could see his face. "Do I?"

He smiled and stroked her cheek with the backs of his fingers. "Without a doubt."

Her breath caught in her throat at the tender look in his eyes, the sweet caress of his hand, and she wondered, wildly, if he meant to suggest that *he* could make her happy.

Say it, she urged. *Say you love me. Ask me to choose you instead.*

"Be patient," he said. "The right man will come along soon enough. You have only to wait."

The hope in her heart flickered and died, snuffed out like a candle's flame, and the warmth in her chest cooled to ice. He had no intention of offering for her tonight. He would *never* offer for her. Not tonight, not tomorrow. Not ever.

She eased out of his arms and stepped back, brushing at her skirts. "I do not need to wait," she said, keeping her voice even. "Paxton is the right man for me."

"In your father's eyes, perhaps. But not yours."

Frustration tensed her jaw, but she did not reply. She did not trust herself to speak.

"You know I'm right, Olivia. Admit it."

"So what if you are?" she said, crossing her arms over her chest. "So what if the duke isn't everything I'd ever dreamed of? Not all dreams come true."

"But some do."

Olivia shook her head, her smile wistful as she turned for the door. "Not this one."

"You don't know that. If you would only wait—"

"Wait for what?" She whirled on him, arms outstretched, her brows forming a frustrated line. "For someone better to come along? For the man of my dreams to swoop in and carry me off to a perfect, blissful future?" She scoffed. "Life doesn't work like that, Griffin. Things don't always turn out as we hope they will. The duke might not be my ideal match, but he is a good man, and he will treat me well. It will be enough." *Because it had to be.*

"No, it won't," he said, the words a low growl. "It will never be enough, not for a woman like you. A woman of passion and wit and fire." His eyes held hers, smoky gray and crackling with feeling. "He will suffocate your flame, Olivia. You deserve a man who will *feed* it."

Her breath caught as he reached a hand out, his fingers cupping her cheek, stroking her lips, setting her blood afire.

"You deserve a man who sees you," he whispered. "A man who sees how incredible you are, who wants to be with you, and will make damned sure you know how much he wants you." His hands found her hips and his fingers bit into her flesh, wringing a gasp from her throat. "And not just your body, petal, but your mind, too. You deserve a man who needs you by his side, in his life. In his bed."

Olivia's skin burned beneath the heat in his gaze and in his words, and her heart thundered in her chest, even as her mind cautioned her to resist. She wanted this man, wanted him so much she ached with it, but she knew she could not have him.

"I—I should go," she whispered, stepping back, away from his mind-muddling touch. "Good night, Griffin."

"Olivia—"

"*Meow.*"

Olivia stilled, surprised, as her gaze flicked to the large armchair by the fire where Artemis sat stretching her limbs. The kitten tromped in a little circle before plopping back onto the mound of blankets and going back to sleep.

"I didn't even know she was there," Olivia said, a reluctant smile turning her lips.

"It's her favorite chair," Griffin said. "She likes to sleep by the fire."

She looked at him, brows raised. "Is she often here with you while you work?"

"She likes it here," Griffin said. "And I like to keep an eye on her. Make certain she stays out of trouble."

He crossed his arms over his chest as if embarrassed and Olivia's heart melted. Oh, how she adored this man.

She would marry Paxton, start a family, and be content in her life as a duchess and mother. Eventually she would forget Griffin and these foolish desires, these impossible hopes, and life without him would be enough. Because it would have to be.

She could not have him, but perhaps she could claim a small bit of him. Perhaps she could leave here with a memento of sorts, a moment to treasure; to remember him by.

But only if she was brave enough to ask for it.

"Griffin?"

His gaze met hers. "Yes?"

"Will you..." She swallowed, battling for courage, her pulse kicking up a frantic beat. "Will you make love to me?"

His lips parted and she could see the surprise in his eyes.

"Please." She stepped forward, closing the distance between them. "Please, Griffin. I want you to make love to me."

"Christ, Olivia, I—" His throat worked as he raked a hand through his hair. "I—you should wait for your wedding night."

Disappointed pricked, and her gaze fell to her fidgeting hands. It wasn't exactly the response she'd hoped for, but it wasn't a refusal, either.

Don't give up yet.

She forced her chin up, found him watching her, his face in shadow, his gaze indecipherable but not indifferent. She pressed on.

"I was fifteen the first time a boy kissed me," she said softly, her lips curving at the memory of that clumsy meeting of mouths. "He was a farmer's son, very handsome, and I fancied myself in love with him. For a while, at least."

Griffin did not speak, though his gaze never strayed from hers. *A good sign?* It was impossible to tell.

Nervously, she moistened her lips with her tongue, and Griffin's gaze flicked to her mouth, tracking the motion with keen interest. Hope surged in her breast.

"I've been kissed many times since, by many different men," she said softly. "But not one of them ever made me burn inside. Not one of them ever left me craving more. Until you."

Tipping her head back, she met his gaze unwaveringly, willing him to listen, to hear her. "You're the only one who makes my body ache," she said. "You're the only one who makes me feel good."

She rose up on tiptoe and pressed her mouth to his throat, wringing a rumbling groan from his chest. "Make me feel good again," she whispered, gripping his arms. "Make love to me, Griffin."

His body was tense beneath her hands as he stared at her, still and quiet for a tortuously long moment, and the only sound Olivia could hear was the hectic beating of her own heart.

Finally, he moved, reaching around her as if going for the door, and for one awful moment, she thought he was going to turn her away, push her from the room, reject her.

But then the soft snick of the door lock clicking into place punctuated the silence, and Griffin's gaze locked on hers. "You're certain?" he asked, his voice husky.

She nodded, her heart thrashing against her ribcage. "Yes. I'm certain."

His gray eyes raked over her face, soft and warm like summer rain, and then he took her by the hand and drew her away from the door.

She followed, her body thrumming, her gaze locked on the chaise longue, which seemed to be their destination. Excitement pulsed through her, swirling in her belly and warming her cheeks.

Griffin turned to face her, still holding her hand, the steady warmth of his grasp doing much to soothe her nerves.

He lifted his free hand to cup her cheek as a smile teased the corners of his lips. "I shouldn't do this," he said, tracing her cheekbone with his thumb. "I should refuse you and send you away, but I don't want to." His eyes blazed. "I want this. I want you, Olivia."

His words scorched her straight through, annihilating her fears, her doubts, until all that was left was a burning desire to touch him, to feel his body against hers.

"Then kiss me," she demanded with a none-too-gentle tug on his hand.

He went to her, his eyes dancing as his mouth swooped down and claimed its kiss. Her eyes fluttered closed as his lips touched hers and she groaned when he deepened the kiss, his tongue sliding into her mouth, his hands sweeping her body against his.

Yes. *Yes.* This was what she wanted. Just for one night, just this once, he would be hers.

Desire pounded through her veins as she returned his kiss, running eager hands up his forearms, his biceps, his shoulders. Reveling in the feel of him beneath her palms, the solid strength of his big, warm body, so different from her own.

She wanted his skin bared. Every inch of it. Now.

Pulling her head back, she met his gaze and slipped her fingers to the buttons of his waistcoat.

"I want to see you."

CHAPTER TWENTY-TWO

THE DESIRE BLAZING IN Olivia's deep blue eyes was more arousing than anything Griffin had ever seen before, and though he knew he should, he was powerless to resist her.

"Loosen the buttons," he ordered, his voice a low rumble. She wanted to see his body. Far be it from him to deny the lady's request.

Olivia dipped her head and went to work on his waistcoat, her progress slowed by unsteady hands, but Griffin did not hurry her, nor did he offer to help. This night was hers—her pace, her preference, her power. He would let her be his guide tonight.

"There," she murmured, pushing his waistcoat from his shoulders and down his arms until it fell in a heap at his feet.

He smiled at the glint of triumph in her eyes. "Shall I remove my shirt, as well?"

She nodded, her gaze already skimming over his body, as if picturing what he would look like. In one deft move, he swept his shirt over his head and dropped it to the floor.

She was silent for a long moment, her eyes skating over his torso, and then she lifted her hands and pressed them to his chest. Griffin held his breath as her fingers began to roam, her skin feather-soft, her touch so light yet so intense it sent shivers across his flesh.

"You told me not so long ago that you think of me sometimes," she said. "When you pleasure yourself." Her gaze lifted from his chest to his face. "I think of you sometimes, too."

God, what was she trying to do to him?

Images of Olivia finding her pleasure at her own hand flooded his mind and his cock surged beneath his trousers.

Gritting his teeth, he guided her to the chaise and urged her to lay down, determined to go slow.

She reclined against the cushion, her fingers laced across her belly, her skirts askew, the most beautiful woman he'd ever seen.

She watched him openly, unabashedly, with curiosity in her eyes, and desire, too. Desire for him.

His breath whooshed from his lungs.

He joined her on the chaise, leaning on one elbow to keep from crushing her as he covered her mouth with his. Olivia arched into him, meeting his kiss with a slow sweep of her tongue along his lip, her hands gripping his shoulders.

Her body was soft and lush beneath his, her scent curling around him, sweet and seductive, just like her.

He skated his hand along the dip of her waist, over her hip, down her thigh, his lips never leaving hers as he hunted for the hem of her gown.

His fingers skimmed satin and he realized she still wore her slippers. He made quick work of them, nudging them to the rug before sliding his hand up her ankle to her calf, caressing her through her stocking. He had just crested her knee when she pulled her mouth from his.

"What about Artemis?" she gasped, glancing over at the kitten's chair, which was turned away from them, facing the hearth.

"She's sleeping."

Her brow lowered. "But...what if she wakes?"

"She won't," he said. "Not if we're quiet." His hand ghosted up her thigh and he nuzzled her throat. "Can you be quiet for me, Olivia?"

He nipped her collarbone with his teeth as his knuckles skimmed her inner thigh, and her breath caught in her throat.

"Griffin," she choked out, her hips bucking, a visceral plea for more. He gave it to her, stroking her softly, her plump, wet heat soft beneath his fingers. Lightly he grazed her nub with the pad of his thumb.

Her groan rent the air.

"You'll have to do better than that," he teased, his gaze roaming over her flushed cheeks and hazy eyes. God, she was gorgeous, so needy and aroused, reveling in her own pleasure. He wanted to give her more of it, even as his own body demanded satisfaction.

"Bite your lip for me, petal," he demanded, his voice ragged.

She obeyed, her gaze locked on his as she drew her lower lip between her teeth, and Griffin's cock throbbed at the sight of it.

"Yes," he murmured approvingly. "Just like that. Don't let go."

He worked his way down her body, bunching her skirts up as he went, his gaze greedy, devouring every inch he uncovered. He bent his head and pressed a kiss to her knee as he settled between her delectable thighs.

The scent of her arousal, sweet and tangy, shot lust through his belly to his groin and he groaned. God, she was so wet, so pink and perfect. He leaned in, craving a taste, and brushed his lips against her sensitive flesh.

Her hand grasped his shoulder and squeezed, but she made not a sound. Not even at the first touch of his tongue.

He worked her over with soft flicks and firm strokes until she was writhing against his mouth, her hips and hands frenzied with her need.

She was no longer mute, but muted whimpers and groans escaped from her throat as she tried, and failed, to keep quiet. He loved her like this, desperate, unraveled.

Unraveled because of *him*.

"Griffin..." His name was barely a whisper on her lips, but he sensed the want in it, the plea to ease her torment.

With quickened strokes of his tongue, he focused his attentions where he knew she wanted them most, letting her body be his guide. She wove her fingers through his hair as the muscles in her thighs began to tremble and as the first tremor took hold, Griffin eased a finger into her wet heat.

She cried out, her body stiffening and clenching around him as she found her release. Griffin nearly joined her, so acute was his arousal, his cock stiff and aching inside his trousers.

But he was no innocent lad. The days of spending in his pants were long behind him.

He sat up and leaned his weight on one hand.

Her eyes opened and met his. "Goodness."

He smiled, inordinately pleased by the edge of wonder in her voice.

"I wasn't quiet, was I?" she said, her expression sweetly flustered.

"Not very. No."

She blew out a breath, as if baffled by her own behavior. "I couldn't help it. Not with your mouth on my..." Her hand flicked down her body, filling in the blanks.

Griffin's smile widened. "Yes, I noticed."

She studied him in silence for a moment, and then spoke. "Would you..." She paused and licked her lips then started again. "Do you think you would suffer the same affliction? If I were to...kiss you the same way?"

God. His grin faltered and he swallowed hard. Just the *thought* of her mouth on his cock made him want to howl, but this night was supposed to be hers, not his. And he was determined to make it everything she wanted it to be.

Even if he perished in the process.

"I can almost guarantee it, petal."

Her eyes sparked with interest. "May I find out for certain?"

His cock throbbed with an interest of its own. "You may do anything you like," he answered, keeping his voice even, though his body thrummed with anticipation.

She rose to a sitting position and chewed her lip thoughtfully, as if plotting out her best strategy.

"Will you lie down?" she asked. "Like I was?"

He did as she requested, trading places with her and leaning back against the arm of the chaise with his legs stretched out before him.

Then, heart thudding, he laced his fingers behind his head and waited for her next move.

OLIVIA HAD NO IDEA where to begin, but she knew one thing for certain. She'd never seen a more arousing sight in her life than the one before her now.

Griffin lay sprawled on the chaise, watching her with patient eyes, the lean muscles in his bare chest and arms gleaming in the low firelight.

An artist's dream subject.

And then, of course, there was the bulge at the front of his breeches, stark evidence of his arousal, though he seemed in no hurry to satisfy it.

Excitement pulsed through her. *Free rein.* He'd given her leave to explore his body and her own curiosity, and she intended to take full advantage.

She scooted forward on the chaise until she was perched beside him, her hip pressed against his thigh. Heart pounding, she laid her hands on his naked chest, and smoothed her palms along the ridge of his pectorals, enjoying the way his dark, springy hair tickled her skin.

"You're hairier than I thought you would be," she murmured as she traced a finger down the slender trail of hair bisecting his firm, flat stomach, watching his muscles leap beneath her touch. "I like it."

"Good."

His voice was rough, his eyes like smoke, and she held his gaze as her hand hovered just above his erection. Finally, she touched him, running her palm down his hard length, stroking him through his breeches.

He sucked in a breath and his hips jerked, thrusting into her hand as if of their own accord. She liked that, a reaction beyond his control. A reaction drawn from her touch.

She undid the fastening of his falls, and his manhood jutted out, thick and hard. She took him in hand, wrapping her fingers around his length and stroking upward in one smooth motion until she reached the head.

He was hot, hotter than she remembered, and she loved that she could see him this time, his nakedness, his shaft in her hand, the pleasure etched on his handsome face.

"I've never done this before," she whispered as she slid to her knees on the rug. "You'll tell me if I do something wrong?"

"There is no—*Christ above, Olivia.*"

She smiled and licked the tip of his shaft again, slower this time, circling the whole of it with her tongue before taking him in her mouth. He groaned and she could feel his gaze on her, watching her every move, but instead of making her feel shy, his attention emboldened her.

His fingers wove through her hair, his hips undulating in short thrusts as she sucked him harder, drawing him deeper into her mouth, one fist holding him captive.

"I can't...last any longer like this," he said through gritted teeth and then he swept her up onto the chaise and covered her with his body.

"This mouth of yours is dangerous, petal," he murmured before taking her lips in a long, intoxicating kiss.

"I liked tasting you," she admitted when they separated to breathe. "I liked making you moan."

He kissed her again, his hands wandering over her body, every touch setting her ablaze and making her ache anew. He eased his lips from hers to kiss her cheek, her jaw, working his way down the column of her throat until she was writhing against him, her hands gripping his biceps.

"How is it that you are still dressed?" he asked as he skimmed his teeth along the slopes of her breasts. "I want to see you naked, Olivia. Sit up."

The low command sent a shiver of heat straight to her core, and she obeyed, lifting so he could access the buttons at her back.

He made fast work of them, his large hands more nimble than they had a right to be, and in a matter of moments he'd divested her of her clothing until she lay before him in only her stockings and stays.

"You're beautiful," he whispered, and the look in his eyes, the frank desire there, brought a flush of pleasure to her cheeks.

"Thank you," she whispered back.

And then she drew his mouth to hers and kissed him, running her hands over his naked back as he settled between her thighs. The feel of his rigid length, hot and smooth against her wetness made her groan and she rubbed herself against him, whimpering into his mouth.

"Are you certain, Olivia?" Griffin pulled back to meet her gaze, his body unnaturally still as he awaited her answer. "I need you to be certain. There is no undoing this."

She raised a hand to his face and stroked his jaw with trembling fingers. "I'm certain," she said. "I want this, Griffin. I will not regret it."

What was there to regret? She was giving herself to the man she loved, the man she would always love. She would never want to undo this night.

He nodded, his eyes fierce as he leaned in to kiss her again, his mouth taking hers in a hard kiss that left no doubt that he wanted this, too.

He skimmed a palm down her belly and eased his fingers into her heat, teasing with strokes so gentle, so *not enough,* he had her arching into his hand, practically panting with need.

"Griffin...*please...*"

He drew back, balancing on his forearm, his gaze trained on hers, dark and intense.

She reached up and stroked her fingers along his hard jaw, needing to touch the evidence of his desire, his loss of control, as if she could keep it in her hand forever.

"This might hurt, petal," Griffin said, sweat beading his brow. "I'm sorry. I wish it wasn't so, but—"

"I know," she said. "It will be fine. I'm ready."

A smile flashed in his eyes, as if he found it amusing that *she* was consoling *him*, but then he sobered, and she held very still as he slowly eased inside. She watched his face, holding her breath as he filled her, and her toes curled as her body stretched to accommodate him.

She gripped his shoulders as she grew accustomed to the feel of him, the sensation unfamiliar but not unpleasant.

He pulled back, then gave another short thrust forward as his eyes met hers. "Is this—am I hurting you?"

"No," she said. "Keep going."

It was starting to feel rather nice, actually, the friction of each thrust sending a little pang of pleasure through her loins, and if he would only quicken the pace, she might finally—

She stiffened as he thrust deep, the twinge swift and sharp, and Griffin held himself very still as he gazed down at her.

"I'm sorry," he said, his eyes remorseful, though the rest of his face seemed carved in stone. "Do you want to stop?"

She shook her head. "I'm fine." There was no turning back now, not when they'd come so far. And the discomfort was beginning to fade now.

He nodded, then slowly edged back then forward again. In and out. In and out. Slow, measured strokes, each one a little deeper than the last, the slide of his shaft an abrasion that was both too much and not enough.

A frustrated noise sounded in her throat, and she arched her hips, rocking into him. Their moans mingled and Olivia wrapped her legs around his hips and thrust again, harder this time, taking in more of him. Still, it wasn't enough.

"You want more?" Griffin rasped, gripping her thigh. "Is that it, petal? Your cunny wants more of me?"

She clenched around him, the naughty word heightening her pleasure, and she gripped his neck, arching up to meet him. He adjusted his angle, leaning into her just so, forcing his long, thick length to drag across her swollen nub.

Her body seized and clenched as she burst into a thousand pieces, keening her pleasure into his ear.

Griffin grunted, quickening his pace, and then, with a low growl, he withdrew from her body and spilled his seed on her thigh.

A long silence followed and then Olivia sat up and sucked in a deep breath, trying to calm her galloping heart. "Oh, my."

Griffin chuckled and sat up, reaching for his discarded shirt. "Indeed," he said, wiping her thigh clean. "I had no idea how persuasive you could be. You would make an excellent barrister."

Olivia laughed, her cheeks warming with pleasure. "Don't be silly. I'm not clever enough to be a barrister."

"Nonsense. You're more than clever enough."

Bemused, Olivia searched his face for a sign he was poking fun, but there was not a glimmer of amusement to be found. "You're serious," she said, hearing the surprise in her own voice.

"Of course," he said.

She looked away, her heart aglow, the compliment and the matter-of-fact way in which he gave it pleasing her more than any praise ever had before. "You're the first man who has ever called me clever."

Griffin leaned back against the chaise and shook his head, chuckling softly. "I find that hard to believe. You must have received hundreds of compliments from men."

She rolled her eyes. "Yes," she said. "On my glorious eyes and beautiful smile."

"How awful for you," Griffin drawled.

She smiled wryly. "Don't misunderstand me, I don't *mind* those compliments. I rather like that men find me attractive. But it would be nice to be praised for my talents or my sense of humor every once in a while."

He nodded. "I hate to speak ill of my fellow men, but we can be astoundingly dense at times."

She huffed out a laugh. "Yes. You certainly can be."

He gave her a half-grin then, the one that always stopped her heart, and then he reached out and brushed his thumb over her smile. "In our defense," he said, his voice husky, "it *is* a beautiful smile."

Olivia swallowed, mesmerized by the warmth in his eyes, the tenderness in his touch. "Griffin," she whispered. "I..."

The words were on the tip of her tongue, words of love, the future, words that would change everything. Words she could not take back.

In the end, she lost her nerve. "I should probably go," she said finally, sitting up.

She dressed quickly, avoiding his gaze, and when she was done she faced him again, unsure of what to say. How did one bring an evening of lovemaking to a close?

"Thank you," she finally settled on. "This was...everything I'd hoped it would be."

Almost everything. But it would have to be enough.

"It was my pleasure," he answered, his voice sincere, though tinged with a dash of amusement she could not fault him for, considering the unusual turn their night had taken.

"Well," she said. "Good night, Griffin."

"Good night, Olivia."

It felt like goodbye, she thought, as she headed for the door. And she supposed it was, in a way. She was bidding farewell to her girlish dreams, the hopeless fantasy she'd held onto these past several years. It was time.

And it was probably for the best. She would marry her duke and lead a full and contented life with him. But she would always have this night to look back on with fondness. She had no regrets.

If anything, she was proud of herself for asking for what she wanted, for taking something for herself, something that had nothing to do with her father or his expectations of her.

And now life would go on as it should, as it was always meant to. And she would be happy with that.

CHAPTER
TWENTY-THREE

THE NEXT SENNIGHT PASSED in relative peace as Olivia settled back into the normalcy of daily life. She attended church service, planted a new rose bush in the garden out back, and even completed the embroidery sampler she'd been working on for the past several months.

Tuesday brought a new letter from Sophie—though, thankfully, she'd received not a word from her father—and on Wednesday, she and her aunt took tea again with the Duchess of Paxton. Not the most enjoyable hour Olivia had ever spent, but the duchess seemed to be warming to her, and her coconut cakes were divine.

Despite how busy she kept herself, her thoughts often strayed to Griffin. How could she help it after the evening they'd shared together? It was an experience she would always remember, but now that it was over, she knew she must let him go.

She'd only seen him once since that night in his bed, and only in passing, a swift 'good afternoon' as they passed each other in the hall. Her heart had stuttered at the sight of him, and for one brief moment of weakness, she'd imagined an alternate version, in which he'd dropped to his knees and begged her to marry him before sweeping her into his arms and kissing her senseless.

It was a fool's fantasy, of course, but she was only human, and an occasionally foolish one, at that.

"Olivia?" Paxton's soft voice drew her gaze to his. "What is your answer? Will you marry me?"

She studied the man seated beside her on the sofa in her drawing room, taking in his hopeful smile, his kind eyes, and she thought of their outing yesterday in a rowboat on the Thames. It was an unusually warm day and the duke, red-cheeked and sweating in his beautifully-tailored suit, must have been miserable beneath the hot afternoon sun, but he never uttered a single word of complaint. He just seemed happy to be with her.

And she knew, if she asked him to, he would do it all over again.

"Yes, Paxton," she said with a smile. "I will marry you."

"Excellent." He beamed and took her hands in his, leaning forward, his eyes dipping to her lips. "May I claim a kiss from my betrothed?"

She nodded and his lips pressed to hers, soft, cool, respectful. A sweet kiss from her sweet husband-to-be.

"Well," he said, drawing back, his brown eyes bright with contentment. "I suppose I should leave you now. I have some news to share with my mother"—he grinned—"and I'm sure you will wish to speak with your aunt straightaway."

She nodded again, her lips tiring from the strain of so much smiling. "Yes, of course. She will be most pleased."

"And I will see you tonight at Almack's?" Paxton asked.

"Yes, I will be there."

"Excellent," he said again. "I cannot wait to dance my first waltz with my betrothed."

He waggled his eyebrows and Olivia widened her smile before rising to her feet, suddenly anxious for him to leave.

The duke bowed and bid her farewell, and Olivia watched him walk from the room, listening for the sound of the front door closing before sinking to the sofa again. She fell back against the cushion with a heavy sigh and closed her eyes.

Good heavens, he could be exhausting sometimes.

But she supposed she would have to get used to it. He was to be her husband now.

Her eyes popped open as the words took root in her mind. It had finally happened, hadn't it? She was betrothed now. She would finally be a duchess. It was everything she'd been working toward, everything she'd hoped for since the start of the Season.

She sat up, nibbling her lower lip as hope and uncertainty crossed swords in her belly. Would her father be happy with the news of her betrothal? Would he be proud?

She pictured his face, imagined him gazing down at her with affection in his eyes, a beaming smile curling up the ends of his mustache. Hope won out and she smiled. *Soon.*

"Knock, knock!"

Olivia sat up with a jolt as Emmy sailed into the room, looking lovely in a muslin morning dress a shade darker than her eyes.

"Emmy." Olivia's gaze darted to the clock on the mantel. "Is it time for our outing already? Where is your mother?"

"She is in the garden with your aunt," Emmy said. "We are a few minutes early." She plopped down onto a chair across from Olivia and stared at her expectantly. "I passed the duke on my way in. He seemed in unusually high spirits."

Olivia nodded. "I...just accepted his proposal of marriage."

"I see." Emmy was silent for a moment and then her hands clapped together, and her lips stretched into a bright smile. "Well! Congratulations, *Duchess.*"

"Thank you, Emmy," Olivia said. "I do appreciate your words of felicitation, even if you don't quite mean them."

Emmy shrugged. "I only want you to be happy."

Olivia noticed her friend had not refuted her charge. "I know you do," she said. "And I will be. You'll see."

"I am certain you're right, of course, but..." Emmy nibbled at her bottom lip, as if debating whether to speak. "I do think you would be happier with Griffin. Why will you not tell him how you feel?"

Olivia sighed, only just resisting the urge to throw her hands up in exasperation. They'd had this discussion before—more than once, in fact—in the days since she made love with Griffin. When she and Emmy met the next day, she couldn't bring herself to tell her the truth. At least, not all of it. She said only that she'd lost her nerve and left without confessing her feelings.

"We've been through this before," Olivia said, as evenly as she could manage. "I told you, it would be a waste of time. He does not share my feelings."

"You don't know that," Emmy said. "And I happen to think he does. If you would only talk to him, I am sure he would—"

"No." Olivia surged to her feet and began to pace, agitation driving every step. "It is done. It is time to move on. Your brother and I..." She shook her head. "It is not meant to be. And I'm engaged to be married, if you remember. I am promised to the duke."

"But you haven't married him yet," Emmy said stubbornly. "You haven't even signed the marriage contract yet. There is still time."

"No, Em. Time has run out on that hope. I am ready to move on with my life." She paused and leaned her arms against the back of the sofa. "Besides, I want a peaceful home, and your brother and I argue far too much to allow for that. We would drive each other to madness before the wedding breakfast was over."

Emmy returned her smile, though it did not reach her eyes. "Perhaps you're right. Perhaps you and Griffin would be miserable together, whereas you and the duke will spend the rest of your days in perfect, polite coexistence."

Olivia nodded. "Precisely. A pleasant, peaceful marriage is exactly what I want."

She would write to her father straightaway, of course. The news that his only daughter would soon be a duchess was sure to please him. At least, she hoped it would.

At the very least, he would be happy to learn she had finally chosen a husband as he wanted her to do, but she hoped her betrothal would mean more to him than that. She hoped her choice of husband would make him proud, and maybe even help to bridge the chasm between them. That would make all of this worthwhile.

And if life with the duke was a little dull, a little prosaic, so be it. She could do a lot worse than a dull duke for a husband, could she not?

And if her husband's kisses left her cold...

Well, there was more to life than passion, and more than one kind of happiness. It would be enough. She would make sure of it.

GRIFFIN LEANED FORWARD IN the large leather chair and rested his elbows on his desk, raking both hands through his hair, certain he must be losing his bloody mind. A week had passed since that night with Olivia—*seven blasted days*—and he swore his study still smelled of jasmine. *Ridiculous.*

Of course, it didn't help that the chaise was in here with him, just feet away, an ever-present reminder of the passion they'd shared.

Needless to say, very little work was done these last few days. The memory of Olivia spread out on the chaise, her gorgeous skin flushed pink with exertion, her mouth parted on a silent scream as her quim pulsed around his cock was simply not conducive to concentration.

Of course, he couldn't blame it all on the chaise nor the room. Wherever he went, whatever he was doing, he thought of her. He ought to be used to it, Olivia under his skin, but this time was different. This time was...lunacy. Madness.

She'd driven him mad with her eager kisses, her soft, curious hands, her gorgeous eyes, darkened to the color of cobalt. The color of desire. And the way she'd moaned his name, as if the taste of it on her tongue pleased her...

Griff groaned. For God's sake, she was a virgin, not some celebrated courtesan practiced in the art of pleasure. He shouldn't be mooning over her like a lovelorn lad.

Then why was he? Why could he not stop thinking of her? Why had their lovemaking shaken him to his core?

Frustrated, he shot to his feet, shoving his chair back with unnecessary force. *Enough of this.* He needed some air, a change of scenery, and then, once this...*fog* had lifted and he was himself again, he would return to his study to work.

Scooping up Artemis from her favorite chair by the hearth, he made for the door, murmuring his apologies to the irritated kitten who hadn't yet finished her nap. He turned the knob and opened the door, stepping into the corridor to find Emmy walking toward him.

"Ah, here's my favorite sister," he said. "Did you have a successful outing at the shops?"

His question was met with a curiously long silence before she finally answered him. "Yes. I suppose I did."

Her voice was cool, her gaze even more so, and it was obvious she was displeased with someone. Probably him, though he had no idea what he might have done to upset her. Truth be told, he rarely knew until she told him.

"Is something wrong, Em?"

"Yes, something is wrong," she said, and the anger in her eyes took him aback. "One of my dearest friends is about to marry a man she does not love because the man she *does* love is a nincompoop."

She cocked her head to one side, her brows raised in challenge. "Or is he a *coward?* I haven't yet decided."

Griffin's lips parted but no words emerged. He was too stunned to form a coherent response, or even to think of one.

"Olivia is going to marry Paxton," Emmy said slowly, as if speaking to a simpleton. "And you are letting her go without a fight. I don't understand you, Griffin. You are obviously in love with her. Everyone knows it. Everyone but you, apparently."

The shock began to wear off as irritation bloomed in its place. Griff inhaled slowly through his nose, wrestling his temper to the floor before he allowed himself to speak.

"I care about Olivia," he said finally, evenly. "But I am not going to marry her. I'm not going to marry anyone yet."

His sister shook her head, as if deeply disappointed in him, and Griffin's jaw tensed with the effort to hold his tongue. Emmy was a meddlesome bother, but he loved her, and he had no wish to say anything he would later regret.

"I understand that you are uncertain of what the future might bring and that frightens you," Emmy said. "It frightens me, too. But, Griff, I haven't met the person I'm meant to be with. *You* have. You've found love and you are throwing it away."

Love? Nonsense. He folded his arms over his chest and shot her a quelling look. "You don't know what you're talking about."

She plopped her hands on her hips and glared at him. "Of course I know what I'm talking about. I *always* know what I'm talking about." She arched her brows. "I know you think you don't love Olivia, and I know you think you're not ready for marriage. But what will happen when you are finally ready? What will you do then, when it's too late? Olivia will be lost to you, Griff. Forever."

Her eyes held his, frustrated and imploring, but Griffin pressed his lips together and said nothing, for there was nothing to say. He could not give his sister the answers she craved.

"Now I understand why she lost her nerve," Emmy muttered. "Who could possibly confess their feelings when faced with such a scowl?"

"What are you talking about?"

"That night in your study," she said, flinging an arm toward the other end of the corridor. "Olivia went there to ask you to marry her. I told her you were in love with her, and that maybe the reason you hadn't confessed your feelings yet was because you thought she would only accept a duke." Her jaw worked. "She went there that night to find out, once and for all, how you felt about her, but she lost her nerve. And I can't say I blame her."

Tossing one final look of disgust his way, she turned on her heel and disappeared up the hall.

Stunned, he watched her go, staring into the empty corridor long after she'd gone, her words settling on his brain, heavy as an anvil.

Olivia loved him.

She'd intended to ask him to marry her.

It was unconventional, yes, but that was hardly the point. She'd gone to him that night, intending to confess her feelings, hoping that he would do it first, that he would marry her. That he would want her.

Guilt swamped him, and something else too. Remorse? Regret?

He did care for Olivia. A great deal, in fact, but he hadn't been lying when he told Emmy he wasn't ready for marriage. Even the thought of shackling himself to another person made his belly roil.

But then, so did the thought of Olivia marrying the duke.

Paxton was a decent enough fellow, but he would never be able to make Olivia happy. He wasn't good enough for her, noble title or not. Hell, no one was good enough for Olivia. He couldn't let her go through with this marriage. Not this like, not when it wasn't her choice. Not when she was doing it for all the wrong reasons.

It came to him then, what he must do, and he strode down the corridor toward the stairs, determination firming his jaw. His club would have to wait for now.

He was headed to Surrey.

CHAPTER
TWENTY-FOUR

OLIVIA LEANED HER BACK against the wrought iron chair and tipped her head up, letting the sun warm her face beneath the brim of her straw hat. She'd come out into their little garden, hoping a bit of sunshine and fresh air would brighten her mood, but so far, it hadn't helped much.

After Emmy left yesterday, Olivia had told Aunt Augusta of the betrothal, concerned it would lead to a row of some sort. She needn't have worried, though. There was a brief flare of disappointment in her aunt's eyes, but she'd given no voice to the feelings. Instead, she'd spouted off a few perfunctory words of congratulations and then she'd asked Olivia where the ceremony would be held and what color she would like her wedding gown to be.

Olivia wasn't stupid. She knew her aunt did not approve of her marriage to the duke, that she wanted more for Olivia than a loveless marriage. Emmy had made no secret of the fact that she shared Aunt Augusta's feelings, and if Sophie were here, Olivia knew precisely what her cousin would say.

You turned down his proposal last Season for a reason, Livvy. Why are you accepting him now?

She appreciated how much her family and friends cared for her, but she was weary, too. Weary of their hopes and expectations for her. Her aunt and cousin, and Emmy, all wanted her to marry for love, and her father simply wanted her to marry and be done with it. He had no specific expectations—at least, none that he'd shared with her—but she knew her own expectations for herself, what she hoped would make her father proud, and that was exhausting, too.

Always trying to please him, to guess at what would make him proud of her, wondering all the while if he even cared. If he even noticed.

When would she be able to do what made *her* happy? When would she be able to act on her own without thinking of others? When would she simply be able to *be?*

The thought made her scoff.

Never.

She was to be a duchess. She would have to fulfill her duties to the title, to the duchy, and to her husband. It was a wife's duty, was it not, to please her husband? To honor and obey?

Of course, Paxton was a kind and gentle man. He would not make unrealistic demands on her. Still, he would be her husband, and he would make her a duchess. It would be a life not without challenges.

Olivia sighed, weariness sweeping over her. She knew she had much to be grateful for, but sometimes she longed to go back to the carefree days of her childhood when she ran wild through the rooms at Keswick House with her friends, exploring the grounds and making mischief.

A smile touched her lips. Those were good times. She'd been happy then, truly happy. Perhaps she would be happy that way again when she had little ones making mischief of their own.

A throat cleared behind her, breaking into her thoughts, and she turned, her eyes widening when they landed on the last person in the world she expected to see.

"Father." Rising to her feet, she stared at him, surprise making her stumble over her words. "Wh-what are you doing here?"

Lord Blakely stepped forward and removed his beaver hat, discomfort etched in every line of his handsome, serious face.

"Olivia, I..." His lips pressed together beneath his salt-and-pepper mustache. "Will you sit with me? I would like to speak with you if I may."

"Of course." Olivia lowered to her seat, her mind whirling. What was her father doing here? He never visited her, and certainly not unannounced like this. What was going on? Had something happened?

For him to leave Caroline in the country in her delicate condition...

Something must be terribly wrong, indeed.

"I understand you are betrothed to the Duke of Paxton," Lord Blakely said as he sat across from her, placing his hat on the table.

"Yes, sir." She kept her expression clear, though his statement discomfited her. How did he know of her betrothal? She'd only posted her letter to him this morning. It would not have reached him in Surrey yet. "We mean to marry as soon as the banns are read," she said. "With your approval, of course."

A hesitant smile touched his lips. "I could hardly object to my daughter marrying a duke, could I?"

She returned his smile with a cautious one of her own. What did that mean? Was he happy with the news? Did he approve?

She studied him for a moment, sweeping her gaze over his face, so like her own. She hadn't seen him in weeks, and he looked largely the same, though his hair was a little longer, brushing his coat collar.

"You're probably wondering why I've come," he said, tapping his gloved fingers on the wrought iron table. "I know I don't visit as often as I should, but I thought an occasion such as this warranted a trip to London. I came today to deliver my blessing in person."

His eyes found hers. "I also came to tell you how proud I am to call you my daughter."

Olivia was silent as her bewildered brain registered the words she'd longed to hear her entire life. She swallowed past the knot in her throat and forced out an unsteady, "Thank you, Father."

Lord Blakely cleared his throat in a blustery way that suggested he was far from comfortable. Still, he was not finished. "I am not a demonstrative man," he went on. "Never have been. But...I should have done better by you, Olivia. I should have told you sooner—and often—how proud you've made me."

She nodded. "That would have been nice," she said softly. "I always thought you resented me. That you blamed me for..." She trailed off, losing her nerve.

"That I blamed you for your mother's death," he finished for her. "You thought I hated you for being born."

She nodded again, her throat too tight to speak.

"I am sorry for that," he said, regret deepening the lines around his eyes. "I had no idea you thought such a thing. Not until—" He broke off with a shake of his head and leaned forward, reaching across the table before pulling his hands back. He sighed. "I don't hate you, Olivia. I've never hated you."

"Then why...?"

"Why did I treat you as I did?" He leaned back in his chair and stroked his mustache as he considered his reply. "The truth is, I did resent your birth at first. I loved your mother very much, believe it or not, and when she died..." He drew in a deep breath, his eyes flashing with pain. "When she died, I was devastated, and I didn't know how to handle it, the pain, the grief. I suppose...I suppose it was easier to blame you."

He frowned and shook his head again, as if his behavior was a puzzle even to him. "Then later, as you grew, you resembled your mother more and more every day and it hurt me to look at you. It was lunacy, allowing myself to give in to that feeling, but I did. And as time went on, the distance between us grew until it was so cavernous I had no idea how to bridge it. Or even how to talk to my own daughter."

Olivia's eyes welled with tears as she gazed across the table at her sire, a man who had caused her so much pain and frustration, a man she barely knew. She had never thought of him as human before, with human weaknesses, never considered he might be unsure of himself or uncertain of what to do. He made mistakes, the same as everybody. And apparently, he was trying to make up for the ones he'd made with her.

"I understand, Father," she said, reaching across the table to take his hand in hers. Had she ever done such a thing? Had they ever done anything so simple as holding hands?

"I mean to do better," he said gruffly. "By your future siblings, and by you, Olivia." He gave her hand a squeeze. "That's why I'm here. It was wrong of me to give you an ultimatum, to force you to choose a husband. I'm sorry for that. Truly I am."

Her lips parted in surprise as her mind struggled to take it all in. "I don't understand..."

He smiled. "I am withdrawing my order that you choose a husband by the end of the Season," he said. "If you still wish to marry the duke, of course you may do so. But if you do not—if you wish to stay in London for the rest of the Season—I will support you. Or..." His smile widened. "You could return to Surrey with me and stay for a while. I would welcome the chance to get to know my daughter better."

Olivia shook her head, baffled by the sudden change in the man seated across from her. Was he in earnest? Did he truly wish to know her better?

"But what about—" She broke off, confusion knitting her brow. "You told me you needed to economize..."

251

"I know I did," he said, his mouth grim. "But my ultimatum was never about money. I just wanted you to marry well, so you would be taken care of. So I could stop worrying about you." He blew out a breath. "The choice is *yours*, Olivia. I will remain in Town for a few days, to give you time to think it over. But whatever you choose, I will support your decision. And, either way, I sincerely hope we can repair our relationship."

He looked at her for a long moment, his blue eyes—*her* eyes—steady and sincere as they held hers. Then he picked up his hat and left.

She watched his retreating form as he disappeared into the house, and in her bemused state she wondered if this was, in fact, all a dream.

"Olivia?" Aunt Augusta stood in the doorway, a look of concern on her face. "Are you unwell? What did your father want?"

Olivia shook her head and drew in a deep breath. The astonishing conversation had barely had time to sink into her brain.

"What is it, dearest?" Aunt Augusta settled into the chair Lord Blakely had just occupied. "Did your father upset you?"

"No. Not at all. I am...stunned, that's all."

She spent the next few minutes repeating what her father had said, her aunt's shocked face mirroring her own feelings of befuddlement.

"I...am at a loss for words," Aunt Augusta said, absent-mindedly rubbing a knuckle along one wrinkled cheek. "What brought on this sudden change of heart?"

Olivia paused, considering her father's words, and then let out a sheepish laugh. "He never said, and I was so stunned, I didn't think to ask."

"Strange..." Aunt Augusta shook her head, her brow clearing. "Still, I am glad to see the man has finally come to his senses."

Olivia nodded, her gaze falling to the wrought-iron tabletop. Absently, she traced the swirls and loops with her fingertips, her father's words looping through her mind.

"What will you do?" her aunt asked gently.

"I don't know." She frowned. "I am betrothed to a duke. Would it not be foolish to throw that away?"

She met her aunt's gaze, seeking affirmation, but Aunt Augusta answered the question with one of her own. "Do you *want* to marry the duke?"

Olivia bobbed a shoulder. "Being a duchess is every girl's dream."

"That is not an answer." Her aunt reached a hand out to still her fingers' movements and Olivia met her gaze.

"You're not a little girl anymore," Aunt Augusta said, her voice kind but firm. "You are a woman grown, and you've just been given something all women should have. You've been given the chance to choose the life you want to live. So...what do you want?"

"I want children. I want a family of my own."

Her aunt nodded. "And do you want those things with the duke?"

No, she thought. *I want them with Griffin.*

But she said nothing.

Her aunt sighed again. "You have a choice now, Olivia. You can become a duchess and give the world the next Duke of Paxton. Or you can leave the duke behind and find someone else to marry. Someone you genuinely *want* to marry."

"And if he does not wish to marry me?" she whispered, her voice wavering.

"Then you will spend the rest of your life surrounded by your friends and family. People who love you." Aunt Augusta smiled. "You are not alone, Olivia. You have me, and your cousin, and Emmy, and Lady Keswick. And you even your father now, it seems."

Olivia nodded and bit her lip.

"I'll not try to sway your decision," Aunt Augusta said. "You already know my opinion. I only want to say this: Think of yourself. Think of what will make you happy and choose *that*."

Olivia gave her aunt a smile, hoping to reassure her, but her lips felt as unsteady as her mind. She knew Aunt Augusta's advice was sound and she wanted nothing more than to follow it, only...

What if the thing that would make her happiest was the one thing she could not have?

OLIVIA WOKE THE NEXT morning after a fitful night's sleep. She'd tossed and turned well into the night, her mind spinning and churning, considering and reconsidering until she thought she would go mad with it.

Even now, hours later, as she strolled up Half Moon Street with Paxton at her side and her chaperoning aunt behind them, she was no closer to making a decision.

Truth be told, she had no idea what she would do.

It was a lovely day for a walk, sunny and warm with only the slightest breeze, and she let her gaze wander over her surroundings—the rows of elegant townhouses, the bustle of horses and carriages passing by on the street—though she barely saw any of it.

You could return to Surrey with me. I would welcome the chance to get to know my daughter better.

She worried her lower lip between her teeth, her father's words echoing through her mind for the hundredth time today. How could she refuse such an offer? How could she deny herself this chance to know him better? To start anew?

But what of your promise to Paxton?

Her heart gave a guilty twist, and she stole a glance at her betrothed, so dapper today in his light green morning suit, his auburn hair flicking in the breeze beneath his beaver hat.

She'd rejected this man once before already. How could she sever their betrothal now? How could she refuse him a second time, after she'd worked so hard to earn his trust again? After *he* had worked so hard to convince his mother it was safe to?

She couldn't.

Or could she?

Oh, she was so confused!

"Olivia?"

Paxton's quiet voice drew her gaze and she found him watching her, as if awaiting her reply to a question she hadn't heard him ask.

"Apologies," she said, her smile sheepish. "I was wool-gathering."

"You've been doing a lot of that this afternoon," he said without a hint of rancor. "Is something troubling you?"

She hadn't told him yet of her father's visit. She dipped her chin, eyeing her cream-colored half-boots as she considered what to say. "My father is in Town," she said. "And he paid me a visit yesterday. I never told you this, but earlier in the year, before the Season began, he gave me an ultimatum..."

She spent the next few minutes detailing her father's demand and his subsequent change of heart.

By the time she'd finished, Paxton's usually-cheerful expression had clouded. "I had no idea you were under such pressure to marry," he said. "But now your father has changed his mind?"

Olivia nodded. "I don't really understand it, but yes, it seems he has. He said he regrets the decision now, and he even apologized for it. And for not being a better father."

Surprise bloomed in Paxton's eyes. "It's about time," he said, nodding his approval. He was well aware of her complicated relationship with her father.

"He wants us to get to know each other better," she said slowly, hesitating over her next words. "He's...invited me to join him in Surrey, to spend some time with him and my stepmother, and I—" She paused on the pavement and turned to face him, half-aware of her aunt hovering a few feet away. "I would like to do it, Paxton. I realize a long engagement is not ideal, but I do hope you are willing to wait for me. I would only be gone for a few months at most, and I..."

She trailed off at the slow shake of Paxton's head.

"No?" she asked, more than a little surprised by his refusal.

"No." His voice held no malice, only resignation and regret.

Olivia frowned. "But...why?"

A half-smile touched his lips, and he drew in a deep breath. "You know how difficult it is for me to deny you anything," he said. "Just as you know I would wait for you forever if you asked it of me. Because I love you."

Olivia blinked, surprise parting her lips. Paxton...loved her? She knew he admired her, and cared for her a great deal, but...*love?* He'd never said that word before.

Paxton's eyes flicked over her face and his smile turned rueful. "But I know you do not feel the same. If you did, you would never have asked me to wait."

She frowned and parted her lips to argue but he raised a hand, staying her words. "That was not an ultimatum," he said. "It was an observation. If you truly wished to marry me, you would ask me to go to Surrey with you. As your husband. You would know you could have both."

His eyes were a mix of affection and frustration as he took both her hands in his, right there on the street for everyone to see.

"Go to Surrey," he said. "Go to your father. Spend time with him. Be happy. It's all I've ever wanted for you."

He was letting her go.

Emotion caught in her throat, and she swallowed hard. "But...what about your mother? What will you tell her?"

Paxton drew in a deep breath, displeasure crossing his face. "I suppose I'll tell her we realized we wouldn't suit."

Olivia pursed her lips. "She will not be pleased."

It was an understatement for the ages.

"No, she won't," he said with a small smile. "But she will forgive me eventually. She always does."

"Well, you *are* her only son," she said, returning his smile. "She hardly has a choice, does she?"

He nodded. "True. Though I suspect she would forgive me even faster if I married Miss Withers."

Olivia regarded him for a moment and then, softly, she asked, "Is that what you mean to do?"

His gaze sobered a bit, and he shook his head. "I don't know. Maybe. But I think I'll nurse my broken heart a little longer before I decide."

Self-mockery tinged his smile and Olivia's heart squeezed with guilt and gratitude and love—the love of friendship. She did not deserve this man's kindness.

And she would miss him.

"Thank you," she whispered, her eyes misting with emotion. "You are a wonderful man, Gregory Paxton. I hope you know that. And I wish you all the happiness in the world. You deserve it."

She squeezed his hands and then gently slipped them free of his grasp.

Free. She was free. The tightness in her chest eased, and it was then she knew with complete certainty that this was right. This was good.

She would have married Paxton, and they would probably have spent many contented years together as husband and wife. But he was right. She did not love him, and if she had married him, it would have been for all the wrong reasons.

No matter what happened now, at least she had that to console her.

CHAPTER TWENTY-FIVE

OLIVIA'S FATHER WAS TRUE to his word. He took her with him to Blakely Manor the very next day and, over the following month, during rides through the countryside and walks in the garden, father and daughter closed the distance between them one conversation at a time.

Olivia enjoyed their time together immensely, learning who he was, his thoughts and opinions, his likes and dislikes, and which ones they shared.

They both preferred coffee over tea, neither was a great reader, and they each fostered a fondness for music, though he preferred Mozart to Beethoven, which had sparked many a good-natured debate between them.

Surprisingly, she'd even enjoyed reacquainting herself with the house. Blakely Manor was only her home for a handful of years when she was very small, but she remembered her time here well enough to know it had been lonely, and she'd wondered if those feelings would surface again. Fortunately, they hadn't and her stay at Blakely Manor proved as comfortable and easy as any visit to the country ought to be.

Now, sitting on the sofa in the morning room one early September day, her stay was nearly at an end, and she was sorry to have to leave. The feeling was still something of a shock to her, that she should miss her father. She'd never missed him before, only the idea of him, the idea of what could be. It was astounding how much a person's life could change in just a few short weeks.

"Oh, Lady Augusta, they're *beautiful*. Aren't they beautiful, Olivia?" Caroline asked, her brown eyes bright with happiness as she held aloft a tiny pair of pale green booties.

Olivia leaned across the chintz sofa they were sharing and stroked the soft wool with her fingers. "They're the sweetest things I've ever seen," she said, smiling at her stepmother.

"I'm so glad you like them, Caroline," Aunt Augusta said from her seat on the giltwood armchair opposite the sofa. "My cousin Mary is quite skilled with knitting needles. I am certain she would be thrilled to knit for you anything you might need for the babe."

It was late afternoon, and the three ladies were gathered in the morning room, catching up over tea and cucumber sandwiches. Aunt Augusta had just arrived at Blakely Manor after a month-long visit to Bath, where she'd stayed with her cousin Mary.

She intended to spend a day or two here at the manor, and then she and Olivia would head to Keswick House, where they would reunite with Sophie before she and her new husband retired to their own estate in Devonshire. Olivia couldn't wait to see her cousin again.

"I still can't quite believe I am to be a mother soon," Caroline said, shaking her dark head in wonder. "I didn't think I would ever have a family of my own. Until I met your father." She flashed Olivia a teary smile, pressing her palm to her swollen belly.

"I am so happy for you," Olivia said, reaching out and giving her stepmother's forearm a gentle squeeze. "You will be a wonderful mother, Caroline."

And she meant it. There was no one sweeter or kinder than her stepmother, and she'd enjoyed getting to know her better these past few weeks.

Caroline was at least a decade older than Olivia and had married Lord Blakely later in life than was common for women. Some might call her plain upon first glance, but she had a lovely smile and the kindest eyes Olivia had ever seen. Her child would be lucky, indeed.

"Thank you," Caroline said, tears misting her eyes. "And you will be a wonderful older sister."

Olivia grinned. "I cannot wait to be a sister."

"And"—Aunt Augusta's crisp voice cut through the soppiness—"as I am already a wonderful great-aunt, this child is destined to be spoiled beyond redemption."

They all laughed, though Olivia suspected her aunt was probably right. She couldn't wait to start spoiling. All the trepidation she'd felt over this baby's impending arrival had vanished. No longer did she feel jealous or worried. She felt only happiness now, for Caroline, for her father. And for herself, too.

After all, she would have a sibling soon. She would be someone's sister. How could she feel anything but happiness over that?

"I've missed you, Aunt," Olivia said with an affectionate smile. "It is good to see you again."

"I have missed you, too, child," her aunt replied. "How have you been these last few weeks? How are you faring with your father?"

"Very well, I think. He's been very kind to me, and I've enjoyed getting to know him better. He is funnier than I expected, and quite easy to talk to."

Truth be told, this visit had gone even better than she'd hoped, and she still couldn't quite believe it had happened.

"They've spent a great deal of time together," Caroline interjected, beaming at Aunt Augusta. "Like two peas in a pod, they are."

"Well, I am very glad to hear that," her aunt said briskly.

"I still don't understand what brought on his sudden change of heart, though," Olivia said with a little shake of her head. "Every time I ask him, all he'll say is he finally saw the error of his ways, but he won't say how or why."

"I know why," Aunt Augusta said, leaning back in her chair. "It was because of Keswick."

"Lady Augusta!" Caroline cried. "We promised not to tell."

Olivia's aunt gave an unrepentant shrug. "You promised. I did not."

"What do you mean, it was because of Keswick?" Olivia asked, her brows furrowed in confusion. "What does Griffin have to do with this?"

Aunt Augusta met her gaze. "It was right after you agreed to marry the duke," she said. "Keswick rode all the way out here to speak with your father. To convince him not to make you go through with it."

Olivia blinked, surprise parting her lips as a thousand questions streaked through her mind. "I don't understand," she said slowly. "Why would he do that? What did he say?"

Her aunt shook her head. "I don't know. I wasn't there. I only heard of the visit from his mother."

Olivia looked at Caroline. "Do you know?"

Her stepmother's gaze fell to the booties in her lap, her lips pinched at the corners, signaling an internal debate.

"Please tell me, Caroline," Olivia said softly and, finally, with a heavy sigh, Caroline caved.

"It was quite late in the afternoon when he arrived," she said. "Your father and I were, of course, mystified by this unexpected visit, but we could hardly turn a marquess away without good reason, so we agreed to meet with him."

She leaned back against the sofa cushion and draped her hands across the swell of her belly. "He was not at all as I remembered," she continued. "He was quite windblown and sweaty, and he smelled of horse. Not at all the elegant marquess I had seen in the past."

"He obviously rode his horse hard that day," Aunt Augusta said. "He must have been in a great hurry to get here."

Caroline nodded. "That was certainly the impression he gave."

Olivia leaned forward, resting her elbows on her knees, not even bothering to hide her interest. "And? What did he say when you greeted him?"

"Well, your father said what a surprise it was to see him," Caroline said. "Lord Keswick apologized for the intrusion and then he said 'I've come to discuss your daughter with you.' Well!" Caroline's hands flew up. "You can imagine how surprised we were to hear those words. I thought he'd come to ask for your hand in marriage, especially after all those lovely things he said about you, but—"

"What lovely things?" Olivia asked, her tone too sharp, but she couldn't seem to help it. She wanted to know everything, etiquette be damned.

"He said you were sweet and clever and beautiful"—Caroline's head bobbed with every attribute—"and then he said you deserved a better father than the one you were given."

Olivia's mouth fell open. "He said that? To Father's face?"

Caroline nodded. "He did."

"And he was right."

Lord Blakely's voice drew everyone's gaze to the door and Olivia watched in silence as her father walked into the room and claimed the chair beside Aunt Augusta's.

"Of course, I didn't want to hear it," he continued, his smile wry beneath the fringe of his mustache. "Especially not from a man I barely knew. I was rather brusque with him, I'm afraid. But then, after he left, I couldn't stop thinking about what he'd said, and eventually I came to realize he was right."

Olivia had no idea what to say. What on earth had possessed Griffin to do such a thing?

And why did he not want her to know he'd done it?

None of this made any sense.

"I owe him a great debt," Lord Blakely said with a smile. "If it weren't for his visit, my daughter would be married to a duke. And I still wouldn't know what a remarkable young woman she is."

Olivia returned his smile. "Thank you, Father."

The conversation turned to other topics, but Olivia listened with only half an ear, her mind otherwise occupied.

Why had Griffin done it? What had compelled him to speak with her father? She was well aware of his less-than-complimentary opinion of Paxton, but marrying the duke would hardly have meant a life of abject misery. She would have been fine. She would have been *more* than fine. For pity's sake, she would have been a duchess.

So why had he interfered?

He cared for her, she knew. She was one of his sister's closest friends and he'd known her since she was a little girl. He probably would have done the same for Sophie, if she'd been in Olivia's place.

Was that all it had been, then? The act of a concerned family friend?

Of course that's all it was, she admonished. *What else would it be?*

His actions were honorable and admirable, but ultimately had been nothing more than a favor for a friend, which probably explained why he'd wanted to keep it from her. He was afraid she would make more of it than it was.

Drawing in a deep breath of air, she willed her racing heart to slow. It had been an act of kindness, nothing more, and she would do well to remind herself of that frequently before she saw him again.

And probably afterward, too.

CHAPTER TWENTY-SIX

TWO DAYS LATER, AFTER a tearful farewell with her father and the promise to see each other at Christmas, Olivia piled into her aunt's carriage and the two set out for Keswick House.

"Did you have a nice visit with your father, my dear?" Aunt Augusta asked from her seat beside Olivia on the plush velvet squabs.

"I did," she answered, an audible note of bewilderment in her voice. "I never thought I would say those words. Or see the day when my father would tell me he's proud of me. To learn that he never hated me, after all those years believing he did..." She trailed off with a shake of her head, still amazed by it, even all these weeks later.

"Your father never was a very expressive man," Aunt Augusta said. "Not even when your mother was alive. Still, that does not excuse his behavior. He should have done better by you. To think of all those years, lost..." She gave her tongue a disapproving cluck.

"It would have been nice, having a father who was more than just an absent guardian," Olivia agreed, settling deeper into the seat. "I don't know that we would have been close—not in the way I am with you—but..." She shrugged. "Still, I am grateful that he's a part of my life now, and that I no longer believe he hates me."

Aunt Augusta gave her a smile of understanding and reached out to cover her hands with one of her own. "He does seem happier since he married Caroline," she said. "I never thought I would see him so content again. He seems to care for her a great deal, and she him."

Olivia nodded. "I agree," she said. "And I'm glad. I hope they're always happy, and I hope their children will be happy."

She meant it, too, with all her heart. It was freeing, feeling this way, feeling happy for her father and his growing family, instead of the resentment and jealousy she'd known before.

She wasn't sure what she would do with her life, or even what she would do after this visit to Keswick House, but it was nice to be able to face such decisions with an unburdened conscience.

The next several hours passed with little ado until finally, around four o'clock, their carriage rolled to a halt in front of Keswick House. A footman handed Olivia down onto the white gravel and then her aunt down from the carriage, the front door to the great house opened and out came Lady Keswick wearing a purple-striped gown and a bright smile.

"There you are!" she cried as she walked toward them, her arms outstretched. "Welcome, darlings! How was your journey?"

"We weren't set upon by highwaymen or ravaged by a rogue snowstorm, so I suppose it went as well as could be expected," Aunt Augusta said, rubbing the sleep from her eyes. She was always grouchy when she first awoke from a nap.

Olivia smiled at Lady Keswick and the two embraced. "You're looking lovely, as always, my lady," Olivia said. "How is your ankle faring?"

"It has healed quite nicely, thank you." The marchioness looped her arm through Olivia's and began leading her toward the front door. "I can move on it freely now, and the tenderness is nearly gone." She leaned in close, as if imparting a secret. "Of course, I shall have to give your aunt a wide berth from here on out. She and that walking stick of hers are a danger to us all."

Olivia's lips twitched with mirth. "Perhaps it would be easier if we simply hid it from her?"

Lady Keswick nodded. "Good idea. I'll distract her while you swipe the walking stick."

From behind them, Aunt Augusta heaved a noisy sigh. "You're never going to let me forget about your ankle, are you?"

Lady Keswick glanced over her shoulder. "Of course I will, Augusta," she said with a beatific smile. "Someday."

Olivia swept her gaze over the great house as they made for the front steps, taking in the welcoming patchwork of white and yellow stone, the tall, narrow windows, the decorative arch above the front door.

She smiled to herself. It was good to be back. The last time she was here, she was almost certain she would never see the place again. Oh, how things had changed since then.

Movement inside the house drew her gaze, and suddenly there was Griffin, standing in the door frame with Artemis in his arms, tall and handsome in buff breeches and a dark gray coat that set off his already striking eyes.

Her heart stuttered and she nearly stumbled on the steps.

Apparently, *some* things hadn't changed.

"Lady Augusta," Griffin said with a warm smile. "You are a vision, as always."

"I am a fright," she shot back, though there was no venom in her voice. "I've been cooped up in a carriage all day, but I appreciate the lie all the same."

Chuckling softly, he moved away from the door to let the ladies into the entrance hall, and as Olivia moved past him, his gaze settled on hers.

"Olivia, welcome," he said. "It is good to see you." His eyes seemed to soften at the sight of her and her heart dipped.

Or was that only wishful thinking?

"And you," she replied. "Thank you for having us."

The politeness between them felt odd, and for some reason she found herself blushing over it. Swallowing, she turned away and began to remove her spencer, resolutely avoiding his gaze.

"Come, ladies," Lady Keswick said. "We are all gathered in the blue salon, and you will find some light refreshments awaiting you there."

"Excellent," Aunt Augusta said, thumping her walking stick on the floor. "These old bones could use a refreshing glass of sherry."

The two older ladies led the way out of the entrance hall, and Griffin fell into step beside Olivia.

"You brought Artemis with you," she said, reaching out to scratch the kitten's ear. The little ball of fluff had grown quite a bit since she'd last seen her.

"Of course," he said simply, as if it had never occurred to him to leave her behind. "She wasn't especially fond of being cooped up in the carriage, but she loves Keswick House."

Olivia smiled. "Lots of spaces to explore."

"And new places to nap in." He cleared his throat as they reached the salon. "Olivia..."

He paused just outside the door, and she did the same, turning to face him with an expectant look.

"How..." He trailed off and cleared his throat again, uncertainty twisting his mouth. "How...was the journey here? Uneventful, I hope?"

Olivia blinked, surprised by the banal question. Was that what he'd wanted to ask? "It was, thankfully," she replied. "And Aunt Augusta slept most of the way, so..." She lifted one shoulder and smiled.

"Ah." He chuckled. "Uneventful *and* peaceful."

"Precisely," she said before clasping her hands behind her back. "And what of you? How have you been since I saw you last?"

"Well enough, I suppose. Glad to be home. Those last few weeks in Town were dull without you." He threw her a teasing smile, his eyes twinkling.

"I think I shall take that as a compliment," she said, arching her brows.

"Good. It was intended as one."

The tenderness in his gaze, the fondness in his smile—what did it mean? Anything? Everything? *Nothing?*

Or was it just a figment of her imagination; nothing more than the yearnings of a wishful heart?

She thought again of all he'd done for her, and wondered, for the hundredth time, what it all meant. She didn't know why he'd visited her father on her behalf, but she knew she had to thank him for it. Whatever his reasons, he deserved her gratitude.

"Griffin..." She drew in a breath and smoothed her palms down her ivory muslin skirt. "I know what you did for me," she said, keeping her voice low. "I know of your visit to Surrey to see my father."

Surprise flashed in his eyes, but he did not speak, though his discomfort showed in his stiffening shoulders. Still, she would say what she must, whether he liked it or not.

"I don't understand why you did it," she went on, "but I am grateful to you all the same. And I will never forget what you did for me."

He said nothing for a long moment, his fingers absently scratching Artemis behind the ear, and then, quietly: "Your relationship has improved, then? With your father?"

She nodded. "It has. Enormously. Whatever you said to him..." She shook her head, a smile turning her lips. "It changed him. It changed my life."

Griffin's gaze softened. "I'm glad, Olivia. That was all I wanted, for your father to treat you as you ought to be treated. For you to be happy."

Her heart dipped at his words, and she could not keep her next question at bay. "Why?" Her voice was barely above a whisper. "Why do you care so—"

"Livvy! At last, you're here!"

Sophie's delighted voice cut through the corridor, silencing Olivia's words, and she turned with a smile to greet her cousin in the doorway. Her talk with Griffin would have to wait, it seemed. There would be plenty of time for answers later, if she chose to try again.

To be honest, she wasn't sure she should.

CHAPTER TWENTY-SEVEN

DINNER THAT NIGHT PASSED in a blur of good food and lively conversation. The small party of seven spent the remainder of the evening in the blue salon, chatting and playing cards before saying their good nights and retiring to their chambers for the evening.

It was nearly midnight when Olivia and her two dearest friends finally found their chance to speak alone in Emmy's chamber, sitting cross-legged in a circle on the bed, just as they had done as little girls.

"Well," Olivia said, leaning forward with her elbows on her knees. "Now that we're finally alone, I demand you tell us everything, Sophie. Do you like being married? Are you happy? Is it everything you thought it would be?"

"And, most importantly," Emmy said, "is James treating you with the deference you deserve? Because if he isn't, you have only to say the word and I will show him the error of his ways."

Sophie laughed, her green eyes sparkling with merriment. "James is treating me very well, thank you," she said, "and I am happier than I have ever been. Of course, I haven't yet had to perform any of my duties as countess, but I've greatly enjoyed everything else." Her smile turned dreamy. "James is a most attentive husband."

"I *knew* you two were meant to be together," Olivia said with a satisfied nod. "Did I not say so last April in this very house?"

"So you did," Sophie said. "And I've never been so happy to admit you were right." She waved a hand. "But enough about me. I want to know what happened with your father. Tell me everything."

Olivia spent the next twenty minutes going over everything Sophie had missed while on her wedding trip, covering all the ups and downs of her courtship with the duke, Griffin's assistance and finally, the surprise visit from her father and the subsequent month spent at his house in Surrey.

"Then your father no longer expects you to marry?" Sophie asked, her dark brows arched in surprise.

Olivia shrugged. "Of course he would *like* for me to marry, but he said he would support me in whatever I wish to do."

Her cousin gave a slow shake of her head. "I can scarcely believe it. I've always thought of your father as something of a villain. This new version will take some getting used to."

Olivia nodded. "I know. Sometimes I wonder if it is all too good to be true." She sighed. "I do regret hurting Paxton again, though. He did not deserve such poor treatment."

"You were only doing what was best for you, Livvy," Sophie said, squeezing Olivia's knee. "He cannot fault you for that."

"I suppose so." But even though Paxton had given her his blessing, she couldn't help feeling a little guilty, even now.

"Speaking of Paxton," Emmy said, her waggling brows a signal of incoming news. "He is no longer in London."

Olivia frowned. "No longer in London? What do you mean?" Guilt sharpened her voice as she thought back to Paxton's jest about nursing his broken heart. At least, she'd *thought* it was a jest. Had he left London because of her?

"Evidently he wished to travel," Emmy said with a shrug. "He never took his Grand Tour like so many young men do, so he's decided to take it now. I believe he is in Greece as we speak."

Olivia did not bother to ask how her friend had come by such detailed information. Emmy worked in mysterious—and effective—ways.

"Did he take his mother with him?" Sophie asked.

"No, he did not." Emmy's tone echoed Olivia's own surprise.

"Goodness," she said. "I never thought Paxton would go anywhere without his mother." When she and the duke were still betrothed, she'd half-expected the dowager duchess to join them on their wedding trip.

"Nor did I," Emmy said. "And I don't think the duchess did either. I saw her on Bond Street only last week and she looked quite cross with the world."

"She always looks like that," Sophie pointed out, displeasure sparking in her green eyes. "She is the most disagreeable woman I have ever met, and I do not like her."

Olivia bit back a smile. Her cousin did not approve of the way the duchess had treated her after she'd turned down Paxton's first offer of marriage, and although Sophie was only two years her senior, she had always watched over her with the fervor of a mother bear protecting her cub.

"Well, I feel sorry for her," Olivia said. "Her son is her life, and he has left her. I don't think he has ever gone against her wishes before."

"It will be good for her," Sophie said with no sympathy whatsoever. "A little humility is good for all of us."

Olivia couldn't argue with that. The duchess was too used to having her own way, and Paxton too often gave it to her, despite what his own wishes might be. Pursuing Olivia was the closest he ever came to a rebellion. Perhaps this trip abroad would lead to some much-needed independence.

"So, what will you do now, Livvy?" Emmy asked, leaning back on her hands. "Another London Season? Or will you hunt for a husband elsewhere?"

Olivia sighed and plucked at her skirts. "I haven't the faintest idea."

"Do you even want to get married?" Sophie asked, her tone curious.

"I think so," she said. "I like the idea of having a family of my own one day." She pursed her lips. "Of course, now that I've been given the chance to marry at my leisure, it seems a waste to marry for any reason other than love, but—" She broke off with a shake of her head, bitterness twisting her heart.

"But you're still in love with Griffin," Emmy finished for her, ever astute.

Olivia's gaze dropped to the quilted counterpane, and she nodded. "I don't know if I will ever stop loving him," she whispered, tracing a finger along the criss-crossed stitching. "And if I can't stop loving him, how can I fall in love with someone else? Someone who will love me in return?"

"You don't know that Griffin doesn't love you," Sophie said. "He obviously cares for you. We can all see it, can't we, Em?"

"We can," Emmy said.

Olivia thought of the look in Griffin's eyes, the tenderness she thought she'd seen there just hours ago, and her heart longed to believe it. *But eyes can lie, can't they? And tenderness isn't love.*

"He will come around, Livvy," Sophie said. "He only needs a little more time to—"

"No," Olivia broke in, her voice firm as her head came up. "No. He's had more than enough time already, and I don't want to marry a man who has to *come around*. If he loved me—*truly* loved me—would he not tell me so? Would he not make his feelings known?"

"Perhaps he already has," Sophie said, her voice soft.

Olivia's brows dipped. "What do you mean?"

"He went to your father, Livvy. I can't think of a more romantic gesture than ensuring your future was your own to decide. Can you?"

Olivia shook her head. "But he asked my father to keep it a secret. If it truly was a romantic gesture, wouldn't he want me to know about it?"

"Not necessarily," Sophie said. "Perhaps he—"

"No, Livvy's right," Emmy broke in. "I don't think it was a gesture."

"What?" Sophie's brows drew together. "Of course it was."

Emmy shook her head as Olivia's eyes darted back and forth between them.

"My brother is the most stubborn person I know," Emmy said. "And he can be astoundingly dense when he chooses to be. There is no doubt in my mind that he loves you, Livvy. His actions more than prove it." She sighed. "Unfortunately, he isn't ready to admit it yet."

Olivia swallowed, her heart giving a foolish little leap. "Why—why are you so certain he loves me?"

"Because he went to see your father with no expectation of a reward, other than seeing you happy," Emmy said, her gray eyes as frank as her words. "I think he wished to keep his visit a secret because he wanted you to believe your father had a change of heart all on his own. After all, would that not have made you even happier than you are now?"

Olivia had no answer for that question, but she thought of little else for the rest of the night as she lay in bed, trying to sleep, her mind a jumbled mass of confused thoughts.

Were Sophie and Emmy right? Was Griffin truly in love with her? Her friends seemed so certain of it and, although the notion sent a shiver of pleasure up her spine, she could not bring herself to believe it. Not wholly.

She'd meant what she said before. She was through with wondering and waiting. He'd had more than enough time to claim her hand and he hadn't.

She could not be certain what her future held, but she liked the turn her life had taken these last few weeks, all the changes forged, and strides made. There was more healing to be done, but for the first time in what seemed like forever she was finally beginning to like herself, faults and all.

When she married—*if* she married—it would be to a man who appreciated those things about her, too. A man who married her because of her flaws, not in spite of them.

She deserved a love like that—every woman did—and she would not settle for anything less. Not anymore.

CHAPTER
TWENTY-EIGHT

IT DRIZZLED OVERNIGHT AND into the early hours of the following morning, but by noon the storm had passed, leaving behind a cloudless sky and the scent of wet forest in the air.

"Where are you headed after you leave Keswick House?" Griffin asked James as he guided his horse, a black Arabian named Rasputin, around a fallen branch lying on the forest floor.

"Falconridge," James replied from his own mount, a handsome chestnut Griffin had recently purchased. "We'll stay there through the new year and then return to London. Unless, of course, some fortuitous event keeps us at home."

Griffin flicked a glance at James, noting the contented smile on his face. It was strange, seeing his normally subdued friend so free and easy with his smiles, so obviously happy in his role as husband. He wasn't sure he'd ever truly believed he would see this day come, or that James would so obviously relish the notion of becoming a father. To be honest, it was a bit surreal.

"I'm glad to see you so happy," he said to him. "Marriage seems to agree with you."

"It does, indeed," James said with a grin. "I'll spare you the dissertation on the merits of taking a wife, though."

"Much obliged."

They came into a small clearing then, and Griff tugged lightly on the reins, slowing Rasputin to a halt.

"It's still intact," he said, his eyes trained on the ramshackle structure a short distance off.

James grunted from beside him. "Mostly."

The fort was in piss-poor condition, but it never was much to look at, even twenty years ago when they'd first cobbled it together.

"Shall we?" Griffin quirked a brow at James, who grinned, and the two dismounted, tethering their horses to the trunks of two sturdy English oaks before heading for the fort.

The 'door' was nothing more than a thick slab of tree trunk propped against the opening to the shack, and Griff moved it out of the way before peering inside. The space was dim and damp, but there appeared to be no immediate danger, so he ducked his head and entered, brushing aside an abandoned spider web with his sleeve.

"Like finding ancient ruins," James mused as he followed Griff inside.

The fortress was dank and smelled of rot. It was much smaller than he remembered. Wild mushrooms and peat moss flourished, filling nearly every crack and crevice, even the giant oak log they'd used for a bench. A rusted tin sat beside it on the ground, as if they'd left it there, intending to return for it the next day.

"Not half so glamorous as I remembered it," Griff joked.

With the tip of his boot, he nudged the tin onto its side. Water spilled onto the already damp dirt floor, carrying with it a heap of 'treasures'—stones and old buttons, chestnut shells, obsolete coins. A collection only a child would value. He smiled to himself. It had taken years to amass.

"Remember that time we nicked a bottle of Cook's sherry?" James asked with a grin.

Griffin nodded. "We drank the whole thing in one sitting, and you fell off the log."

"*You* fell off the log, and took me with you," James shot back, slipping his hands in his pockets. "God, was I sick the next morning."

Griffin chuckled. "My mother called the doctor, and we spent the remainder of our holiday confined to our beds." He glanced at James. "Think she knew?"

James grinned. "Without a doubt."

After one final glance around the dilapidated fort, the two exited and made their way back to the horses.

The two mounted and began the short journey back to the house, keeping a leisurely pace as they cleared the forest and crossed the wide, green fields, still wet from the early morning rains.

"So," James said some minutes later, "I understand you journeyed to Surrey last month. To pay a visit to Olivia's father, I believe?"

Griff threw him a look, surprise slackening his jaw. "Does everyone know?"

James shrugged. "Lady Augusta told Olivia and Olivia told Sophie and, naturally, Sophie told me."

Griffin gritted his teeth in annoyance. "It was meant to be a secret," he muttered, guiding his mount around an abandoned fox hole.

He'd told no one about his visit to Surrey. How the devil had Lady Augusta found out about it?

"You know there are no secrets in this family," James said with a chuckle. "So, what did you say to the man? And why did you do it?"

Griff blew out a slow breath. "I don't know. I just..." His jaw clenched. "It wasn't right, her marrying a duke to make her father happy. Especially when he'd done nothing to deserve it. I didn't like it." *A gross understatement.*

"Hm."

Griff lowered his brows. "What?"

"Are you certain that's the only reason?"

"Of course."

"Hm."

Griffin sighed. "Will you stop grunting and say what you wish to say?"

James looked at him. "Could it be you want her for yourself? That you went to her father in the hopes it would end her betrothal and leave her available for you?"

Niggling doubt scraped at the nape of his neck, but he ignored it. "I have no interest in marrying right now, as you well know."

"Perhaps you hoped she would wait until you are interested."

Griffin grunted his disagreement and reached down to pat Rasputin's neck.

"So, what did you do when you met with her father?" James asked a moment later. "Demand he treat her better? Take back his ultimatum?"

"Yes."

"And? What did he say?"

"He was...unreceptive," Griff said, recalling the pinched expression on Lord Blakely's face. "So, I offered him five thousand pounds."

"Five thou—" James broke off and whistled his surprise. "That is an awfully large sum of money, Griff."

He shrugged. "He refused to accept it. And he assured me he had no idea Olivia felt the way she did. He said he would work at mending the rift between them and apparently, he has." He cleared his throat. "I would ask that you keep this between us. I don't want Olivia to know about it."

James raised one brow. "Why not?"

"Because it doesn't matter. Because I want her to have a decent relationship with her father." *Because it makes her happy, and I need her to be happy.*

He glanced at James, who nodded and said, "Of course. You have my word."

Satisfied, Griffin looked forward again just as the stables came into view. He gave Rasputin's neck another rub. The curiosity in James's eyes suggested there were other questions he wanted to ask, but being the excellent friend he was, he kept them to himself.

The two rode back the rest of the way in silence, and as they reached the stables, Griff asked James if he would join him for a game of billiards.

"Not now," James said after they'd dismounted. "Later, perhaps."

Griff handed the reins over to a groom before following James from the stables toward the house. They had just walked through the door when Lady Keswick met them in the corridor.

"There you two are," she said with a smile. "You're both looking windblown and red-cheeked. Did you enjoy your ride?"

"Very much," James said, smoothing his hair. "Can you tell me where my wife has got to?"

Her smile widened. "She's out on the terrace, James. All of us ladies are."

"Excellent," he said with a grin. "I'll see you out there, then." And with that, he set off, a noticeable spring in his step.

Lady Keswick chuckled and looped her arm through Griffin's, tugging him along with her. "I've never seen James so happy," she said. "Marriage obviously suits him."

"*Sophie* suits him," Griff said dryly. "He can barely keep away from her."

His mother nodded as they stepped onto the terrace and paused just outside the door. "It is sweet, isn't it? They are a good match."

There was no arguing with that. The two were obviously in love, as evidenced yet again by the way the two were smiling at each other as Sophie handed James a glass of lemonade.

A stab of envy shot through Griffin's chest, its intensity surprising him, and before he knew what he was doing, his gaze had shot to Olivia.

She was standing with Lady Augusta at the edge of the terrace, her pale pink gown rustling in the breeze, the late summer sun warming her hair to an even richer shade of wheat. God, she was lovely today.

Of course, she was always lovely, whether she wore pink silk, peacock feathers, or nothing at all.

Especially when she wore nothing at all.

"When are you going to marry the girl, darling?"

Griff stiffened and glanced at his mother, feigning ignorance, though she'd clearly caught him staring. "I beg your pardon?"

"Olivia suits you," Lady Keswick said quietly. "The same way Sophie suits James. And it is obvious you're in love with her."

He drew in a steadying breath, resisting the urge to look to the sky. First Emmy and now his mother. Why was everyone so bloody certain of his feelings when he didn't know them himself?

"I don't know how you can say that," he said, keeping his voice even. "I've done nothing to suggest it."

"Nonsense. Your feelings are right there for everyone to see. It's the way you look at her." A small smile curved her lips. "It's the same way your father used to look at me."

Was it? He remembered how his parents were with each other. *Did he really look at Olivia that way?*

"Your story is special," he argued, crossing his arms over his chest. "It was love at first sight for you."

She hooked a brow. "For your father, it was, but I wasn't so certain of my feelings. Or of marrying your father, for that matter."

Griffin glanced at her in surprise. "Really? That isn't what he told me."

Lady Keswick smiled. "Your father was a romantic, bless him. And love at first sight makes for a far more romantic tale than the real story."

"What was the real story?"

His mother motioned to an empty bench abutting the house, and after they sat and she'd adjusted her skirts just so, she continued.

"I loved your father dearly," she said, "but our beginning was anything but romantic. It was a match arranged by our parents, and we met only a handful of times before we were married, but your father always said he knew the moment he laid eyes on me that we were meant to be. That it was divine intervention that brought us together."

She laughed softly. "I liked to tease him that it was our parents who brought us together, but he would only smile and say we would have found our way to each other, with or without their help."

Her smile softened and her eyes turned wistful, as if seeing the memory anew.

"Do you think he was right?" Griff asked.

"Oh, without a doubt," she said, waving a hand in the air. "It took me a little while to realize it, but eventually I came to agree with him. And, day by day, I fell more and more in love with him. With his kindness, his quiet strength, his infectious laugh." She flashed Griffin a wry grin. "And, of course, the way he spoiled me with gifts and flattery did help sway me to his way of thinking."

Griffin smiled, leaning his elbows on his knees. "I don't remember you two together as much as I'd like to, but I do remember bits and pieces. His arm around your waist, your hand on his cheek. A kiss in the corridor when you thought no one was around."

His smile faded a bit. He missed that. He missed when they were whole.

"You can have that for yourself, you know," his mother said, her gaze on his face. "Marry the girl, Griffin. Marry her and make her as happy as your father made me."

Griff's jaw clenched and he gave a sharp shake of his head. "And if I do, how long will her happiness last?" he asked. "Fifteen years? Ten? Five?"

Lady Keswick's head tilted to one side. "What do you mean by that?"

"Father gave you ten years of happiness. And fifteen years of missing him. Fifteen years and counting." His gaze dropped to the floor, his heart thudding in his chest. "What if I do the same to her? What if we marry and have children and then I—" He broke off, working his jaw. "I care for her too much to risk hurting her like that. The way Father hurt you." *The way he hurt* us.

"Oh, Griffin..." His mother reached for his hand, and he sat up, meeting her pained gaze.

"I wouldn't trade those ten years with your father for anything in this world," she said quietly. "When we first lost him, in my grief, I did sometimes wish I had never met him, but that feeling didn't last. Yes, I still miss him every day, even now, but I know how lucky I am, too, to have had those years with him."

She squeezed Griff's hand. "He gave me his love—a love I never thought possible—and he gave me you and your sister. How could I possibly regret knowing him?"

She held his gaze, her blue eyes unflinching yet gentle, and he could see the truth of her words staring back at him.

His throat tightened and he looked out across the lawn, swallowing hard as memories and feelings assailed him, even as the knot between his shoulder blades began to ease.

His mother did not regret knowing his father.

"You cannot let fear dictate what you will or will not do, darling," Lady Keswick said. "Life is a risk. Marriage is a risk. It's a frightening thing, binding oneself to another person, not knowing what the future will bring. But, Griffin..."

She gave his hand a tug, seeking his gaze, and he turned to look at her.

"Even if you avoid all risk," she said, "the future will always be unsure. And wouldn't it be worse living with the regret of what might have been? Of watching the woman you love bind herself to someone else?"

Griffin drew in a deep breath as his gaze found Olivia again, and he thought of her marrying another man, of living with him and bearing his children. He thought of her gone from his life.

His chest hollowed. He could think of nothing worse.

But it wasn't his own future he was thinking of. It was hers. He cared for her.

Damn it all, he might even *love* her.

Could he really ask her to marry him, to give him her love, her *years*, when he knew he might leave her one day? When he knew he could not promise to keep her happy, no matter how desperately he wanted to?

On the other hand, could he live with himself if he didn't try?

HOURS LATER, GRIFFIN SAT alone in his study, slumped before the fire in a leather wingback chair, an untouched glass of brandy cradled in one hand on his knee.

It was well after midnight—the rest of the party had gone to their beds ages ago—but here he sat, wide awake, gazing into the fire as if it might reveal the answers he sought.

Wearily, he rubbed at his eyes and let his head fall back against the chair's supple leather. His gaze flicked to the large portrait hanging above the fireplace, and he stared up at his father's face, at the mischievous half-smile so perfectly captured, the kindness in those warm gray eyes peering down at him.

"What should I do, Father?" he murmured, his low voice mingling with the snap and crackle of the fire. "What would *you* do?"

No answer came, of course, but then, he didn't really need one. He already knew what his father would say. He would tell him to face life's challenges without fear, and to fight for what he wanted. He would tell him to go after the girl.

Griffin blew out a frustrated breath and drank from his glass. *Go after the girl.*

It was what everyone seemed to want him to do, what they all seemed to think he should do. Were they right? Should he *go after* Olivia?

Did he even want to?

He cared for her a great deal, of course, and there was no denying he wanted her. He wanted her to be happy; he could admit that. After all, he'd gone to see her father, hadn't he? He'd gone to Surrey on her behalf, to secure her freedom and ensure her right to make her own choices. He'd done it because he cared for her, and because it was the right thing to do.

Could it be you want her for yourself? That you went to her father in the hopes it would end her betrothal and leave her available for you?

James's words slithered through his mind, and he shifted in his chair, his gaze slipping from his father's portrait to the fire. Uneasiness pricked at the back of his neck.

Could James be right? Had he been fooling himself this entire time, telling himself he'd gone to Surrey for unselfish reasons when, in fact, he'd gone because he'd hoped Olivia would wait for him?

Uncertainty warred within him, even as a guilty flush bloomed in his cheeks.

Damn it all. It was true, wasn't it? He hadn't gone to Surrey for her at all—at least, not entirely. He'd gone there for himself, too, in the hopes she would wait until he was ready to marry her.

He raked a hand through his hair, disgust burning his insides. Jesus, he was a selfish cur. A cowardly cur.

He *loved* her, for God's sake.

He surged to his feet and set his brandy on the mantel with a sharp thunk of glass on marble. Then he began to pace, back and forth, back and forth, marching an agitated path in front of the fireplace, his mind alive with realization.

He *loved* Olivia Blakely.

Of course he loved her. He wanted to marry her, too, and spend the rest of his days with her at his side. Why was he only now realizing it? Why had he resisted for so long?

"Because you're a ruddy idiot," he grumbled, his mouth a twist of agitation.

He'd told himself he wanted his freedom, that he wanted to enjoy his life as a single man for as long as he could, when in reality, he was simply scared. Scared of the future, of the uncertainties of life, of the vulnerabilities that came with being human.

These vulnerabilities were felt by everyone; *faced* by everyone. No one was immune to them. He knew that. So why was he acting as if he didn't? Why was he acting as if he were the only man on the planet coursing through life without a safety net?

Why was he so bloody scared?

He halted before the fire and stared up at his father's portrait again, determination setting his jaw.

He was through with it, with living like a frightened man. He was done. Life was much too short to live it in fear of what might be, and if his father's death had taught him anything, it was that time was our most precious commodity.

He owed it to himself, and to his father's memory, to make the most of every second he was gifted, and he wanted to share them all, every last second, with the woman he loved.

He only hoped he could convince her to take them.

CHAPTER TWENTY-NINE

"Oh, you are such a *sweetheart*," Sophie cooed the following afternoon in the gray salon as she bounced Artemis on her knee. She turned to the large, serious man sitting beside her on the sofa, and gave him an expectant smile. "Isn't she a sweetheart, husband?"

"Absolutely adorable," James agreed with a smile for his wife that could only be described as smitten.

Olivia watched their interplay from her seat on an armchair opposite the sofa, hiding her own smile behind the rim of her sherry glass, as twin jolts of envy and joy shot through her. The love Sophie shared with her husband was there for all to see, and she was thrilled for her cousin—of course she was—but she couldn't help being a little envious too.

"I can't believe how much Artemis has grown since I saw her last," Olivia said, shoving aside the pesky pang of longing. "Only a month ago, she could fit in the palm of my hand."

Sophie scratched her fingernails down Artemis's spine and the kitten arched into her touch, purring loudly. It was just the four of them gathered around the sofa table. Aunt Augusta sat in the farthest corner of the room, playing chess with Lady Keswick, and Emmy and Griffin were nowhere to be seen.

"Emmy told me Griffin found her on the street," Sophie said. "Is that true?"

Olivia gave her a small, uncomfortable smile. "That is...what he told us."

"How kind of him to give the poor little thing a home."

"Yes. Immensely kind." But she was thinking of Mrs. Morris, Griffin's former mistress, the beautiful widow who didn't like cats. Had he renewed his arrangement with the lady, or did he have a new lover now, one even more beautiful than the last?

Jealousy shot through her, and she wondered yet again if he ever thought of her, of that night they spent together, in his study, in each other's arms.

She drained the last of her sherry, frustrated with the path her thoughts had taken. He'd been a distraction all day, his behavior conflicting, confusing, as he avoided her like an illness and yet, every time she looked at him, he seemed to be watching her.

Dratted man. He wasn't even in the room and, still, he was on her mind.

"Olivia?"

Lady Keswick's voice broke into her thoughts, and she looked across the room at the marchioness. "Yes, my lady?"

"Be a dear and fetch Emmy for me, would you? I believe she is in the family library."

Olivia smiled, pleased by the unexpected errand. She could do with a distraction.

"Of course, Lady Keswick," she said, setting her glass on the sofa table before rising to her feet and quitting the room.

Walking up the corridor with measured steps, she took in the familiar pattern of the Turkish rug beneath her feet, the watercolors and pencil sketches lining the walls, and she smiled to herself. She adored this house. It was like a second home to her, had been ever since she was a little girl, and it had seen her through many seasons of her life.

She hoped it always would.

After she'd made her way up the single flight of stairs and down one more corridor, she reached the family library. The door was slightly ajar, so she knocked softly before nudging it open with her knuckles and walking through.

Her steps faltered just inside the door as her gaze fell on Griffin standing across the room before the hearth, his hands clasped at his front, as if he'd been expecting her.

"Griffin. I wasn't..." She cast her gaze over the room, looking for Emmy. "Is your sister in here with you? I was asked to—"

She turned at the sound of the door clicking shut behind her, and her brows dipped in confusion. "Is something amiss?" She turned to face Griffin again. "Your mother sent me here to look for Emmy."

His smile was rueful. "A ruse, I'm afraid."

"A ruse? For what—" Her eyes caught on something dangling from the hearth above his head, something green and leafy, held together with a strip of bright red ribbon. "What is that?"

"A mistletoe ball, of course."

She looked at him, her heart beginning to thump in her chest. "It's September," she said faintly. "And that isn't mistletoe."

"I know it isn't. But it was the best I could do."

The best he could do? The best he could do for *what?*

Olivia crossed her arms over her chest and frowned at him. "What is this, Griffin?"

He drew in a breath, and then he crossed the room toward her, his eyes locked on hers.

"This is me trying to right a wrong," he said gruffly, halting inches away from her. "Doing what I should have done—what I wanted to do—last December in Lord Stevenson's library."

Olivia swallowed, slowly sweeping her gaze over his face, searching for the answer to her question before she voiced it. "And what did you want to do?" she whispered.

"Kiss you senseless. Throw myself at your feet." His voice was a caress. "Love you."

Her breath hitched.

"I love you, Olivia," he said softly, drawing her trembling hands in his and stroking his thumbs across her knuckles.

"Do you?" she whispered, afraid to believe him. Valiantly trying to guard her heart.

"I do. Very much." He smiled. "I have for quite some time, if you must know."

"Even when you thought me a silly, shallow flirt?" she asked, her own smile wry, self-protective.

His gray eyes dimmed, regret lining his face as he slowly shook his head. "I'm sorry I said those words to you. I shouldn't have. But when I saw you standing there with that teasing smile and Christmas punch on your lips, I saw only danger. I saw how easy it would be for you to take me apart, piece by piece." His lips quirked. "Even more terrifying was the fact that I wanted you to do it. Because I wanted *you.*"

She dropped her gaze to their joined hands, the sight of his bare skin on hers sending a thrill straight through her, even as her mind reeled.

"You didn't want to, though, did you?" Her eyes lifted to his. "You didn't want to want me."

It wasn't a question. It was an accusation, driven by the need to hear the truth, as if the truth would keep her safe.

"No," he said quietly. "I didn't."

The answer did not surprise her, but it stung all the same. Gently she withdrew her hands from his and folded her arms across her belly, desperate to put some distance between them.

"But now you do?" Her brows knit. "Why? What has changed? I know it wasn't me. I am the same as I've always been."

And, for once, she felt no inclination to apologize for it.

"Yes, you are," he said, his eyes soft with fondness, as if he liked her, just as she was. "I, however, am not."

She shook her head. "What does that mean?"

Griffin turned away, raked a hand through his hair before letting it fall to his side. "I...thought I knew you," he said slowly. "I thought you were a spoiled, title-chasing flirt without scruples yet, still, you tempted me. Still, you were in my thoughts. Under my skin."

He faced her again, and her heart dipped at the naked feeling in his eyes, the self-deprecating smile curving his lips.

"I tried to stay away from you," he said. "God knows I tried. But then my mother injured her ankle, and I could no longer avoid you. And as I began to know you better, I realized how wrong I was. There is nothing shallow or silly about you, Olivia. You are clever and funny and sweet." His gaze pierced hers. "You are the most remarkable woman I've ever known."

Pleasure flowed through her, swift and stunning, even as her mind cautioned her to hold fast.

She swallowed, her lips twisting. "I tried to get close to you," she whispered. "So many times, I tried. But you always pushed me away."

"I know. I know you did." He shook his head, his mouth grim. "I was afraid, Olivia. I was afraid to let you in."

The admission stunned her. Griffin was always so confident, so self-assured. The vulnerability she saw in his eyes rocked her to her core.

"Afraid?" she asked. "Afraid of what?"

He drew in a breath, as if shoring his courage. "Of disappointing you. Of hurting you, the way my father hurt my mother. To be honest, I still am."

Olivia stared, trying to make sense of his words. "I don't understand. Your father—"

"He left her." Griffin's gaze fell to the floor, his throat working. "He loved her, and still he left, long before he should have. And I'm afraid I'll do the same to you." His eyes met hers. "I don't want to hurt you, Olivia. I never want to hurt you."

"You wouldn't," she said, stepping toward him, her heart in her throat. "You *won't*."

His brow creased. "I might."

"But not intentionally. You would never hurt me on purpose, Griffin." She reached up and cupped his face in her palm. "Foolish man. Don't you see? I would rather have you for only a little while than never at all."

GRIFFIN'S HEART WAS BEATING so fast he thought it would burst from his chest. He bent his head and pressed his lips to hers, rejoicing when she kissed him back.

"I love you," he said against her lips, then he pulled back and repeated the words. "I love you."

Her beautiful eyes searched his, roving over his face, lingering on his mouth. "Is that why you went to my father?" she asked softly. "Because you loved me?"

He nodded. "Of course, I didn't know that at the time. All I knew was I couldn't bear the thought of you unhappy. I couldn't let you marry Paxton, not if it wasn't your choice. Not unless it was what you really wanted."

Olivia smiled. "It was the kindest thing anyone had ever done for me."

He shook his head. "It wasn't kind. It was selfish. I wanted you for myself, only I didn't realize it then. I told myself I was helping you."

"You did help me," she said simply, and the way she was looking at him, the acceptance, the *love* shining in her beautiful blue eyes nearly undid him.

"All I want is for you to be happy," he said. "And I want to spend the rest of my days ensuring it. I want you to marry me, petal." He smiled. "But first, I want to court you. You deserve a good courting."

"Do I?" Olivia asked, smiling back at him.

"Oh, yes." His nose bumped hers. "I intend to treat you like a queen. Kneel before you and kiss your feet in deference." His lips brushed hers. "Until I convince you to make me your king."

He kissed her again, lingering over the task this time, and her arms looped around his neck as she returned his kiss eagerly. God, she was delicious. Deliciously *his.*

He scooped her up in his arms and carried her to the desk, setting her gently on the edge. Then he pressed his palms on the desk at either side of her and leaned into her warmth, his lips meeting hers in slow, worshipful kisses.

She pulled him closer, and he went, stepping between her thighs and closing his arms around her until he could feel her everywhere.

With a stilted moan, she pulled back and gazed up at him with hazy, honeyed eyes. "Yes," she said huskily, her lips gorgeously plump. "Yes, I will marry you."

Cupping his face in her hands, she leaned in and pressed a kiss to his mouth. "I love you, Griffin. I've always loved you. I—"

He swooped in with a low growl and stole another kiss, cutting into her words, relief and joy sweeping over him in waves. She had said yes. She would be his.

She *was* his. And he was hers.

"Of course, I will only marry you *after* you've properly courted me," she said a moment later through wet lips and ragged breaths. "I shall expect regular trips to Gunter's and *at least* three picnics in the park. And don't think for a moment I will allow you to renege on that promise you made to kneel before me and kiss my feet." She arched an adorably imperious brow. "I think that ought to be a daily occurrence, don't you?"

Griffin grinned. "I'll kneel before you as often as you like, petal," he said, nudging a slipper off her foot with his thumb. It tumbled to the floor with a satisfying thud. "I'll begin here, at your toes then work my way up your ankles to your calves, pausing to rest for a time at your delectable thighs, of course, and then..."

His hands skated up her legs in time with his words, squeezing and shaping through the fine silk of her skirts.

"And then?" she prodded, her eyes dark as midnight.

He drew slow, sweeping circles at the tops of her thighs with his thumbs, teasing her without mercy. "And then," he murmured, "if you ask very nicely, I might consider doing it all over again. *Under* your skirts."

His lips found her earlobe, drawing a gasp from her lips.

"Define *nicely*," she said, her voice a near moan.

"Begging. Pleading. Panting with need."

"I might plead on occasion, but"—she gasped as he shoved her skirts to her knees—"I will never *pant.*"

A wicked smile turned his lips. "Never?"

"*Never.*"

"Hm." He clucked his tongue. "That *is* a sobering thought. Still, no one has ever accused me of being a quitter..." He slid his palms up her thighs until he reached her stays, and then he gave her delectably creamy flesh a squeeze, his thumbs brushing the tender skin at her inner thighs.

"Touch me, Griffin," Olivia pleaded, her eyes begging. "Please."

And then she panted it.

EPILOGUE

THERE WERE NO TRIPS to Gunter's Tea Shop in the weeks leading up to their wedding, but Griffin courted his lady with the ardent and faithful devotion of a man besotted beyond reason, and Olivia soaked up every moment of it like it was her due. Which, of course, it was.

Standing in the entrance hall at Keswick House with their friends and family gathered all around, Griffin watched his new bride as she laughed and chatted, looking happy and utterly gorgeous in her pink silk wedding gown.

As promised, he'd taken her out on the picnics she'd asked for—not three, but five, just to prove how serious he was—and it was on their fifth picnic that their wedding date was finally set.

A satisfied smile touched his lips. He'd wooed her with wine and cheese and several long, languorous kisses beneath the warm autumn sun, employing every persuasive tactic he could think of to finally convince her to marry him as soon as the banns were read.

And now, finally, she was his. As she was always meant to be.

"It was a lovely ceremony," Lady Keswick said quietly as she drew up beside him, her words for his ears only. "I'm so happy for you, darling. I'm so happy you're happy."

He smiled. "Thank you, Mother." He took her hand in his and pressed a kiss to her knuckles. "I owe so much of this to you. I am who I am because of you."

Her eyes misted and she gave him a watery smile. "And your father, too," she said softly. "You knew him for such a short time, but I see so much of him in you. And that is the highest compliment I could ever pay." She squeezed his forearm. "He would be proud of you. Just as I am."

Emotion thickened Griff's throat and he cleared it away. "You were always there to prod me down the right path and talk sense into me when I needed it. Thank you for that."

Lady Keswick shrugged. "Any mother with an injured ankle and an unusually clever mind would have done the same."

A smile tugged at the corners of her lips and Griffin blinked at her. "You *faked* your ankle sprain?"

She shot him an offended look. "Don't be absurd. I did not *fake* anything. Although...I might have exaggerated it a bit."

Griffin laughed. "And you call me incorrigible."

"I'm a mother," she said with another elegant shrug. "There is nothing I will not do for my children."

She had the grace to look mildly sheepish but made no apology for her actions. Not that he wanted one. He might not be here now, married to the finest woman in England, if it wasn't for his mother's machinations.

"I'll have to think of a new scheme for your sister, of course," Lady Keswick said, her gaze trained on Emmy's smiling face. "I was willing to confine myself to my bed once for my children, but I cannot bear it a second time."

Griffin grinned. *Poor Emmy.* "I'm going to pretend I didn't hear that," he said before leaning down to buss his mother's cheek. "Thank you again for everything. And for looking after Artemis while we're away."

She smiled at him and patted his cheek. "It is my pleasure, darling," she said. "Now, you and your bride had best be off. I hope you two have a marvelous wedding trip and do remember to write, hm?"

After giving his mother his assurance that he would do just that, he whisked Olivia through the front door, and the two dashed down the steps toward their awaiting carriage, dodging flying rice and satin slippers on the way.

Breathless and laughing, they tumbled into the carriage and then Griffin rapped his knuckles on the roof and with a jolt the carriage set off down the street.

"Goodness," Olivia said as she fell back against the black velvet squabs, pink-cheeked and gorgeous. "I'm glad that is over with. I'm exhausted."

Griffin edged closer to her on the seat, only satisfied when their hips were touching. "Exhausted?" he teased. "But the day has only just begun."

She sighed. "For you, perhaps. I've been awake since dawn."

"So have I, but I'm not tired at all." He took her hand in his and pressed his lips to her gloved knuckles, his smile full of mischief. "I've finally got you all to myself. I spent all morning thinking about this moment, about you and me, alone in this carriage." He lowered his voice. "About an afternoon of utter debauchery."

Olivia's head dipped to his shoulder, and she let out a noisy yawn. "Can the debauchery not wait until after I've had a nap?"

Griffin shot her a look of exaggerated disapproval. "First I discover my new bride's middle name is *Ursuline* of all things, and now this. Falling asleep only moments after the wedding." He shook his head. "Not a very auspicious beginning to our marriage, petal."

Olivia's head came up and she peered down her nose at him. "Ursuline was my grandmother's name," she said with a haughty sniff. "And those who live in glass houses should not throw stones, Griffin *Barnabas* Keswick."

"Barnabas is an excellent name. A powerful name."

She arched her brows. "Well, if you like it so much, perhaps I shall call you Barnabas instead. Or Barnaby, maybe? No, no. *Barney.*" She gave Griffin's nose a playful tweak. "Shall I start calling you Barney, husband?"

"Only if you wish never to see me again."

She laughed, the sound merry and sweet to his ears. "All right," she said, her eyes twinkling. "I'll only call you Barney when I'm cross with you."

Griffin frowned at her with faux displeasure.

His wife responded with an impudent smile. "Think of it as an added incentive to ensure I am always happy."

Laughing, Griffin tugged her into his arms and pressed his lips to her forehead. "God, I love you," he said and then he pulled back and gazed into her eyes, his smile sobering. "And I hope you will be happy, always. I will do everything in my power to make it so."

She cupped his cheek, her eyes happy. "I know," she whispered. "And you're off to a very promising start, my lord. But there is one thing you can do that would make me even happier."

He smiled. "What's that?"

"Kiss me."

She angled her head up, those dark blue eyes of hers drawing him in, drawing him under her spell. He dipped his head, capturing her lips in an ardent, reverent meeting of mouths that left them both breathless and wanting.

"I love you, husband-mine," Olivia whispered against his lips. "And I'm not sleepy anymore."

Grinning now, Griffin tugged off first his own gloves and then his wife's before sweeping her into his arms and kissing her again, slowly working his lips down her throat until she was writhing against him, her hands clutching his shoulders.

"With my body, I thee worship," he murmured into her deliciously soft skin, inhaling the sweet scent of jasmine as he nipped her with his teeth. "I made a promise this morning, petal, and I mean to make good on it. Every day of my life if you'll let me."

Olivia's breath hitched as he tugged her bodice down, freeing her breasts. "Griffin..."

He dipped his head and pressed his lips to one rosy nipple. "With my lips, I thee kiss..."

He flicked his tongue over the pebbled peak, drawing a gasp from deep in her throat. "With my tongue, I thee taste..." He sucked her nipple into his mouth, and she arched into him, groaning his name again, her hands threading into his hair as his own inched down her thighs.

He slipped a hand beneath her skirt. "With my fingers, I thee—"

"Griffin!"

He brought his head up, his expression all innocence. "Yes, petal?"

Hazy blue eyes scolded. "You talk too much."

He grinned. "Forgive me, wife."

And with that, the Marquess of Keswick went back to work, ensuring his marchioness was happy that day and all the days of his life.

ABOUT THE AUTHOR

Sylvie Sinclair cut her teeth on the Sweet Valley Twins, Sunfire Romances, and L.M. Montgomery before inevitably graduating to the classic bodice rippers of the 80's and 90's (which she kept hidden under her bed from her disapproving mother for years).

The romance and adventure in these books inspired her to create her own love stories with strong heroines who know their own mind and the heroes who wouldn't have it any other way.

She lives in California with her cinnamon roll husband and their cantankerous-but-adorable Siamese cat. When she isn't writing or reading, she can usually be found watching Melrose Place with a glass of red wine in hand, or puttering around in her flower garden. Visit her online at www.sylvi esinclair.com.

Printed in Great Britain
by Amazon